Broken Souls

D1519029

Broken Souls

Little Hope Series, Book 3

Ariana Cane

ARIANA CANE

ASIN: B09KXCCCHR

Any references to historical events, real people, or real places are used
fictitiously. Names, characters, and places are products of the author's
imagination.

www.arianacane.com

Editor: Anna Noel.

Proofreader: Lauren Alexander.

THEY SAY YOU SHOULDN'T LET THE PAST DEFINE YOU. BUT WHEN THE PAST BECOMES ALL YOU ARE, SOMETIMES YOU JUST NEED A BLANK PAGE.

Broken Souls

Little Hope Series, Book 3

ARIANA CANE

To all who went through hell.

Author's Note

Please READ BEFORE diving in.

This book is darker than the previous two because it takes on a very heavy subject. Please, read the trigger warning (TW).

The first ever person to see this book was someone who went through what Alicia went through. Even before sending it to my editor, I sent the story completely unedited (a truly shameful moment for me) to someone who could relate and help me make this book a *healing* one.

After helping me with a few sensitive lines, this person emailed back the following (inserted here with her permission): *"Thank you for making me feel heard."* I cried the whole evening. Everyone who goes through hell like that, no matter the gender, deserves their story to be heard *if* they choose it to be. And if this book helps even one person, I'll be over the moon.

We are not our past. We are the future.

TW: SA (the heroine suffered in the past, not from the hero, but the whole book circles around it). Adult language and adult situations.

If you find yourself in a similar situation as certain characters, please speak to someone. There's help out there.

The National Sexual Assault Hotline in the US as of fall 2022 can be reached at 1-800-656-4673.

Prologue

"Nobody will get to you on time." A heavy breathing assaults the back of my head. "Nobody." I hear a disgusting sound from behind me, like a hyena cackling. I squeeze my eyes shut, trying to drown it out. I'll never look at that animal the same again. He presses my face into the bed and drags my pants down. "Nobody will come. You're all alone here." His whisper drops. "With us."

I wake up to my sheets completely soaked in sweat. It's the same nightmare that has been haunting me for years. It's always the same moment of that night. The same words. The same people. And the same no-escape situation. They haunt me in my waking moments and in my sleep, even all these years later.

Today is a lucky day for me; I woke up a little earlier, a few breaths before my life was forever changed, so I don't have to relive it again. I check the time. It's four thirty in the morning—no way I'll go back to sleep after that. I never do.

I look around my room to ground myself. My shelf is stacked with some of my favorite books, some of which have been there for years... some since, well, eight years ago. I'm twenty-six and still live with my parents. Still have the same nightmare. The same furniture since I was a teenager. The same paint on the walls.

And the same sleepless nights.

I take a deep breath, closing my eyes and falling back against my pillows. Something needs to change. Anything. I'm not saying I'm ready to move *on*, but I think I'm ready to move *away*.

I sigh, accepting the fact it won't be easy. For any of the members of my family.

But it's time.

Chapter One

ALICIA

"Are you sure you wanna do this?" Kayla, my older brother's girlfriend, asks, carrying a box to the kitchen. My first kitchen, which will belong to *only me*. I look around with pride. I won't be sharing the space with my mom anymore. I love my mom—I do—but I want to do things my way.

Kayla's perfect ash-blonde hair sticks to her sweaty forehead, and she has raccoon mascara smudges under her eyes, yet she's one of the most interesting people I've ever seen. Her colorful tattoos play peekaboo from under her long sleeves as she unboxes the silverware my mom packed for my new home. Sometimes I stare at them in wonder. I love her tattoos, but I'm not sure I could handle getting one. To let someone keep touching my skin for hours? I don't think so.

Kayla notices me watching her art and covers it with the sleeves of her sweater, sending me a playful wink. She is such a beautiful woman. Mixed with Justin, she'll make me the cutest nephews and nieces in the universe, so I can spoil them rotten.

Despite our rough beginning, I think about how lucky I am to have her now. She didn't have to forgive us for how we treated her, but she did. She's the type of person who shines despite everything. I judged her wrongfully before, and I'll be ashamed of that for the rest of my life.

Plus, she's so good for Justin. He finally took that pretty-boy mask off, and now, surprisingly, he's a decent human being. Almost. Well, he's getting there.

"Yeah, I'm sure." And I'm sure that I'm sure. It was time to get out from under my parents' wings.

My parents love me to death, but sometimes it can be crippling. With my history, it's understandable to a certain degree. At least Justin got off my back after Kayla talked to him.

I support myself and make decent money, but still I've been living in my childhood bedroom, scared to venture into the real world again. Today is my first day living independently at the sweet age of twenty-six.

I look around the house. The building is old, built in the nineteen hundreds. I don't think there have been many renovations ever since. It's one story, with shallow ceilings, one bedroom, one bath, a living room with a vintage fireplace, and an oversized eat-in kitchen.

The kitchen is what sold me. It's never been updated, which I think gives it a certain charm. All the appliances are old besides the fridge and the stove. The original molding on the cabinets is broad and highly detailed. The island is oval. I never thought I'd love a weird, oval-shaped kitchen island, but I can already imagine sitting here with a laptop and a steaming cup of coffee, typing all my wild fantasies away.

Another thing I absolutely adore is the fireplace. Built with the house, its red brick and beautifully detailed iron cover give me shivers of pleasure as I imagine curling up in front of a crackling fire during late, cozy winter nights. Good thing cold nights are frequent here, deep in Maine. I let out a dreamy sigh.

If I'm completely honest, Little Hope, our charming small town, doesn't have many renting options available, so I've been waiting for Mrs. Jenkins's daughter to move her mom in with her. Mrs. Jenkins is a wonderful old lady but a little too old to live independently. So when Justin had mentioned months ago that he wanted to call her daughter and explain how bad things were getting, I got excited. And I've been waiting patiently ever since for it to happen.

"The place is dope." Kayla saunters over to me, looking around. "I can't believe you scored it." She shakes her head, digging into the bags on the counter.

"Me neither. It's pure luck." It's not. I'd been lurking in the bushes, waiting for the perfect moment to ambush the scary old lady with my proposal.

"I'd say it is. You charmed the hell out of Mrs. Jenkins."

"What can I say? I am a natural-born charmer." I wink. I'm so not. A long time ago, maybe. But not anymore. Now I just hide behind this facade of a total bitch or a fluffy bear, depending on the mood. We Attleboroughs all have that in common. We seem to all like hiding behind our own masks. Yeah, we're blood-related, for sure.

Kayla laughs. She's one of the few people who knows

what happened to me, so she doesn't believe my veneer for a second. "Also, Justin's been fixing her car for years for almost nothing. I may have reminded her of it." I shoot her a sheepish smile and shrug.

"You hussy!" She points her finger at me, laughing. "For real, though, how did you convince her to rent it out to you and not someone else?"

"It wasn't easy. The lady is tough, man." I shiver, remembering every conversation I tried to start. She always sent me on my merry way with a cute, very grandma-like *"Screw you, Alicia, go bother your parents; they got money and can get you anything."* But I wanted this old house. I've been watching it since I was a kid as we drove by. It looked like a fairy cabin, nestled deep in the forest, from a story about a long-lost princess who finds her prince and has her happily ever after. Something I'll never have. *That's* why I wanted the house, so at least I can have *that*.

"I know. I'm scared of her. Whenever she comes to the diner, I feel like I'm at military school, about to get busted for something." Her eyes widen like she's seen a ghost as she remembers.

"Even after Marina?" Her employer and the guardian angel of sorts is a tough, old-fashioned woman and probably the trendiest person in Little Hope, with her sleek bob and fancy makeup. For a small town in Maine, she always looks so expensive. Marina took Kayla in when she had no money and nowhere to go. Even though Kayla is a highly sought-after tattoo artist and does fine money-wise, she still helps Marina on her days off. Marina's diner is like a family business for them and a homey place for everyone in Little Hope.

To be honest, *I'm* a little scared of Marina. Reasonably, she's not my biggest fan after I've been a bitch to Kayla on a few occasions, so I guess it's well deserved. But still, I'm half expecting her to add some laxatives to my order. Again, well deserved.

"Nah, Mrs. Jenkins is like a pit bull with a bone, while Marina is a Chihuahua with a bow. No, thank you." She shudders visibly, and I laugh.

"She's not so bad. She did promise to put a chastity belt on me if I organize any orgies here, but otherwise, I should be good."

"See!" She laughs, throwing her head back. "Scary."

Yeah, she is. She threatened to do all sorts of things if I destroyed her house, but I really needed to get out from under my family's roof, and her house was my dream home. I promised to keep her house free of orgies—an easy deal on my end, since I'm not my fun-seeking brother Justin—and parties. It's not like I have friends to throw crazy celebrations because I don't. I have Josie, but she's an internet friend. You know, one you talk to every day but never meet in real life. Kayla considers herself my friend, but I don't deserve her. Sometimes it's hard to think I deserve anyone.

Maybe I'll make some friends eventually. This first step on the path of accepting my new self might be what I needed.

Mrs. Jenkins gave me endless instructions, including attaching a photo update of her houseplants with every monthly money transfer. She has quite a few of those, and I already know how I'll set up a green corner in the living room next to the wide window, a beautiful collection of all those plants scattered all over the place. Mrs. Jenkins took all the furniture but left the plants. It doesn't make any sense to me, but who knows what quirks I'll have at her age.

"Did you meet your new neighbors?" Kayla asks,

placing cleaning supplies in the cabinet underneath the sink.

"Not yet. I'm sure they'll be great." I pause and add with a chuckle: "If I ever talk to them."

"Right." Her laughter is forced, and I do a double take to ensure I haven't missed anything. She's standing in the same spot, rocking on her heels and watching me with a weird look on her face.

"I think that was the last one." Justin walks down the stairs, drawing my attention away from Kayla. "Jake's bringing pizza if that's alright," he tells Kayla while heading to the bathroom, and she rolls her eyes.

I quickly glance at her. I know she hasn't made amends with Jake after his evil actions nearly cost them their relationship. Well, it's more like *he* hasn't made amends with *her*. He should start by begging her for forgiveness for the years of torment. In his defense, he thought she was to blame for what happened to me that night. He was wrong, though. We all were. And now we all have a lifetime to make it up to her.

She never brings up the years of hate we sent her way. We don't deserve her. She's a bigger person than any of us will ever be.

As for Justin, he's still mad at Jake, and it pains me. No matter what happened, they're still my brothers, and I love them. I wish they would bury the hatchet so we can return to being a big happy family. Justin tolerates Jake at family gatherings, but I think the biggest thing stopping Justin from accepting Jake is that his meek apology to Kayla didn't seem sincere. It didn't seem genuine to any of us, to be fair. I understand where Justin comes from since Kayla is his person, but it still hurts to see our family so fractured.

Jake's our little brother, and we all look so much alike.

Anyone can tell we're related. We're all blond with baby-blue eyes. The boys have athletic builds, which is the one difference between us. I have huge boobs and a few extra pounds that I could survive without nowadays. I used to be told I was pretty, and I liked to believe that, but I've grown to resent it.

"I bought these new hair bands. You know, I think they'll look absolutely amazing on you." Kayla notes as she bends to drag a giant box marked 'clothes' to the exit, murmuring, "How the hell did this box get into the kitchen? Men." She rolls her eyes, and I chuckle. "So anyway, wanna try these bands? I can drop them off if you want." She glances at me while dragging the box onto the floor.

"I mean, yeah, sure." My eyes dart around as my palms turn sweaty.

"Awesome!" Kayla finally drops the box as Justin returns. "Be a dear and carry this to the bedroom, please." She walks to stand behind me and suddenly touches my ponytail, making me jump. She instantly drops her hand, and my cheeks turn hot.

"Sorry," I murmur, avoiding her eyes.

"Don't be!" She waves her hand dismissively. "I have this tendency to startle people. Not a good thing when I have a pen with ink in my hand, if you ask me."

I finally manage to meet her eyes, and she winks at me. "Yeah" is all I can squeeze out. I'm grateful to her for not making it weird.

"Go, Justin. The box won't carry itself." Kayla shoos him away, knowing he won't leave on his own. Whenever he sees me triggered by something, he goes into this overpro-tective-brother mode. I adore him—I do—but I'm being suffocated a little. And to be honest, I think he is too.

"Yeah. Thanks, Justin. I mean it, *thank you*." I find and

hold his gaze, silently showing him my gratitude for everything. He helped me convince our parents to let me live alone. They're overprotective. Not without reason.

"Welcome, Tiny." He strolls over and throws his arm around my shoulders.

I punch him under his ribs. "I told you to stop calling me that." I'm anything but tiny. I'm five-eleven, for heaven's sake.

"You did?" He snickers and I punch him again. He lets me go with a loud *oof*, smiles, and heads toward Kayla. I can feel their love in the air. Thick with passion. It's where I find inspiration, in people like them. Their chemistry and life stories. It's also where I feel overwhelmed with guilt, remembering how I nearly ruined everything for them. He leans in for a kiss, and within a second, their perfect Disney-worthy kiss turns into something you'd find on Pornhub. I instantly cover my eyes with my hand.

"Jeez! Stop it!" I yell. "You can't christen my kitchen before me!"

Justin jumps from Kayla immediately. "What the hell are you talking about? You aren't having sex here." He thinks for a moment. "Or anywhere else, for that matter." He looks horrified, like the actual idea of me having sex with somebody makes him sick.

I almost want to tell him it makes me sick too.

Kayla laughs, turning slightly red as she starts putting my silverware inside the drawers.

The front door opens, and Jake comes barreling in, holding five pizza boxes.

"I see you're hungry." I quirk a brow.

"I'm a growing boy." He winks, putting the pizzas down on the counter. "I met Freya and Alex at the store. They're stopping by later. Do you mind?"

"Not at all," I tell him with a shrug. Alex is Justin's best friend, and Freya is his girlfriend. I like them both, especially Freya. She's changed this town for the better since she's been here. Talk about how one person can change the world.

Justin and Alex served together in the military and have always been close. But Jake was at odds with Alex for a while. I guess Jake started to grow on Alex when he saved his fiancé by shooting her crazy ex. Jake can be hard to like, but he's also a lifesaver. Quite literally.

We're almost done putting everything in the kitchen away when there's a knock on the door. "It's my first guest!" I cry, jumping up and down like a happy toddler before rushing to open the door. Freya and Alex are standing on my doorstep—*my*—with two huge boxes in Alex's arms. Something long and wrapped in gazette paper sticks from the corner. "We came bearing gifts!" Freya exclaims, and I let them in with a smile.

"Come inside, guys. Pizza's getting cold."

"Good thing we brought a microwave," she says with a toothy grin, and I laugh.

"Thank you, guys! The best housewarming gift ever!"

I find plates in the cabinet where I just stuck them and put them on the island next to the boxes. Within minutes, the pizza is devoured, with only a couple of slices remaining. Suddenly, I'm grateful Jake was hungry enough to bring so much.

Once everyone is happy and fed, I decide to ask about the gifts.

"What's in the other box?" It sits between her feet, and she looks like she's guarding it like Cerberus. I lean closer to them and try to pick at the side for clues. Freya smacks my hand away and orders Alex to put them on the counter.

When he's done, Freya pushes one of them toward Jake. "Open that one, will ya?" She beams at him. For someone so short and tiny—to be fair, many people are short next to me—everyone always listens to her command. She's a force to be reckoned with.

Jake opens the box and starts setting the microwave up while Freya pushes the other box toward me.

"Can I touch it now?" I ask, smiling at her. "You're not gonna beat me up again, are you?"

"Only if you don't like it. Now open it." She nudges the box toward me and impatiently claps her hands.

I take a knife and cut the box open. It's huge. I have no idea how Alex could have carried both boxes simultaneously, even considering his Godzilla size. I have no idea what could be in here.

When it's finally open, I laugh until tears start streaming down my face. "You guys. It's perfect!"

Justin tries to peek around me, but Kayla nudges him aside. "Lemme see."

The box is filled with single-life necessities: a six-pack of ginger ale (because I don't drink alcohol since that night), a gift card for the one Chinese restaurant in Little Hope (we need more, in my opinion), a box of condoms, a mighty bat, a bag of mint gum, and a massive ten-inch dildo.

"What the hell, Freya?" Justin yells, turning red. "That's my little sister." Even the tips of his ears are crimson.

"Right. Like you don't rub one out here and there." She mocks him.

I throw my hands up. "Stop, just stop. Both of you. I'll be traumatized after today, for sure." I pull the bat out and weigh it in my hands. Living alone has its perks, but I'm also a little scared. What if someone tries to break in? I haven't lived on my own since... well, ever. I only attended one year of college, but I lived in the sorority house. I was never alone. I'll need this bat more than I need a dildo. Though, judging by the size of it, it could cause some serious damage. No way I ever let that monster near my lady parts; it'd split me in two. Why did Freya buy it? Is Alex the same size? Eyeing him from the side, I wouldn't be surprised. Poor woman. Or... a lucky one? Bless her soul... and lady bits.

Kayla chortles to my right and pushes Justin to the side. "It's time to go, people."

"What? Why?" Jake asks.

"Because Alicia needs to get comfortable and ready for bed. It's late, dummy," she explains, annoyed she even has to explain. "We're overstaying."

Jake looks dumbfounded, glancing between us. "She's our sister. It's practically our house. We can stay as much as we want. Right, Alicia?" He looks at me for support. Support I'm not going to give him. Knowing my overprotective brothers, they'd be camping here. Taking turns out front, shotgun in hand, ready to take on any windblown leaf that threatens my peace.

"Yeah, no," I answer with a shake of my head. "I love you, Jakey, I do, but go home."

He looks offended.

"Because I'm about to use Freya's gifts."

He looks at me with dead eyes, not understanding.

I widen my eyes and add, "All of them."

Now, he's terrified.

"Okay, people, gotta go." He collects his jacket and practically runs out the door. Everyone gathers their purses and jackets and swiftly follows him.

We all share good nights, I thank them for helping me move my furniture and endless boxes, and they leave, but

Justin lingers on the porch for a moment, rocking on his heels. "Are you sure you'll be okay?"

It nearly breaks my heart. Justin still blames himself for what happened to me; no matter what I say, I can't change that. He must forgive himself first. Until then, he'll never *hear* me trying to tell him I've never blamed him.

I wrap my arms around Justin and rest my cheek on his chest. He smells like my childhood hopes and security. "I love you, big brother."

A choke sounds from above me, but I don't look up. I don't want him to feel embarrassed. "I love you too, little sister." He nearly croaks his words, walking to his truck. Kayla's in the passenger seat, looking the other way, giving us privacy.

I can't believe I ever thought ill of her, following the masses and... well, my own prejudice. She's so pure. Probably the purest of us all.

I take a deep breath, trying to calm my emotions. It's the first day of my new life.

I'll get better soon.

Chapter Two

MARK

I wake up to a loud beeping sound. Lost between sleep and wakefulness, I pry my eyes open in an attempt to understand what's happening. My last two back-to-back shifts have left me groggy and disoriented. Little Hope isn't very big on firefighters—or emergencies, for that matter—and yesterday, we got called to help put out a massive fire in an apartment building in Copeland, a neighboring town. One whole crew went to fight the fire, and the other remained in Little Hope, both pulling double shifts.

Someone is licking my fingers, and it takes me a while to figure out it's Ghost. He's whining as he gently pulls on my hand. I try to force my eyes back open, but they don't listen. I haven't slept in days, and I'm fucking exhausted.

When I finally get my wits together, my brain clears, and I am finally able to force my body to move, I realize the sound seems familiar. Very familiar. A fire alarm. I jump from the bed, wide awake, and grab my pants from the floor. I've seen far too many dicks during my firefighter career. Enough to last me a lifetime. People get caught in weird states of undress during emergencies more often than you might think.

I run downstairs, trying to figure out where the sound is coming from. It only takes me a moment to realize it's coming from Mrs. Jenkins's house. She had just rented her place to somebody. Just fuckin' awesome—the perfect welcome party on the first night they moved in.

"Stay," I command Ghost as I grab a fire extinguisher from the wall next to the door. I run toward her house. I have manners, so I knock on the door once, but I don't hear an answer, so I kick it in with my foot in one go. I've been telling Mrs. Jenkins for ages that her door's flimsy, and I've asked her to let me fix it on more than one occasion, but she's a stubborn old lady. Looks like she'd foreseen the current disaster.

As soon as the door is out, the smoke comes out thick. The fire must have been running for a few good minutes. And then I hear a child shrieking.

My blood runs cold, and I rush toward the screams. But there's no child in there, not at all. Only a tall, blonde lady running around Mrs. Jenkins's living room, waving her arms and yelling like a banshee as smoke barrels out of the fireplace. I'm next to it in two big jumps, spraying the foam all over. I'm so glad I grabbed the extinguisher because Mrs. Jenkins never had one. Watching the smoke die down, I'm thankful the fire wasn't a real house fire. This idiot must have started it without knowing how the fireplace works. *Fuckin' spoiled princess.*

She keeps yelling, clutching her hands to her chest.

My head is killing me, and her shrieks threaten to break my skull in two. "Shut up!" I bark.

To my surprise, it works. She closes her mouth and looks around nervously with her big blue eyes. Fuck me for noticing their color.

"Did you open the damper?" I growl.

"What?" she asks, finally shifting her attention from the fire to me. She's crying, her face black from the thick smoke, with two clean paths down her face made by tears.

"Did. You. Open. The. Damper." She's obviously an idiot, and my tolerance for stupidity has run out by now, so I accentuate every word.

She whimpers. "What is a damper?"

Oh, fuck it. I turn to the kitchen, grab a few towels, and wrap them around my hands. Returning, I dive inside the fireplace.

"What are you doing?" she shrieks again. "You're going to burn!" She makes a beeline toward me, but I'm already done. I open the damper, and the smoke flows up the chimney. It will get rid of it faster than if I just opened the door or the window. Chimneys are made this way, so the house won't burn down. The ancient and trusty-as-shit technology is clearly wasted here on this ridiculous creature.

"Why did you do that? You'd burn!" Her eyes dart around my torso, and I become too aware that I'm half-naked in a stranger's house.

"I wouldn't. The fire was out already," I explain but glance down at myself just in case. With the amount of body hairs I have, a few may have gotten scorched.

"But the surface must still be hot!" She's still yelling, and although it's like sandpaper against my brain, I'm grateful to find a drop of common sense in that head of hers.

"I didn't touch any of it. See?" I spread my arms wide. "I'm fine."

Her eyes rake over me, but I can't see her facial expression behind all that soot. Her eyes survey me one more time, narrowing as if not happy with what they see. She quickly averts them. I'm not prince charming, but I'm not *that* ugly to look at. Her obvious disgust causes acid to settle in my stomach. This is why I don't mess with rich girls anymore, the ones who can only paint their nails and aren't capable of anything else.

The sound of a fire engine roars outside. Just great. Thirty seconds later, three people in full gear burst in, stopping short when they notice me. One comes toward us while the other two hover by the entrance.

"Dang, boy, you're fast," Austin says after asserting the situation. He's the oldest at the station and is like a father figure to everyone he works with. We respect him tremendously, even when he's busting our asses. Especially then.

I grab my extinguisher and get ready to go back home. There's no way this chick would know what to do if a fire really did break out, so I'm her best bet for survival here. This thing goes with me wherever I go, within reach in case of emergency. It's a necessary precaution, or she'll burn down the whole neighborhood.

"What happened here?" Austin asks with a whistle, looking around.

"This idi... *lady*..." I gesture at the blonde, "decided to light the fireplace without opening the damper."

"Oh, ma'am." Austin coughs, trying to hide his laughter. "Are you alright?"

The woman shoots me a dirty look and turns toward Austin. Trying to maintain her pride, her posture is so proper and intense that she might as well be the queen of England. "I'm fine, thank you very much," she tells him, a thankful smile on her lips.

"Yeah, good thing Mark lives nearby," he says, a proud smile on his lips.

"You're here just as fast as he was, so I'm sure you'd have been able to save me anyway." She gives him a sweet, megawatt smile, and her pearly white teeth look ridiculous on her smokey face. In fact, her eyes and her teeth are the only places not covered in soot.

I briefly assess her attire: oversized—like four sizes over-sized—pajama pants and a long-sleeve shirt of an unknown color. Her long blonde hair falls in a tangled mess down her lower back, covered in soot. My sister wouldn't be caught dead looking like that, even at home alone on a Sunday night.

"Yeah, you got a point there. We need to check every-thing to ensure the fire didn't spread." He looks around, wonder in his eyes. "Damn, the old bat really kept all this beauty to herself? Hmm." He proceeds to check the building.

As he does, the two other guys come closer. They're new and from a different shift. I don't even remember their names yet.

"'Sup, man. Heard a lot about you," one says with a nod, turning toward Austin before leaving. "We'll be outside. Shout if you need us."

I look around and see that Mrs. Jenkins took all the furniture with her and left her houseplants. She hated those things with passion. Her kids thought she loved them, so they kept giving them to her as gifts. She had to keep them.

I bet she was more than giddy to dump them on this woman.

I turn my attention to her and catch her checking me out. My torso, to be precise. She's so focused, I look down to ensure I don't have a nasty burn or something I don't know about. No, everything looks just fine. I glance back at her, and when she notices my eyes on her, she sheepishly averts her eyes to her naked feet. It would be adorable if I wasn't annoyed as fuck by getting awakened after a double shift. Plus, her disgust a few minutes ago didn't exactly stroke my ego.

Austin comes back. "All good. Do you need an ambulance, ma'am?"

The blonde shakes her head. "No, *the gentleman* stopped the fire on time," she says, still looking at her feet. After a few moments, I hear a "thanks." It comes out of her mouth like it physically pains her.

Fuckin' spoiled princess. Even from here, I can tell the potato bag she's wearing costs more than any piece of clothing should.

"See you tomorrow, Mark," Austin says with a wave, getting ready to walk out the door.

"Nah, I'm off tomorrow. Have some errands to run, finally," I say, following him. Whatever happens here now is the blonde's problem, not mine. "You staying for another shift? It will be what? The third for you?"

"The fourth," he says. "Mary isn't speaking to me, so I'm in the doghouse. I figure if I spend this time at work and let her miss me, she may properly greet me later." He winks as he laughs at his own joke.

I chuckle and smack his shoulder. The escapades between him and his wife are legendary. They spend more time fighting than making up, but they love each other. I guess it's their foreplay. Regardless, I wouldn't know what a normal relationship would look like if it bit me in the ass.

Austin leaves the house and saunters over to the new guys outside. I throw one last look at the woman, making sure she's really all right. As annoying as the idiot has been, I still have some empathy for her. She stands in the middle of the room, looking around at the mess and biting her thumbnail. Her eyes seem lost, as if she's mentally somewhere I can't see, and she isn't moving.

"Are you sure you don't need an ambulance?" I ask her.

She blinks a few times, her eyes clearing. "Yeah, I'm okay. Thank you."

I nod and leave. My job for tonight is done.

Outside, the crew is getting ready to leave. They'll probably stay for a few more minutes just to be sure everything is all right.

I get home and place the extinguisher back where it belongs, making a mental note to replenish it. Ghost nervously moves around my feet, nearly knocking me down with his massive frame. "Easy, boy. We have a new neighbor. I have a feeling our quiet days are over."

He whines and presses his wet muzzle into my hand, his big brown eyes looking up at me.

I reek of smoke but don't have the energy to take a shower, so I go back to my bedroom. Before mindlessly falling into bed, I peek outside. My window is across from Mrs. Jenkins's window. Well, from her new tenant's. Her curtains are open, and the light is on. She's standing in the middle of the room, her face covered by her hands. I step closer to the window, trying to get a better look. Her shoulders are shaking. She's crying. Fuck. *Fuck!*

Not your problem. Not your problem.

Even if she's annoying as fuck, I'm a firefighter, and she

21

might be in shock. The sour taste in my mouth is impossible to ignore, and I'm about to go to her again when she turns, notices me peeping, and jumps to the window to close the curtains. What do I do now? Just as I'm about to turn back to my bed, an elegant hand, covered in grime, pops up between the curtains, middle finger raised. I chuckle. I guess that's my answer.

"Watch our new neighbor tonight, Ghost. Daddy was rough and kicked her door out," I say to him as my head hits the pillow.

He lets out a low bark and patters to the window overseeing her front porch. He'll let me know if someone comes around. Heaven knows I can't watch it tonight.

Chapter Three

ALICIA

I wake up groggy and puffy from crying. The first day of my new life didn't exactly go according to plan. To almost burn down the house on my first night... I couldn't even make that up for one of my books.

Speaking of my books, one positive is that I got some good inspiration from my next-door neighbor. He's very tall, a few good inches taller than me, and as I've mentioned, I'm not petite. His brown hair was in a messy, low man-bun, and he has abs I'd describe as washboard in any of my novels. And his arms? Huge. Real deal arm porn. I can't stop thinking about his chest either. He's hairy. Very hairy. I was never the one to like hairy guys, but this particular one pulls it off like a champ.

Perfect inspiration indeed—until he opened his mouth.

Oh, I saw the judgment in his eyes. For multiple reasons, I've become well acquainted with people's convictions over the years, so I recognize it when I see it.

And how much embarrassment can one person handle? A firetruck outside my new home on my first night. I groan and cover my face with a pillow, wishing I could erase the humiliation. If Mrs. Jenkins finds out, I'll be out on my ass faster than I can sneeze. So I need to make sure she won't. I have a very long day ahead of me.

I took a shower before I went to sleep to wash all the soot and grime off my body, but I need another one now. I still feel dirty, so I hop under the hot water and scrub my body, ridding it of the invisible dirt. The more I scour it, the more I remember another time I tried to scrub off filth. A different type of filth. Dirty, sweaty, wandering hands on my skin. I scrub faster. The hands slither up my arms, and I scrub them fiercely too, wanting nothing more than to purge my brain from the memories. I scrub my skin so vigorously, it bleeds. But I don't stop. I can't stop. The hands make their way down my back and push me down. I can't breathe. I'm suffocating. I claw at the hands—the door handle—and run out of the shower. Here, I can breathe again. I'm alone. I'm safe.

It's been nearly eight years. *Why can't I move past it? Why?* I smack the tiled wall. And again. And again.

When I'm done, and the panic is taken out on myself and the wall, I dry up and do my skincare routine. It's the constant in my life, keeping me grounded. It might seem superficial for some, but for me, it's the only thing that still makes me feel like a woman.

24

I might have joked about vibrators earlier, but I don't use them. I don't have a use for them. My libido's been dead ever since that night. My doctor says it will come back when the time's right, but I don't think it ever will. At least, it feels that way. It's had a lot of time to find its way back and still hasn't done so.

I'm broken, and I accept it.

After applying my seven-step morning routine to my face and body, I get dressed in my typical gray oversized sweatshirt and sweatpants and go to the kitchen to assess the damage.

Smoke is still everywhere, especially on the walls and ceiling next to the fireplace. The front door hangs on a hinge. One. It must have been moved by the wind at night. After my neighbor left after saving my bacon, the fire-fighters came back and tried to put screws back in there, but the threshold was destroyed. They did their best. The entrance was somewhat covered by the door, but not well, and it won't hold up for long. I need to call one of my brothers to come help me. The cold will be here before I know it, and I'd like to be able to shield myself from the Maine elements.

I cover my face with my hands and groan loudly. Man, I can hear it now. I'll never hear the end of "I told you so." Not until the day I die.

I start the coffee machine and get to work. Everyone in my family is a self-proclaimed proud coffee snob, so I can't do anything without a cup of good, sweet caffeine.

A few hours later, the front door bursts open, almost falling, nearly startling me to death.

A glass of tall, messy, and angry comes in without knocking. He's wearing his brown hair in a low bun, his beard neatly trimmed. A tight white T-shirt fits his impressive chest like a glove, and worn-out dark jeans cling to his narrow hips and muscular thighs. I wonder if he forgot his jacket. It sure is cold outside. It's mid-September, but it's uncommonly chilly out there—with the amount of muscle he has, he probably doesn't even know he's supposed to get cold.

His shoulders are broad, even wider than my small door, fit for a fairy—or a very old woman. He has to step in sideways to get in. I'm not kidding. It's the only way he fits. I always wrote those characters, but I've never seen one of them in real life. Well, maybe Alex fits the bill a little, but I've never seen him stepping through any doorway sideways. I gulp, freezing on my knees, my scrub brush forgotten on the floor.

And then it hits me like a ton of bricks. There's a big man in my space. A *very* big man in my space. I look around for an escape route. If he comes charging in, I'll run for the back door and outside to the front of the house, where other neighbors can see me. I'll be yelling all the way. I will not be quiet. Not this time.

I turn my attention back to him as he carefully watches me. Assessing me? Thinking about how easy I'd be to overpower?

I'm shaken from my thoughts as he lifts a box of tools in his hands to show me. "I'm gonna fix the door."

I let out a breath, gulping again but not with fear this time. Instead, with embarrassment. "You don't have to."

"I know," he says as he puts the tools on the floor. He checks the door out before standing upright and turning to leave. "You need a new lock."

"I wouldn't need it if you didn't break the door." I stand and follow him outside.

"I stopped the fire. A simple thank-you will suffice." He

comes to a halt on the stairs outside my home, turning toward me. Folding his bulging arms across his chest, he narrows his eyes.

"You could have knocked." I mimic him by crossing my arms, but it lacks the energy he has.

"I did, but you didn't answer. You were too busy shrieking like a banshee. It could have cost you your life." His large brow quirks up, challenging me to argue.

My mouth hangs open. "I was not!"

"Were too." He annoyingly clicks his tongue.

My chest swells, puffing up like an angry dragon about to burn a village. I never scream like a banshee, never. I'm calm and collected.

"Thank you for stopping the fire and saving my ass. Bye!" I say, running back inside and smacking the door shut behind me. Well, I try to smack it closed, but it doesn't work. Part of the frame is missing. I sigh. I'd be in enormous trouble if it was winter. But it's still fall, thank God.

Wait a minute. Bad people don't care if the weather's good or bad; they just come in and do bad stuff. I shiver at the thought. I was sleeping with an unlocked door the whole night. I never do that, ever. I must have really been in shock.

I continue my mission to scrub the house clean of soot, resuming in the kitchen when the front door opens again.

"You there?" an already familiar voice calls in. I groan and go to meet him.

"What are you doing here?" I stand in the living room, arms folded across my chest, just as he did before. Looks like it's a default pose of mine nowadays.

He's on the floor next to the door with his tools and a brand-new lock. "Come 'ere."

"Why?" I narrow my eyes.

"So you can take the lock from the box and make sure it's sealed and never been opened." He stretches his hand out, the clear plastic package containing the lock looking so small in his giant hands. I swallow the lump in my throat. And then another.

With no snarky remark—or any, for that matter—I walk to him on wobbly legs and carefully take the box from his hand. The factory seal isn't broken.

"Good?" he asks, and I nod silently. He takes the box from me, cuts it with a pocketknife, and passes the set of keys to me. I take it with another nod and murmur, "Thanks." I can't say it any louder. If I do, tears will burst from my burning eyes.

Do I give off a vibe that I'm miserable and scared? Why did he do that? There is no way he did it just to be benevolent, right? Nice guys don't exist.

I walk to the kitchen and start the coffee machine again. The good one, not the drip thing. I fix a mighty strong americano and debate whether to put sugar in it. He seems like a guy who doesn't take his coffee sweet, but looks can fool, so I decide to spice it up a little with just one spoonful and bring it to him. He's still fixing the door, but the missing pieces in the frame are back in place.

Silently, I pass the mug to him. He looks up at me, then at the mug and takes it with a nod. I wait for his reaction, scared he'll be disgusted. I'd be disappointed if he hated it. I put one perfect golden spoon of organic brown sugar in it. It's exactly how I take it, and nobody likes when somebody doesn't like our favorite things. He studies the cup for a moment and takes a careful sip. He pauses for a moment, and the sip grows into a big, healthy gulp. *Me likey.*

He nods silently and puts the half-empty mug on the floor next to him as he returns to work. I do the same. After about thirty minutes, I hear him clear his throat. "Lock the door behind me," he says, just loud enough for me to hear him but not loud enough to be considered a yell.

In the short time it takes me to walk to the living room from the kitchen to thank him, he's gone. A phantom of the opera. A ghost.

I check the lock, and to no surprise, it works perfectly. Tonight I can sleep peacefully, not worrying about strange people breaking in. I still can't believe I hadn't thought about that yesterday. I must have been exhausted; there's no other explanation. Even when I lived with my parents, I sometimes locked the door to my room. Absurd, but necessary for me regardless.

Hours fly by as I clean and clean and clean. By the time I'm done, it's long been dark outside, and I'm starving. I have a few slices of pizza left over from yesterday that I decide to warm up. It's September, and it's time for lit fires and cozy socks in Maine. I look outside and, for a second, I consider starting the fireplace. This time I know what to do to avoid disaster. But this idea quickly vanishes when I stretch my arms and feel a pinch of pain in my back, reminding me of how I've spent the whole day and why. No, thank you. I'll use a cozy throw and be good to go.

I usually don't like reheated pizza, but today it tastes like the nectar of gods, and I moan as I take my first bite. While I chew this delicious cheesy goodness, I think about my day. My first real, whole day of living alone. It went well, I'd say. Of course, it could have been better, but I've always dealt with problems on my own. Fudge, I didn't deal with them on my own this time, did I? I wish I did, but without my neighbor's help, I'd have had to call my brothers.

I jump when my phone rings. Somehow, they always

show up in some way the second I think of them. Ever since that night. I already know who it is without even checking the screen.

"Hey, Justin," I say as I hit 'accept' without even looking at the caller.

"How's my favorite sister doing?" I hear a smile in his voice.

"I'm your only sister. And I'm doing great," I answer as I stop chewing. I loathe open-mouthed chewers and try to extend the same courtesy to people around me.

"You're not scared to stay there by yourself, are you? Because I can come and stay with you for a couple of days." I hear the metallic rustle of keys, and I'm almost positive he's halfway out of the house to start the truck.

"No, please don't," I groan. "I'm fine, I promise. In fact, I'm very proud of you."

There's a pause as he stops walking. *"For what?"* He sounds confused.

"For waiting a whole day to call me." *Duh.*

I can hear Kayla chuckling, and Justin clears his throat. *"Yeah, well, that's me, the best brother."*

Kayla guffaws.

I can't help but chuckle. "She stopped you from pestering me, didn't she?"

"Maybe," he answers sheepishly.

"Thank you, Kayla!" I call louder so she can hear.

"No problem!" she shouts back.

"Are you sure you're okay?" he asks again. There's a hidden meaning behind his words.

I take a deep breath before offering a response. I want to make sure I believe it myself before I sell it to anyone else. "Yeah, I'm good, Jus. Really good."

"Okay." I hear him drop the keys. *"Promise you'll call me when you need me?"*

"Of course I will." I nod, even though I know he can't see me.

"Okay, good. Love you, little sister."

"Love you, big brother. Now go chill with your woman and stop worrying about me," I say and hang up the phone. Knowing him, he'd start looking for an excuse to stay over and guard me.

No can do—if he asked too many questions, I'd let the story about the fire slip at some point, and all hell would break loose. He'd be here in a minute, throwing all my stuff into his truck.

I throw the dishes in the sink, trying hard to overcome the urge to not wash them immediately. I'm so used to trying to have control anywhere I can. It's a loud shout-out —and a fuck you—to the night I lost control over my life. Even small things like washing dishes make me feel like I have a grip on my life and what's happening in it.

But the dirty plate keeps bothering me, looking at me from the sink with judgment on its perfectly dirty surface. I take a deep breath and decide to take a shower just so I can break this soul-draining eye contact. Letting control slip here and there might be another thing missing in my perfectly routine life.

Instead of a shower, I fill the bathtub with hot water and not one but two bath bombs. I'm spoiling myself rotten today.

In a house like this, I honestly expected an old-fashioned clawed tub, but in reality, it has an average tub that can barely contain my long frame. It works for me either way. A tub is a tub. I sink my tired body into the water and decide to spend a few minutes by myself, without scrolling through social media or reading a book. Just me and my thoughts. A scary place sometimes, if I'm honest.

I lean back and close my eyes, hoping to get a moment of peace. But instead, I get a mental visit from my neighbor. His broad chest pops into my mind and doesn't leave. I open my eyes and vigorously shake my head, but the image of his naked torso doesn't go away. I shake my head some more, but it's still there.

I groan in annoyance and bump my head on the back of the tub. *Why? Why are you in my head?* His wide, beautiful chest, covered in dark hair... I hate hairy men. I can't stand them. The characters in my books are always hairless with perfect, smooth chests, and yet this one in particular—this... yeti can't get out of my mind.

His arms are the size of thick, old trees. Probably even bigger than Alex's. When I was a teenager, of course I had a crush on my brother's best friend. It's a given, duh. A right of passage of sorts. Because of this, I've observed Alex's body many, many times throughout the years. Of course, I'd outgrown this stage by the time he left to serve, but still, in my sensitive mind, Alex was a hero. Plus, he's really huge. Like tank-size large. Always has been. So maybe it's why I'm comparing my new neighbor to him. Because I seriously think this guy's arms are bigger. And hairier. That's for sure. And surprisingly, I find it hot. His pectorals are so pronounced, and his dark pink nipples... *How on earth do I even remember the color of his nipples when my house was on fire? How did I even focus on them?* My fingers itch to touch them, to see if they're as smooth as they seem. Or maybe he has other smooth parts? Now I'm itching to know.

My thighs slap shut on their own accord, water splashing everywhere with the movement. Embarrassment creeps up my cheeks. A weird feeling between my legs makes me squirm, and I move around some more, trying to get rid of it. It's a feeling I lost so long ago, I don't even remember what it is.

Why, universe? Why now?

I groan and submerge myself into the water, attempting to keep myself there as long as possible, long enough for my lungs to start burning and my brain to become busy with other thoughts—anything other than imagining the hot man next door barreling right in here, asking if he needs to put out another fire. Yeah, I'm not sure I'll be able to escape those thoughts.

I rise above the surface and breathe the air in. My lungs do in fact burn as planned, but my brain is still hung up on my night visitor.

The tingling between my legs is still there but subsides a touch. It's so unfamiliar and long forgotten that I honestly don't know how to react to it. I don't even know why it's here now. My therapist said it would come back at the right time when my body is ready to respond to the *right someone*. It wouldn't respond to the yeti, right? Because the look he gave me was anything but sexy. I've seen that look around town, from people who don't know me and only see a version of me I let them see. Not this time though, no. This time I didn't even have the chance to open my mouth, and he already formed an opinion about me. And it was not a favorable one.

I groan again and get out of the bath—my me time is ruined anyway—and finish my evening routine. A weird noise coming from the pipes makes me pause for a second. Is that normal? It sounds like a wounded beast howling inside them, and an uncomfortable shiver runs down my still-wet back, causing goose bumps to rise all over my body.

Do I live here alone? Do I want to live here alone? Or anywhere, for that matter?

For the first time since the idea of moving out entered my brain, I'm unsure if it was the right choice. I mean, I'm not equipped to live alone per se, but I'm scared of anything with more than four legs—meaning if I see a spider, I'll get an aneurysm. I don't know how to unclog the toilet if it happens, and I don't do grocery shopping because there are too many people in those stores, rubbing against me in the aisles. On the other hand, I have horrible nightmares, and most nights I wake up screaming, covered in sticky sweat, so having no one giving me looks of pity in the morning is a huge bonus.

The howling stops after a few moments, but my elevated heartbeat remains. If it comes back, I'm calling Jake or Justin for a sleepover, hoping Jake is still in town. I wish I had a nearby girlfriend so we could do girly stuff together, but I don't. That's my own fault. My closest friend is Josie, who lives in New York. We FaceTime almost every single day, but it's not the same. It's not like I can fall asleep on a call with her; unlike me, she has a life.

I pull on an oversized white T-shirt and red plaid pants and walk to the kitchen. A nice warm cup of peppermint tea sounds relaxing, and it's exactly what I need. I take out my kettle, turn on the faucet, and shit hits the fan.

Well, not quite so literal, thank God, because that would be a disaster. But something breaks under the sink with a loud *pop*. I duck under to investigate, and when I open the doors, water starts spraying everywhere. Under the water pressure, my million-step skincare routine washes away from my face in a second. My T-shirt clings to my body for dear life, and my pants almost slip off; that's how powerful those angry pipes are.

"Fuck!" I yell, trying to get closer and see if I can close something in there or, at the very least, wrap a towel around the pipe. That should help, right? But the pressure is so intense, it keeps beating onto my face without letting me get an inch.

You dirty bastard, you're the howling beast who nearly made me shit myself?!

By the time I reach the offensive pipe, the kitchen is wholly drowned in icy water—it's about an inch and a half deep—and there is not a single dry patch left on my body. Turns out the pipe burst.

The water hose looks rusty. I try to collect all of the kitchen towels to wrap them around the pipe, but it doesn't work. At all.

"Fuck me!" I kick the cabinet with my foot and howl in pain. "Fuck you!" I yell as I smack the pipe with my fist, causing my knuckle to split. Just great. *Just keep it coming, universe, would you?* I dive inside the cabinet again, but the moment the cold water reaches my split skin, I jump back and yell. "Fuckity fuck!" As I fall on my ass. What in the ever-loving hell is happening right now? Who did I piss off in my previous life?

I can't contain it anymore. I just yell. I let all of my frustration out as loud as I can. "*A-a-a-a-a!*" as I remain seated in the pool of water on my kitchen floor while the pipe still showers me from under the sink.

Chapter Four

MARK

To say my morning sucks would be a colossal understatement. I'm beat from back-to-back shifts and not sleeping nearly enough after last night since I had to rescue my new neighbor, who is surely going to be a pain in my ass going forward. I can already tell.

I walk Ghost in the morning, make myself breakfast, and go to do some grocery shopping. Before I leave, I check the annoyance's door, just to be sure of what I need to buy. I'm well acquainted with the door after all of the issues Mrs. Jenkins had with it and don't need to see the hinges in order to buy new ones. Good thing I can do that from outside. It's too early to face the banshee again.

A couple of hours later, I fix her door as silently as I can, because if I open my mouth and say something to her, she'll say something back, and I'll likely strangle her. The woman has the insane ability to wake carnal urges in my body by being this ice-cold queen. I want to shake her, just to prove she has red blood running through her veins like the rest of us, even though she clearly thinks of herself as better than us lowly animals.

I leave quietly when I'm done, without saying a word. I have so much stuff to do, but I've wasted two hours driving to the store for parts for the door and then fixing it. I could be doing other things. It pisses me off and ruins my day, but a fucking hero-syndrome makes me put everything aside and run to a rescue, whether she want it or not.

* * *

Thankfully, later that evening, I relax a little. I'm home and relatively calm. Tomorrow I have another shift, and I'm still groggy from the days I've had.

I took a shower and am about to let Ghost outside before we go to bed. I'm walking to the fridge for a well-deserved beer in anticipation of a nice, relaxing dinner when a blood-chilling scream pierces the air. Ghost's ears go up and he whines. I run outside with him hot on my heels. Another piercing cry comes from the neighbor's house, and I don't hesitate when I rush to her door. It's locked. Figures.

I step back and kick the door open with one hard push of my boot. I'm so fucking glad I put boots on before walking Ghost. Kicking doors out while wearing slippers is an ungrateful job. The moment the door is off the hinges, Ghost is inside.

We run toward the sound coming from the kitchen. My

38

body tenses, ready to fight with whoever I'll find there. When we reach the kitchen, the cry intensifies.

My new neighbor is sitting on the floor, resting her elbows on her bent knees, her butt almost submerged in the water that completely covers the floor. The water is spraying from under the sink like a fucking fountain.

Ghost stops abruptly, and I nearly fall, stumbling over his body.

I drop to the floor next to her and ask, "Who's here?"

She's still yelling, so I shake her elbow lightly.

"Is anyone in the house besides you?"

She stops yelling, but her eyes are terror-stricken. Ghost nudges her cheek, and she moves her attention to him, finally blinking.

I take a deep breath before asking again, "Is anyone else in the house besides you?"

She shakes her head with a quiet "no."

"Are you hurt?"

She shakes her head again.

I don't know what the hell happened here, but in the ten seconds I've been in her house, I've gotten completely wet. "Stay here."

I hurry to the basement, shutting off the main valve. When I turn to go back up, I notice Ghost hasn't followed me downstairs. Hmm, that's unusual.

When I return to the kitchen, the scene greeting me nearly knocks me to my knees: my new neighbor hasn't changed her sitting position, but now her hands are resting on her soaked feet, her knees bent to her chest while she stares ahead, unblinking. My loyal dog sits behind her, resting his head on the woman's shoulder. His butt is in the water, and he hates cold water. The spoiled little shit always waits for me to warm it up before I clean his paws. His eyes are sad as he notices my approach.

Ghost got his name for a reason. We never see him coming; he's stealthy and mean. He knows how to hold a grudge and isn't friendly to anyone. He doesn't even like my sister, simply tolerating her presence, even though she's been bribing him with treats for years.

I got him from the K-9 unit in Boston. He was my friend's dog for a few months of training as a puppy until they deemed him unsuitable for the job. My gain. The friend couldn't have two dogs at the same time—his unit rules—so he had to find him a new home. I gladly accepted the pup since I'd been looking into shelters by then anyway.

Since then, Ghost has been my best friend, a part of my family, and my therapist. Sometimes, a very mean one. He doesn't bite, but he can give anyone a stink eye, sure to make them understand how little their worth is. It's precisely why I give my new neighbor and my dog a moment before I burst in. I've never seen him try to comfort anyone but me.

And it's fucking annoying.

"What happened here?" I ask, managing to calm my voice despite the adrenaline rushing through my body.

She finally moves her attention to me. Those big blue eyes are full of pain, sadness... and something else. Something that's been lingering there for a long time, but I just noticed it. Something I can't name yet. "The pipe burst," she says quietly.

"Why were you yelling?" I ask, calmer now.

Her voice is barely above a whisper. "I got tired."

"Tired?" I ask, annoyed. I'm back to being pissed off. What the fuck could she have gotten tired of to yell like someone was killing her? "Of what?"

"Of living like that." This time, I have to strain my ears

to hear. I'm not even sure I was meant to hear it. My annoyance evaporates. Ghost whines, nudging his wet nose into her neck. She shudders, blinking rapidly. Her stare becomes more focused and present. Only now she understands she has a huge German shepherd sitting behind her back, nuzzling his big head into her neck. "Of the pipe fighting me. That's what I got tired of."

"It fought with you?" I raise a brow.

"It did." She nods and turns toward Ghost. The bastard is eager for attention and hangs his tongue out the side of his mouth. She carefully strokes the fur behind his ear, whispering something meant only for him.

I'm jealous. I'm fucking jealous that she bewitched my dog, a mean bastard to everyone. But not her. It took him months to warm up to me after the betrayal of his first daddy.

"I turned the main pipe off. I'll check what the problem is." I dive under the sink. The pipe has given its last breath, and there's no way I can fix it without replacing the whole thing. "The hardware store is closed, obviously, and I don't have anything I can replace it with now. You can call tomorrow for someone to come and fix it or wait for the day after tomorrow. I'll be off shift and can do it. Your choice."

"I'll call someone," she answers quietly. "Thank you."

I nod in acknowledgment of her decision and whistle to Ghost. He whines but follows me. Thank fuck, or I'd be super pissed.

When I'm about to walk outside, I notice the door is toast. Damn it, how can I leave her alone, sleeping at night like this when a lot of weird shit has been happening in Little Hope recently? Last night I was too exhausted to think about it, but now, when my brain is functioning, I can't just close my eyes to it. I sigh and walk back. She's still on the floor in cold water.

"Do you have anywhere to stay tonight? I thought someone was here killing you or something..." I notice her slight flinch, but I keep going. "So I kicked the door to get inside."

Her eyes go round, but she's quiet.

"So yeah, no door," I say, feeling a little guilty. "Do you have anywhere to go tonight?"

"Sure," she mumbles as the corners of her lips drag down. She's the picture of pure sorrow.

Fuck my life. "You can stay with me."

Her eyes widen even more if that's possible, and I'm about to drown myself in those deep blue oceans like a fool, led by his dick.

"I'm okay." She wipes her nose and finally rises from the floor.

"It's almost midnight," I say after glancing at the clock on the wall. "Call them now so you can go there."

"Sure, I will," she says, still sitting without making any movements. She must sense me waiting because she adds, "When you leave."

I look up, calling for patience. I take several level breaths. "You won't be calling anyone, will you?" I ask when I'm able to speak calmly.

She shakes her head, not meeting my eyes.

"Why?"

Her voice is so small. "I can't because I'll never hear the end of 'I told you so.'"

Yeah, I knew this was going to happen. With a dreadful feeling in the pit of my stomach, I make her an offer. "My house is almost the same layout as this one, and I have a big

42

couch. You can sleep there, and Ghost will keep you company."

There's hesitation written all over her face. It's clear as day. She's confused. Hell, even I'm confused about why I offered, but it's too late to back out now.

"I don't want to impose," she tells me, meeting my gaze. Her voice drips with concern and melancholy. But she shouldn't feel concerned. I've been so used to people sleeping at my place growing up, and later sharing a space with other firefighters, that sometimes I feel weird when no one is around—hence getting a dog.

"You won't. In fact, you'll be doing me a favor. I'll be up at the ass crack of dawn for my shift, and you could do me a favor by walking Ghost in the morning." I glance at the dog, his tail wagging vigorously, too excited at the prospect. I send him a look. *Traitor*. He just hangs his tongue out, mocking me.

"He has a cool name." Her voice sounds shy, which is weird, considering her being a spoiled princess and all. She had to be; otherwise, she wouldn't have scored this house. Mrs. Jenkins, the lady from the local elites, is notorious for being picky, and someone must have pulled a few strings to get her this place. "And he's so cute," she says, even shier. Where did her confident voice go from last night, talking like she owned the world? She sounds like a normal person today. She looks at Ghost and cracks a smile, the very first one I've seen on her face. My breath hitches. It's fucking breathtaking.

Suddenly, I notice other things too, like the way her soaked white shirt clings to her body, completely see-through. And her tits are gorgeous—big and supple. My fingers itch to touch them. She's got curves on her under those baggy clothes. In all the right places. Just how I like them. I can see her narrow waist under her generous chest. Her pants hang low, clinging to her for dear life, and my eyes travel long past her belly button. All through her shirt.

My dick stirs, and at that moment, I know it was a terrible idea to invite her over. I turn around, subtly pretending that I don't have a raging hard-on. "Get your stuff and come over." I move to leave, but her voice calls out from behind me, stronger this time.

"Can Ghost stay with me while I get ready?" She rushes as if embarrassed to ask. And she should be. It's my fucking dog. I turn around to remind her of it when I see her face. Her request isn't one of a spoiled brat but necessity. She's probably scared to stay at some dude's house or even stay here, an evening on her own with no lock.

Even in Little Hope.

I keep forgetting I'm a large man with different fears. I swallow my sharp remark and nod.

"Stay here," I command Ghost, and I walk away.

I can't pinpoint why exactly, but her guarded aura nudges me inside, and I don't like it.

Chapter Five

ALICIA

I watch him leave my destroyed kitchen. Did I just agree to spend a night at the house of a guy whose name I don't even know? I guess I did. That's not just out of character; it's out of my mental capacity, yet here we are.

I've never spent a night with anyone but one of my family members under the same roof, and here I am about to walk into my neighbor's house. No one will know where I am. Should I call one of my brothers and admit defeat? They'll haul me away from here before I even end the call.

Do I want to stay on my own so badly though? I look around. The kitchen is a catastrophe. I'm sitting on my ass on the floor covered in inches of water. Some water seeped into the living room, but most of it stayed in the kitchen. I'm so grateful to whoever built this house with such a tall threshold. I nearly kissed the floor this morning when I stumbled over it, sleepy and groggy from the night I had, cursing it with all the words I know, but now, I'm thrilled it's here.

Ghost whines, drawing my attention to his dancing from paw to paw. He clearly isn't enjoying the cold water.

"Yeah, it sucks." I stretch my arm to pet him, and he leans into my touch. His fur is so thick and soft. Surprisingly so. I expected him to be... prickly, maybe? I don't know. I've never had a dog. Mom is a cat person, so we always had those fluffy egoistic bastards at home. They absolutely hated me and used to pee in my shoes. I don't have a good track record with pets.

Ghost is something else entirely though. His eyes, currently staring into mine, are intelligent—almost on a human level or even brighter (yep, you got that right). He feels my pain, the one I've been burying all along. I've heard that dogs are empaths, and now I'm sure they are. No creature that has these compassionate eyes can stick to a bad person. And to be honest, I don't know why, but the grouchy man doesn't set off any of my triggers. In fact, it's the opposite. I'm calm when he's around.

Yes, I yelled when I saw him in my kitchen. Who wouldn't? A huge man, knocking down the front door and barreling in? Yeah, that's part of my night horrors. Until I realized it was him. Well, I didn't *see* him until he walked into the kitchen; at that moment, all I saw was a repeat of my nightmares. Until he was beside me with his dog nudging my cheek with his nose. Only then did I comprehend who was in front of me: a person I met no more than twenty-four hours ago and who already saved me. Twice.

Plus, he's a firefighter. The people from yesterday clearly knew him and worked with him, it seems. *So I should be safe, right?*

Ghost nudges my neck with his muzzle, reminding me of our current situation.

"Yes, boy. Let's go."

He jumps up and sprints to the living room, far from the water, not waiting for me. Shaking his enormous paws as soon as he steps on the dry surface, he shoots me a worried look and proceeds to dry himself.

Me though... It takes me a while to lift my wet, battered body from the floor. I'm soaked. My hair is a disaster. My clothes cling to my body like a sleazy second skin.

Wait a minute! I look down and groan. My nipples are on full display. And the hot man had seen all this mess, everything I've tried to hide for years. Everything I never planned to share. *Why, universe? Why?*

I slowly walk toward the shower. I'm cold to the bone, and even though my skin looks wrinkly, like I'm two hundred years old from marinating in the water for so long, I still need a shower. And I need to warm myself up ASAP before I catch pneumonia.

I strip and get inside...

And no water comes from the showerhead. I groan as the cold sends painful shivers down my body. I forgot Mark shut off the main valve, and so there will be no hot water—or any water—for me in the foreseeable future. So I pull one of the towels from the hook by the tub, wrap myself in it, and enter the nothingness of my mind. I go there often since that night. Sometimes, my mind enters a stage where it can't take anymore and just erases everything and thinks of nothing.

I don't know how long I've been in here, but a loud

barking brings me back. I blink rapidly, trying to clear the fog and look at the dog. He stops barking and watches me with a slight tilt of his head.

"You're a good boy, aren't you?" I smile at Ghost, and I swear he smiles back. "Also, you're a bit of a pervert."

I step out of the shower and dry myself with a big, fluffy towel. Then I dry Ghost as much as I can with the same towel. He deserves his own, but I don't have another available at the moment. The bathroom is a decent size, but there is almost zero storage here, so I put all my towels in the dresser in the bedroom.

I throw a sad look in the direction of the kitchen. I don't even want to think about how much I'll have to pay to fix this water damage.

I sigh before walking to the bedroom. I climb on the bed and put on another pair of pants and a T-shirt, both extra big of course. Folding the pants up at the bottom just in case, I climb out of bed and motion for Ghost to follow me. I grab a few towels on the way and a pair of fuzzy slippers because it's cold outside. I'm not psycho enough to walk barefoot, even in this state.

When I pass the kitchen, I throw the towels on the floor so more water won't slip through. I stop for a moment, contemplating if I should just get rid of the water in the kitchen now or wait till later. It won't go anywhere. I'm about to drop my slippers and get to work when I feel exhaustion eating my muscles and bones. My knees crack like I'm ninety-nine, and I give up on the idea of doing anything but sleeping tonight.

We slowly walk toward my neighbor's house. Ghost's letting me know he's here with me by pressing his big, warm body to my leg. I drop my hand and touch his fur. He's still wet, but at least water isn't dripping from him anymore.

As I slowly move my feet, I think about what the hell I am doing here. Why did I agree to go to a stranger's house? What if I have a nightmare? What if he's like *them*?

I shake my head because no, he is not.

Despite my attempt at relaxing, I still stop. I look back at my house. Maybe I'm safer in there, even with a busted door.

A fluffy body moves behind my legs, pushing me forward, and I laugh. Squatting to the dog's level, I say to him, "Can you read my mind, good boy?"

He blinks at me with his beautiful, intelligent eyes.

"Do you think I'll be alright?"

He sticks his tongue out and gives me a long, slobbery doggy kiss on my cheek, making me giggle. The old Alicia would absolutely hate it. She was so squeamish. But I'm not her anymore. This moment with him is something special. I cherish every single interaction I have in my life now. They don't come often because I never have the guts to be around people. I guess dogs are my buddies now.

I continue my walk at a snail's pace to the neighbor's house. I guess I should call him by his name. *Mark.* That's what the other firefighter called him. Such a short yet strong name. I like it.

When we finally make it to the house, the door is slightly ajar, and Ghost runs inside. I slowly step over the threshold, expecting a bachelor's den, like my brother used to have before Kayla moved in: beer cans, dirty clothes, dishes everywhere. But something different greets me.

The house is simple but beautiful. He was right; it's got the same layout as my house. The only difference is that it mirrors mine. It has the same ancient fireplace, but his looks better. More polished. The kitchen has a rectangular marble island. The backsplash is a work of art, like the most difficult mosaic of abstract figures, yet the simplest one. The cabinets are wood. The molding around the house is spectacular, so many tiny details merged into one gorgeous pattern. An oversized, worn-out leather couch sits in the middle of the living room, and a ginormous flat-screen TV hangs on the wall in front of it.

I gasp as I look around.

"It's so beautiful," I whisper to myself.

"Thank you." A low voice comes from behind me, and I jump.

Mark steps back, throwing his hands up in front of him. "Sorry. Didn't mean to scare you."

"No, it's fine. Sorry," I answer. When will I stop jumping when a man talks to me? "I didn't expect your house to look so..." I can't find the right word.

"Clean?" He raises a brow.

"Perfect." That's the word. His house is what I picture when someone says *home*.

His pupils dilate from the unexpected compliment, and his cheeks turn pink beneath his beard. We both feel super uncomfortable with the deep but short conversation, so we look around.

"I'm Alicia, by the way." I give a small wave with my hand.

"Hi, Alicia." He swallows nervously and says, "I'm Mark."

"I know," I admit with a smile.

"How so?" His eyes narrow, but there's no malice.

"The other night, the firefighter called you that." I wave behind me like the other night is right there.

"Oh. Austin." He nods in understanding.

"Is he your friend?" I don't know why I'm asking, but I'm curious to know tiny bits about him.

"Yeah, he's a good guy. Set to be the next chief. A well-deserved promotion." He nods and steps back when Ghost bumps into his legs, looking for daddy's attention.

"Cool." I don't know what else to say. It's more than I've spoken to anyone besides my family and Josie. My social skills are nonexistent at this point, and I forget how people usually do small talk.

He feels awkward too; I can tell. Maybe he's reconsidering his offer.

"Look, I can just go home. It's fine."

"No." He cuts me off and pauses before adding more gently, "No, stay. It's fine. You can take my bedroom. I just changed the sheets." He points at the bedroom door. I know because mine is made the same way.

"No way," I answer, carefully eyeing him. This close, he looks even more massive than he was entering my door sideways. "I'll sleep on the couch." *Because the couch is closer to the door.*

"Take the bed." He pinches the bridge of his nose, looking tired. "We can spend all night arguing, or you can go to bed, and I can sleep here." From his body language and the true exhaustion written on his face, I can tell he's being a knight by offering me his bed, not a creep.

"Alright. Thank you." I contemplate saying something else, anything to dissolve this awkwardness, but nothing comes to mind. "So it's in there?" I nod toward the bedroom door.

"Yeah." He lets out a loud yawn. "I'm wiped. If you can let Ghost out to the backyard tomorrow and let him back in, that would be great."

"Of course," I promise, but he's already headed toward the couch. He falls on it, folding his arms under the pillow and turning away.

Well, I guess this is it. I search for a switch and find it in the same place as mine, by the kitchen. I turn it off and walk to the bedroom, curious to see what will greet me there.

I can't help but gasp when I step into the room. Where did he find furniture like this? It's amazing! A huge king bed takes up almost the whole room, which is tiny to begin with. The headboard is made of dark oak and has the most incredible and detailed artwork. I walk closer, wanting to see what it is. *Are those Celtic symbols engraved into the dark wood?* It's the most beautiful bed I've ever seen, and I'm actually happy he didn't let me argue. Even if I felt bad—still do— about taking his bed when he clearly isn't very comfortable on the couch, it is a little too small for him. I'm glad I got to see this. There's no other possible scenario where I can witness his bedroom.

No. Other. Scenario.

I will not be seeing anyone else's bedroom besides mine, and I'm okay with it.

I kneel on the bed and touch the carvings, tracing the symbols with my finger. Its smooth, lacquered surface speaks to my skin. It's gentle and sexy and calm and passionate. I feel like I'm reliving the days the carver had. Closing my eyes, I feel how their callused fingers moved along the edges, smoothing it with every stroke. I'm overcome with the urgency to sniff it, so I bring my nose to the wood and breathe in.

The calmness of a forest with a hint of lightly burned chemicals envelopes me in a hug. That combination shouldn't be so wonderful, but it is.

I lean against the headboard and look around. Two nightstands with the same Celtic carvings as the bed adorn each side. A tall, skinny eight-drawer dresser sits in the corner. All of them are clearly pieces of the same set, made by a person with golden hands.

Suddenly I feel a weight on the bed, and I jump. Ghost's whine anchors me back to the present. He settles next to me on top of the covers.

"What are you doing? Are you even allowed up here?" I rub his ears as he crawls closer. "You look too guilty, so I'll go with no."

He hides his nose under the comforter and wiggles his big tail while looking up at me with the biggest, most adorable eyes. I never really knew what people meant by puppy-dog eyes. Now I do.

"Fine. Stay tonight." I settle into the fluffy, comfy pillows and warn him, "Don't make me stink like wet dog tomorrow."

He lets out a cute doggy fart and falls asleep.

Not me though. I lie awake with my hand in Ghost's fur, looking at the shadows dancing on the ceiling. I don't know what to make of it—what to make of this situation and of my weird trust in this guy. Is it because he's a firefighter and supposed to help me? Maybe.

I don't feel panic with a stranger sleeping in the next room. I'm not terrified that I haven't locked my door, and more than that, I haven't even checked if there's a lock. Probably for the first time in years.

Lying here in a stranger's bed and looking into the darkness makes me think that despite recent events, I might have made the right choice by trying to move on.

Chapter Six

ALICIA

I wake in a cocoon of warmth, fluff, and fur, a woodsy scent intruding my nostrils. Not that I minded. I take a deep breath, settling into the fur with a content sigh.

Wait. Fur?

"Ghost!" I cry, my eyes shooting open as I move the heavy head from my chest. He lets out a tired, whiny yap. He's whiny for a dog of his size. I look down, observing his drool all over my shirt, forming a huge wet spot. "Ew, disgusting." I try to wipe it clean with my hands, but of course, it's useless. "Why is your drool everywhere?" I eye him suspiciously.

He stops complaining and gives me a stink eye. "Oh,

c'mon!" I glare back as I stretch to grab my phone from the nightstand.

My phone that isn't there. I never took it with me.

I freeze. I never forget my phone. Ever.

I must have been in so much shock yesterday, I didn't even think about it. It's weird because every night, when I wake in a pool of sweat, I grab my phone and scroll through social media to distract myself.

Wait a minute—

I didn't wake up covered in sweat this morning. I woke up well rested and dry. Well, besides the giant wet spot from the big furry baby next to me.

I look at him with a sigh. He glances at me for a second, his head tilted slightly, like he knows what's going through my brain. We connect just a moment before he bends over to lick his jewels. He does it a lot, so I remind myself never to let him give me a sloppy kiss ever again.

What time is it? I look around and see a clock on the dresser. It's vintage and well loved, if the worn-out metal is any indication, matching the rustic, handmade furniture adorning the room. It shows twenty minutes past nine.

What? I've never been able to sleep this late. Night-mares keep me up. Justin and I are similar in that way. He developed insomnia too, after that night. Only, he can't fall asleep, while I wake up after a couple of hours, not having nearly enough rest my body needs.

He thinks I don't know, but I do. Mom does too. She's been super worried, but he seems better now. Since he's been dating Kayla, the ever-present dark circles around his eyes have all but disappeared, and the corners of his lips don't point downward anymore. Before her, we could always tell no matter how much he tried to hide his unhappiness, even when he was smiling. But the sadness isn't there anymore.

Ghost must have sensed the shift in my mood. He crawls closer and licks my hands. Just like that, I forget I swore to never let him just a few seconds ago.

"Aren't you a good boy?" I ask him, my voice unrecognizably high-pitched, as if I'm speaking to a baby. I play with his ears, paying special attention to scratching behind them. It seems to be his favorite spot. He lets out a whine and looks at the door. "Ah, nature's calling."

After climbing out of bed, I walk to the door and open it. The moment I do, he sprints into the house, and I'm forced to follow him. He stops at the kitchen door, the one leading to the backyard, and scratches at it, so I let him out. While he's doing his doggy business, I curiously look around.

The place is pristine, a far cry from my slob brother. Before Kayla, it was dangerous to step foot inside his place without risking stitches or breaking a limb while trying to navigate everything strewn about. It was that bad. His place is really the only bachelor's den I've seen to compare Mark's to.

Kayla has been like a magic fairy who cleans his place and makes it livable. I've been to her trailer, now parked behind Justin's place since she's moved in with him (don't ask me what they're using her trailer for now—I don't want to know), and it looks so cozy and homey. She seems to know how to make everything look nice and welcoming. Unfortunately, I sure as hell don't possess such a gift.

I think of the state I left my home in last night and sigh. I destroy everything. Time after time.

Today I need to call all the contractors I can find, beg them to help me, and beg them not to tell Mrs. Jenkins or my brothers. I might have to call someone from Springfield and cross my fingers that they don't know anyone here.

I'm awakened from my thoughts when Ghost paws the door from outside, and I let him in. He runs to his plate and digs into the food Mark must have left before he went to work.

I watch him happily eat, looking over Mark's house once more, and yawn. I need coffee... but not here. Mark's kitchen is so pristine, I don't want to ruin anything. And I'm sure I will if I touch something. The last two days haven't exactly proven otherwise. Besides being an intruder—and I am an intruder—I can't bring myself to overstay my welcome by using his kitchen for my own needs with my kitchen right next door.

A ruined kitchen. A submerged kitchen. Oh, man. I groan and rack my brain, trying to remember if I have bottled water back home. Hoping I do, I head for the door.

"Okay, Ghost, I'm leaving. See ya." I glance back at him, already at the door. Big mistake. A big fat mistake. Those pitiful puppy eyes peer back at me. They have the power to shred anyone's armor into smithereens with just one look, and I feel my heart filling with astronomical guilt.

"Oh, c'mon, don't do that to me."

The corners of his eyes droop as he licks his lips and lies on the floor, placing his big head on his crisscrossed paws and boring his sad eyes into mine. A picture of misery and desperation.

I groan. "That's so not fair."

He lets out a tiny whine, and my heart officially breaks.

"Fine, you can come with me."

His ears instantly perk as he jumps up.

I let out a soft chuckle, shaking my head. "You're a good

actor. I see what you did in there." I direct a pointed finger at him, mentally reprimanding myself for being so sapless.

I sit at the breakfast table, waiting for his majesty to finish his food, and continue to ogle my surroundings. There's so much art. So many beautiful wood carvings. The molding on the cabinets and along the walls is superb. It's detailed and pristine, like the bed. The table I'm sitting at is perfect too. It's so smooth, and yet it's clearly made by hand. So much love's poured into the carving under the lacquer that I lean in to look closer.

It must have cost a fortune, this level of handiwork. It's amazing. I need to ask Mark where he got all of this because I want a chair from the same place. I've always dreamed of a wooden rocking chair, an old-fashioned one from a child-hood fairytale. One I can curl up on, with a book and a cozy blanket during long Maine winter nights. My room at my parents' place was too small, and my mom was a bit of a control freak about what types of furniture came into the house. I didn't want to interfere with her design.

Well, Jake was still there too. But Jake is a guy; I'm sure he'd be happy to live in their basement till he's forty. I wanted my own kitchen and my own yard. My own dishes and my own mistakes. The only thing I've gotten from that list so far is the latter.

Ghost nudges my hand, letting me know he's finished and it's time to go.

"Are you sure you want to come with me? It's wet every-where over there." I give him one last chance to save himself, but he runs toward the door, wagging his fluffy tail. I shrug and follow him. "Alrighty. Suit yourself."

I check the lock to make sure it can close if I click it before exiting. I make sure to do so, understanding that Ghost is staying with me until his dad is back. I don't like dogs. I've never had them, and here I am, a babysitter to this enormous-ass monster of a dog with intelligent eyes and a slight ball-licking habit he should kick. Josie won't believe me.

I silently remind myself to call her. She's been bombarding me with messages about my move since the moment I'd made the decision. With everything going on, I've been only giving her halfhearted responses. She doesn't deserve that.

When I open the door to my house, the humid air hits me like a wall, and I almost fall back. *Probably should have cleaned up yesterday,* I think with a wince. Ghost trots past me to the living room and jumps on the couch, making brief eye contact with me before licking his jewels again. I roll my eyes. Typical male.

The kitchen is in the same state of disarray as I left it. There's about one inch of water covering the floor. For what feels like the tenth time, I find myself expressing immense gratitude to the engineers of this beautiful little home for making the thresholds as high as they are.

I change into shorts and a tank top and bring out more towels to mop the water. But before I can, I need to figure out who will help fix this mess to make the place livable again.

I fetch my phone from my room, wincing when I see a string of unanswered messages from Josie, and dial Kayla.

"Hey, Alicia!" Her voice cheerfully greets me after two rings.

"Hey, Kay. I was wondering if you could help me." I chuckle sheepishly.

"Sure. What's up?"

"Before I ask, can you promise it will stay between you and me? Justin can't know. Please?"

There's a heavy pause on the other end. *"Alright. Shoot."*

I sigh. "Do you know of a plumber who can help me with something on short notice?"

Another pause. *"A plumber? You just moved in. What happened?"*

"A small hiccup with the sink." I'm not technically lying. The break is one inch in depth.

"If it's small, Justin or Jake can fix it."

"I can't ask them. You know why."

She lets out a loud exhale. *"I know. Alright, let me see if I can find someone. I'll call you later once I know something."*

"And a contractor too."

"Alicia..." Her voice starts to remind me of my third-grade teacher, who caught me throwing balls of paper at the boy I had a crush on. *"What's happening?"*

"Kayla, please, just let me know if you know someone." I lower myself to pleading. "Please."

I can hear her chewing her lip. *"Alright. I'll call you."*

"Thank you! You are the best sister-in-law I've ever had!"

"I'm your only sister-in-law."

"Ha!" I cry out. "I knew it! You set a date finally!"

"There's nothing to know yet. Bye!" She hangs up with a chuckle. I think Justin is running out of patience. Kayla's been wearing that ring on her finger for... what, a year now? And still, she hasn't set a date. I think he may just handcuff her to his wrist and drag her ass to elope soon.

I understand though. They'd been stuck in that wheel of hate for so long, it was hard to get out. They did, thank God. But it was more complicated for Kayla after years of torment.

My next task to tackle is Josie. I have a dozen missed FaceTime calls from her and about two dozen messages. I sigh as I click call.

"Bitch, you'd better be in a sex coma because that's the only excuse I'll accept right now!" she yells. Her face fills my phone screen, her eyes bright, makeup perfect as always. She's walking, her shiny black hair in perfect sixties waves bouncing with each step. I touch my hair, becoming all too aware of its current ratty state.

"I'm sorry, Josie." I wince. "I ran into some trouble."

"What sort of trouble stops you from picking up your damn phone to shoot me a short message? I thought you could have died! I was about to call a SWAT team on you!" She shakes her head.

"Well, glad you asked." I point my phone camera to show her the disaster in my kitchen.

"Oh, shit." She whistles.

"Shit, indeed. Now you see?"

"I see it, but I still don't see why you couldn't pick up your phone." She sat down, scratching her cheek with her perfectly manicured middle finger.

I laugh and flip the camera back around. "Because I left my phone at home."

Her eyes, previously looking straight ahead, snap toward me, closely resembling the owl I saw in my backyard the other night. *"And you were—"* She clears her throat before continuing. *"Where were you?"*

"At my neighbor's house," I answer proudly.

"As in, for the night? The entire night?" Her eyes somehow widen even more.

"Yep," I reply, popping the *p*.

"What?" She jumps from her chair with a shriek.

"What the fuck?" someone says in the background.

62

She turns her attention to them and says, *"Oh, you shut it, party pooper,"* and then back to me. *"Like you spent the whole night at her house?"*

I pause for dramatic effect, knowing she's about to lose her shit. "His house," I tell her, a smile playing on my lips.

"What?" she cries even louder, followed by someone's voice in the background.

"Psycho."

But she ignores him. I stunned her into silence, an impossible task. *"You spent the night at a dude's house?"* she nearly shrieks.

"I did."

Her eyes turn misty. *"I'm so damn proud of you, girl. So proud."* She dabs the corner of her eyes with a white napkin she produced out of nowhere and sniffles.

"We didn't do anything," I assure her, sighing.

"Bummer." She scrunches her nose. *"But it doesn't make me any less proud."* The corner of her lips turns upward in a knowing smile.

She knows about my situation. Well, she knows what happened to me, but she doesn't know the chain of events that took place for it to happen. No one does. But she's aware of my nightmares and my fears. In fact, she's one of the only people who actually knows about them.

We met in an online book club five years ago and seemed to instantly click. At the time, everything was still so fresh. My nightmares came often, and I was having a hard time accepting them. It turned out she was also going through a rough patch.

Josie was born in a small town in Arkansas. It's the kind of town where everyone conformed to certain beliefs, and no one was allowed to show any type of original thought. They couldn't contain her creative nature. She has too much personality for the small town to handle. Because of this, the locals weren't exactly kind to her, always treating her with prejudice simply for stepping out of the stereotype they had written in stone as law. Colorful clothes, crazy makeup, and big hair—she always had a distinct style.

I've always been jealous of how she's embraced her uniqueness with unfettered confidence. She was my opposite, and opposites attract.

Since moving to New York City, she's surrounded herself with people who love the same things and have the same free spirit. She's finally been able to be *herself.*

We met—online via chat, as most people seem to do nowadays—the first year there, and we've been inseparable ever since.

"So, who's the stud?" Her brow lifts as she eyes me.

My eyes narrow. "How do you know he's a stud?"

"Please, I've been to Maine." She rolls her eyes. *"Everyone there is a stud. All flannel-clad hairy men with big muscles from chopping wood all day to keep their houses warm. They all definitely know how to use their giant, sexy hands."* She closes her eyes, pure bliss flittering across her face as she enjoys the image.

I can feel my eyes start to bug out of my eye sockets. She's not wrong. Mark is both hairy and sexy. A warm shiver tingles at my thighs.

"Well, yeah, he's super attractive." My cheeks heat.

"Book boyfriend attractive?" she asks, waggling her brows.

I sigh dreamily. "Yeah," I confess.

"Ahh!" she squeaks. There's a mumble in the background, and Josie turns to flip them off before returning her attention back to me. *"Speaking of Maine; I have a big job in Portland in a few months and was thinking maybe it's time*

we meet up." She glances to the side, looking shy all of a sudden. I've never seen Josie shy, ever.

"Portland? As in Portland, Maine?" I feel a nervous pinch in my chest.

"Well, yeah. A big-shot developer I've worked with in New York just bought an old house there and is planning to completely remodel it. I'll be spending a few months gutting the place, and I was wondering if maybe we could meet up for a coffee or something." She pushes a lock of hair behind her ear. I become all too aware of how her cheeks have pinkened.

Josie is a popular interior designer whose calendar is booked for the next two years. It must be someone close to her if she suddenly made room for them, unless she's known and didn't say anything to me.

"Do you think it's weird?" She bites the inside of her cheek, looking unsure.

"Are you insane?" I roll my eyes. "It's about time. I want to meet you in person before you're an age you'll need to wear diapers. Again."

Josie snorts. *"I was at Times Square when the ball dropped last year. Let's not talk about diapers."*

"Fair enough." I giggle.

"Alright then. I gotta run now, but I'll—" A loud bark interrupts us, and Josie whips around to face me again. *"What the ever-loving fuck was that?"*

I flip the camera again. "That's Ghost, my new friend."

"Did you get a dog and not tell me?" She rears back, sounding offended.

"I'd never do that to you!" I bring my hand to my heart, making her chuckle. "It's Mark's dog."

"The hot neighbor?" She rolls her lip inward, trying to suppress whatever's clearly on her mind.

"Yeah, that's him." I nod, walking over to Ghost. He lies on the couch with his posture straight, front paws hanging off the front.

"So, the guy's a dog dad. Does he wear flannels?"

I scour my memory but can't remember if he has. "Actually, so far, I've only seen him in pants." Then I remember that he fixed my door. While wearing more clothes. But it's too late to say anything because the Josie-train is gaining speed.

Her mouth hangs open, shocked. *"You go, girl,"* she laughs. A loud *thud* behind her captures her attention. *"I gotta go now, or they'll throw me out of this gallery. Everyone seems to have a stick up their ass."* She rolls her eyes. *"Give that pretty boy a belly rub from Auntie Josie. Talk to you soon. And bitch, don't disappear on me like that again!"* She points a finger at me before she disconnects.

I make do on my promise and give Ghost a belly rub before turning to the kitchen with a sigh. What a disaster.

It takes me a couple of hours to remove the water from the floor. By the time I'm done, I'm sweaty and stinky. The floorboards are raised, so they'll need to be replaced. It certainly wasn't on my list of things to spend money on, so I'll have to dig into my savings. I was hoping to use them to put a down payment on a house. I silently pray I'll still have enough.

My phone rings. *Kayla.* I pick it up, praying for good news.

"Sorry, Alicia, we have two plumbers, and they're both in Copeland, working on houses that recently had a fire. They say they'll be there for a while. I think they're trying to fix the place next to it too, since it was damaged or something like that. I'm not sure. How urgent is your problem?"

"Not that urgent," I tell her, trying to sound optimistic. Inside, I'm deflating like a spent penis.

"You sure? Maybe Justin can come and take a look?"

"No!" I say way too fast and too loud. I sigh. "No," I say calmer, "I'll wait until they're done. It's totally fine."

"Alright. I know Justin wanted to visit you tonight. I can tag along too."

A feeling of pure horror spreads through my chest. "Nah, I'm still unpacking," I lie. "Let me make it look pretty first, and I'll have a housewarming party."

There's a pregnant pause on the other end of the phone. Kayla isn't an idiot. She knows I'm hiding something, but she also understands the desire to be left alone. *"Alright, there's a new movie I've been dying to see; I think I'll make him go tonight."*

"Yeah, you should do that." I sigh in relief. "Thank you."

"No problem. Call if you need me, alright?"

"Will do. Thank you, Kay."

I think she's unofficially adopted me as a big sister. Even though we're about the same age, Kayla is far more mature, considering she's been living on her own forever. Plus, I don't know what I'd do if I didn't have her to avert Justin's attention from me here and there. My big brother is super overbearing.

I look behind me to the family room, seeing Ghost curled up. He senses my gaze, picks his head up, and lets out a lazy yawn. I walk to him, dropping down beside him as I let out my own yawn. He instantly places his head on my lap, and my hands dig into his fur of their own accord. I think rubbing his ears is comfort for me more than it's a pleasure for him.

I think about what I should do now. I have no plumbers

and no contractors. I can't call my brothers or father because I'm scared I'll be dragged back to my parents. It's a shame, really, two days after I've moved out.

I pull up Google, search for plumbers and contractors in neighboring cities, and make a few phone calls. None of them are available immediately, and I needed the work done yesterday. I don't even have water, for God's sake. I can't take a shower or flush the toilet. All I have is a case of bottled water.

Mark offered to take a look at my pipes—I make a mental note of how dirty that sounds and promise I'll use it later in one of my steamy series—and I just might have to accept his offer. I didn't want to accept it at first because it's so embarrassing, but I may not have any other choice. And I need a shower. But I have no water. I can't go into town looking and smelling like this. I cover my face with my hands and groan.

Chapter Seven

MARK

The morning after the pipe situation, I wake up with pain in my back. That's what happens when you pass the thirty-year-old mark (ha-ha, a corny joke here) and sleep the whole night on the couch. The next stage is aching knees when you stand up too fast; thank God I'm not there yet, but carrying heavy shit all day, every day, has undoubtedly taken a toll on my body.

It feels weird not to have Ghost's body next to me. He went to sleep with our guest yesterday, so I woke up alone, grumpy, and in pain.

I glance at the bedroom door, trying to recall the events of the evening before and figure out how she ended up at my place. She's the type of girl I stay the hell away from. After everything that happened in the past, messing with girls like her is never worth it. They are used to getting everything handed to them from birth. Everything comes easy for them, and I want nothing to do with her—a cold-blooded, gorgeous woman, too beautiful and perfect despite the state of total disarray I found her in. Her head was held too high and the clothes on her confident shoulders probably cost more than a car. She has the attitude to match. *Yeah, I don't think so.*

And yet, here we are. I gave up my comfy bed for her. My perfectly made bed with perfectly fluffy pillows and that goose-down comforter that Ghost and I love so much. I curse a little that the little bastard still got to enjoy them.

My sigh is loud. *Why? Why did I do that?* For fuck's sake, I've never even liked my girlfriends staying the night. So much so that I always tried to meet up at their places. I like guests, but I don't like women as guests. They tend to bring too much trouble, and I have the stories to prove it.

And yet, remembering this does nothing to bring my morning wood down. It actually does the opposite. When I recall yesterday, my blonde neighbor appears in front of my eyes. Her see-through shirt... clinging to her breasts. All my blood rushes south, and the sensation in my dick turns painful. I give it a hard squeeze, hoping to ease it a little, but it makes it worse. I bury my face in my hands and groan. I brought trouble into my own house.

I know from experience that my little situation won't go away on its own. If I ignore it, I'll risk ending up with blue balls for my whole shift, which is not fun. I glance at the bedroom door one more time and stand, hoping she won't walk out. I sneak to the bathroom, mentally thanking myself for keeping a spare change of clothes in the bathroom cabinet. It's a habit from the firehouse I picked up over the years I've been there, and it comes in handy from time to time.

While I wait for the water to warm, I brush my teeth and try to pee. A useless fucking task with a hard dick that refuses to subside. I consider taking a cold shower. It would work for the time being, but I remember the last time I decided to skip my morning jerk-off session.

I lean back, silently cursing my desperate need to get off every day to stay sane. None of my girlfriends could keep up, and honestly, I didn't share my problem with either of them—didn't want to risk sounding like a psycho.

I can't precisely pinpoint the exact moment it started. When I was younger, I only cared about having willing pussy at my door whenever I wanted. It's why I went for those girls. The 'good' girls from the good side of town only wanted to see how it would be on the wild side with a guy from the bad neighborhood.

I needed sex like I needed water. Maybe it was a control thing. I'm not sure. I'd have my way with whoever came my way and then add a solo session at night to fall asleep.

Since then, I have learned to control it. I don't require as much sex anymore, but I still crave it. I love the feeling of a woman in my hands, their soft bodies, their perfect curves... My cock gets harder at the thought. To think of it, the last memory was far too long ago, which might be contributing to the steel rod in my pants.

These days, it's just my hand and me. Sometimes having a girlfriend is complicated, and I ran out of those in Little Hope long ago. My last girlfriend was from Springfield, and we broke up six months ago. She wanted more than I was willing to give. My history is far too messy for me to be in a healthy relationship, let alone even be in the same room where marriage is being discussed.

So the moment I realized she was pointing out rings, I was out. In my defense, I was open from the beginning about what was or wasn't going to happen between us, so it shouldn't have come as a surprise. Yet it still did. She threw a fit.

I'll never get married and will never have kids. I don't know shit about raising kids, much less kids I won't fuck up with my own issues. I raised my sister, ten years younger than me, and I still can't be positive she doesn't have a few screws loose.

I step in the shower, sighing into the hot water beating down on my aching shoulders. In pain with a raging hard-on... Not a good way to start a twenty-four-hour shift.

My dick is somewhat softer. Remembering my childhood tends to deflate everything in me. But I know I have to get it out of the way, or the only thing I'll think about the entire shift is how my neighbor's shirt clung to her the night before.

I grab the base of my cock and squeeze it, making the head turn a dark shade. Blood rushes to it in an instant.

I squeeze some shower gel into my palm and try to recall the last porn video I watched. It works for a moment. Two hot chicks in high heels go at each other, their tongues intertwining with intensity, their hands exploring farther and farther south... but the moment I close my eyes, the picture changes.

Now, there's a tall blonde girl with curves for days in a wet T-shirt standing in front of me. She brings her hands to her nipples and pinches them as her head falls back, her eyes closed. I squeeze the head of my dick even harder, my breathing picking up. As she moves her hands down her stomach, my hand moves up and down my length. Her hands dip between her thighs, and I speed up the tempo.

She dips her finger inside her dripping pussy, and I squeeze the base of my dick so hard that it turns purple. Just how I like it. Rough.

My stomach muscles start clenching, my thighs jerk forward, and I move my hand faster. She bites her full wet lips, and I cover the head with my hand, spreading the pre-cum all over. A few slow, teasing circles around the head before I go all in. She comes closer, and I pant. She drops to her knees, and I place my hand on the wall, trying to keep myself upright. She looks up at me from under her long lashes, and my lower belly tightens unexpectedly. I start jerking my dick faster and unload my aching balls a few short seconds later with an embarrassing groan. I try to suppress it the best I can, considering *she's* right there, sleeping in the next room, and I'm here, jacking off to the image of her on her knees in front of me. I'm a sick fuck.

I'm a sick fuck who doesn't remember the last time he came so hard, his knees shook.

I wash away any evidence of my insanity from myself and from the wall, and for the millionth time in my life, I curse myself for this fucking increased libido.

I quickly finish my shower, praying she isn't awake. I can't face her now, minutes after I imagined her stroking her pussy in the shower with me. I just can't. I don't know what would happen if she showed up right now; I'm so lost between dream and reality. I can't even say her name in my head. I feel too ashamed. I offered her my house as a safe place. The last thing she needs is to figure out she's the main character in my morning fantasy.

I quickly get ready to leave the house without even a cup of coffee. I can get one on the way to the station. In fact, I'll get breakfast too. I'll have time, since I'm not making anything at home.

I stop by the bedroom door, trying to hear if Ghost is making a ruckus, attempting to get outside. It's quiet in the room, only the soft, comfortable snoring of my dog, which I'm used to.

Well, I'll have to rely on Alicia here and hope she'll let him out. She seemed enamored by him earlier, so I hope she won't leave him inside, or I'll have to come back home to a stinky surprise on the floor.

I quietly close the front door and go to my truck, throwing sneaky glances at the bedroom window. I don't know what I'm expecting to find there, but I want to see *something*. A peek. I see nothing and leave a little disappointed.

I park at Marina's diner, where Kayla, my old neighbor from the trailer park, works, and go inside. We've grown up together. She's a few years younger than me, and her living situation was just as shitty as mine when she was a kid, so she spent a lot of time in our trailer whenever her mother brought her boyfriends over. Our place wasn't the best option per se, but it was better when predators visited hers.

My father was an abusive son of a bitch, but it was never sexual in nature. Our shithole was a better option for her. I grew up looking after her and never saw that girl as anything but another little sister. It's why I went off the fucking rails when I spotted Kayla outside Justin's garage, crying her eyes out with that tool Jake hot on her heels. *An officer of the law,* my ass. A damn bully, that's what he is.

They reconciled after that. She never told me why he'd hated her so much, and I never pursued the subject. She's a grown person, and I have my own stuff to worry about. Love makes people do stupid things, like forget years of bullying and harassment.

Love. I snort to myself. My sister is the only person I've ever loved, and I'm intent on keeping it this way. I'm incapable of loving a woman romantically. I learned way too early that no woman would love me, but they'd use me until they were done with me. I'm not good enough for anything else, so why should I let myself love someone and get hurt. Love just isn't in the cards for me.

"Well, hello to a local hero!" Kayla exclaims as soon as I step a foot through the entryway.

The heads of every patron turn my way. I roll my eyes at her theatrics. She lives for this shit.

"What are you here for, my friend?"

"A breakfast," I answer as I take a stool at the bar.

"For the station?" she asks as she gets her notebook out.

"No, just for me," I answer, knowing how many questions will follow.

She quirks an eyebrow. I never come for food for myself. I usually come during my rotation to get breakfast for the team.

"Don't get me wrong, I'm happy to see your hairy face, but is everything okay?" she asks, concern lacing her cheerful voice.

"Yeah, sure," I shrug a shoulder, "just decided to change things up a bit."

"Alright." She places a mug in front of me. "And it's nothing to do with your new neighbor?"

My eyes dart toward her. "How do you know I have a new neighbor?"

"P-p-please." She rolls her eyes. "It's Little Hope. Everyone knows everything."

"Which reminds me..." I tap my chin. "What are you doing here today? I thought you're in Springfield on weekdays?" Kayla has been a waitress here for as long as I can remember, but recently, she went to school and followed her passion by becoming a tattoo artist. Her boss has a parlor in Springfield, where she works during the week.

"I switched to weekends for the fall. Marina needs more help during the fall and winter since everyone wants to visit Maine when it's a tits-freezing temperature. Go figure." A lazy, bemused smile spreads across her face. "And since Freya opened the PTSD center, we get even more loads of customers, and Marina needs more help here. Even though she'll never admit it to me," she says quieter.

"Why doesn't she hire another waitress?" I ask, looking around. It is indeed unusually hectic. Almost every single table is taken. "And I don't know, expand, maybe? Seems like business is doing fine."

"Tell me about it. We already hired two, but she doesn't want to close the place because she doesn't want to lose a few months, since she's saving money for a down payment for *my* place." She rolls her eyes as she pours coffee for me. "The stubborn woman refuses to understand I'm finally able to take care of myself."

"I heard you!" Marina yells from the kitchen, making me chuckle.

"I sure hope you did!" Kayla yells back. They bicker all the time, but it's out of mutual respect. They're a weird family that formed later in life.

She switches her attention back to me. "Don't think you're getting off that easy. Why are you here?"

"Can't a man get a breakfast at the breakfast place?" I ask, throwing my hands up.

"Why, a man can, of course." She dramatically presses her open palm to her chest. "But really. Is everything okay?"

"Why wouldn't it be?" My eyes narrow at her. She knows something she's not telling me. Her gaze darts to the side as she bites the inside of her cheek. It's something I've seen so many times, all the way back when she used to come to my place when her mom brought another boyfriend home. I'd ask her what happened, and she'd say nothing and start chewing on her cheek.

"Just—" She gives a slight shake of her head. "Never mind. Do you want the usual?"

I almost want to press for what she was about to say, but I know it wouldn't end well for me.

"Nah, let's do something new. What would you recommend? I'm kind of short on time here."

"Well..." She taps a pen on her lips. "Everything will take time, but—" She gives me a conspiratorial smile and looks around. "I might be able to snatch a Lonely Kurt for you from someone's order. You're a hero, after all. They can wait."

"Won't you get in trouble?"

"Please." Her eyes roll so far into her head, I'm scared they're stuck there. "It's Freya's to-go order, and I don't remember her ever picking it up on time."

"Sounds good then." I've never tried the Lonely Kurt, but I've heard from the guys that it's incredible. And very, very fattening. A fatty meal is just what I need after my morning session. I feel heat rising beneath my beard, and for the umpteenth time, I'm glad I've grown it out. It's so easy to hide behind it.

Kayla runs to the kitchen and returns with a full plate. An excellent breakfast to satisfy any man. I dig into it while she flies around, delivering plates and refilling coffees. Once she makes her rounds, she returns and leans on the bar, propping her chin on her hands.

"So, how's life?"

"Same old," I answer between bites. I'm really short on time and am definitely not worried about manners.

"How is Ghost?"

"He's fine. Being a pain in my ass as usual. How's your life?" I shoot back; I've never liked being the target of questioning, even from a friendly face. "Did the asshole mess up again?"

"Nah, he's doing fine so far." There's pure adoration in her voice, and I nearly choke on a piece of bacon.

"He'd better be, or I'll rearrange his face," I announce through a mouthful of food.

"I'll pass that on to him. I'm sure he'd love to hear it." She giggles, her lips rolling back.

"You do that." I nod.

Her smile fades, and she bites her lip nervously. "Honestly though, I don't think I ever thanked you."

I stop eating and look up, confused. "For what?"

"Justin told me it was you who explained to him what happened and why I left. If you didn't tell him, I don't know how long we'd have been apart." She shrugs. "You know, like the more the distance between people grows, the more difficult it is to step over it once the issue is resolved." She starts fidgeting with a lock of her hair. "So yeah, thank you."

"He'd come around eventually anyway. His puppy eyes make me wanna vomit." I remember how he came to the bar seeking a fight and how the night ended with him gearing up to get his girl back. I still have no idea what possessed me to even talk to him.

"You just wait, Mark." She laughs and refills my cup.

"For what?"

"For the right woman to snatch you." She points a finger at me again.

I snort loudly. "That's not going to happen. You know my story. No, thank you."

"You just watch." She releases a devilish laugh. Chills

78

run down my spine. I don't like where she's going. "I think I know what type of woman can breach this hard facade, and I'll be right here to enjoy the show." She winks and walks away, humming a song under her breath.

Women and their charades. I finish my food, drop cash on the counter, and leave the diner, waving at Kayla. I love her like a sister, I do, but sometimes she acts like an annoying little pest, and I need to get away.

The station is quiet; everyone's moving at a snail's pace, gearing up for the next twenty-four hours. We love mornings like this, but no one would ever say it out loud. The moment we do, that's it. We're getting the craziest shift of our lives. Jinxing is a very real thing in our profession.

"'Sup, Mark. Got a minute?" Austin walks out of the chief's door and calls out to me. A heavy weight settles in my stomach. No one likes that type of question from the boss this early.

"Sure." I follow him as he gestures for me to join him. "What happened?"

"Oh, nothing. Chill, man." He laughs and slaps my shoulder. "I just wanted to ask how your new neighbor is doing."

A wave of irritation washes over me. Why is everyone so concerned with my neighbor all of a sudden?

"She's fine." I clench my teeth, not wanting to go there.

He gives me a curious look, looks around, and asks, "Where's Ghost?"

"Stayed home." My jaw is so tight, I'm about to crack a tooth.

His brows shoot upward. "Alone for the whole shift?"

I usually bring him here so everyone can dote on him. The bastard always pretends to be grouchy, but I know he secretly loves it.

"I have someone to watch him." Do I? I didn't explain jack shit to her, and it's my dog we're talking about. The dog I left with a complete stranger... "But I'll need to go and check on him before the end of the night. Maybe I'll bring him back with me."

"Alright."

Time has never moved slower. I swear the oldest snail in the world could move faster than time moves right now. I itch to go check on my dog. I'm a tool to leave him with a total stranger in my bed.

At 1:30 p.m., I tell Austin I'll be back and run to my truck.

When I walk inside my place, I notice the harrowing absence of sloppy kisses. My dog isn't here. I check the house just to be sure and look out the window. My neighbor sits in a plastic lounge chair in her backyard, laptop on her lap and my idiot dog at her feet. She's feeding him little pieces of something she's got on a plate next to her. Ghost looks incredibly happy.

I walk outside and toward her. Finally, Ghost notices my approach, and I give him two seconds to react before I give up on the traitor and our friendship. He senses my not-so-sunny mood and jumps to greet me. Nearly knocking me down with his massive body, he slumps into me with the full force of his doggy happiness. I crouch next to him, patting his ears and feeling my anxiety melting away.

"Hey." Her soft voice reminds me she's there.

"Hey," I respond grouchily.

"I thought you were working today." She closes her laptop and places her hands over it. She's wearing black-rimmed glasses, and I get a pinch in the bottom of my stomach upon seeing them.

"I am." I keep playing with Ghost, who's trying to lick my face.

"I see. Didn't trust me." She chuckles. "I left your house as soon as I woke up."

"I'm not worried about the house." I look away.

"Oh. Okay."

The silence that follows is uncomfortable, and I look for a way to get my dog and get the hell out of here.

She breaks the silence first. "Thank you for letting me stay at your place yesterday."

"No problem," I respond gruffly. "Did you fix the pipe?"

"Not yet." Her face turns cloudy.

"Who did you find?"

"Actually, I haven't found anyone yet." She taps her laptop with her fingers. "That's what I'm doing right now. Turns out Little Hope is low on contractors and plumbers. Everyone here knows how to fix everything, but only for themselves."

"Small-town life." I shrug.

"Yeah." Her voice is flat.

"Did you grow up in a small town?" I ask out of nowhere, not knowing why I suddenly need to know.

She shoots me a weird look. "Yeah, born and raised." Not in this one though, I'd know. She'd be hard to miss. A woman so ripe for the taking.

"Cool." I glance at her house. "How are you planning to fix it?"

"I'm still looking for options. I was hoping neighboring towns had something available, you know." She fixes the glasses on her face, and my dick stirs. Of course it does, at the worst time imaginable. I have no idea why I find her thick-rimmed glasses so fucking sexy. I was never into nerdy girls.

81

I try to imagine old Mrs. Jenkins in her nightgown, which I accidentally witnessed one time, forcing my dick to relax a little, and I look at my watch. "It's past two; none of them will come today."

"Well, nature is right here." She waves at the woods with a forced smile.

Yeah, sitting on the ground with a bare ass won't be fun as it gets colder. I feel bad for a moment. "Are you staying with someone tonight?" I ask her.

She vigorously shakes her head.

"Why?" I ask, confused. "You've mentioned you have someone in town."

"Family." She swallows. Family? Who is her family? I'd probably know them, wouldn't I?

"So why don't you stay with them until you fix your place?" It's an obvious choice to me.

"Because they *are family*," she answers as if it's the dumbest question in the whole world.

"Makes no sense to me." It truly doesn't. I mean, my family is fucked up, but most families aren't. People tend to help each other in difficult situations. Isn't that what family is all about?

"I know it wouldn't. I'm just—" She sighs. "I just can't tell them about this only two days after I've moved out."

"I see." I stand. "No friends here either?" She shakes her head, biting hard on the inside of her cheek while her eyes go misty.

I internally groan. Looking up, I ask the sky for the strength I sure as fuck will need when I offer her my solution. "You can stay at my place. I'll be on my twenty-four, so you'll have the place to yourself."

"No!" she cries, a little too loud for my liking.

I offered her my hospitality, for fuck's sake. It's not like I asked her to drop on the ground and suck my dick.

"I mean, thank you, but I'll figure something out."

"Why are you being stubborn?" I ask tiredly.

Her pink cheeks turn even pinker. "I put you out of your bedroom, and I can't imagine you had a good night's sleep."

My anger dissolves a little. "I won't even be home, and you don't even have a lock on your door."

She lets out a defeated sigh before straightening. "I don't. But I can bar it, maybe." Her nose scrunches with concentration.

"Bar it?" I'm genuinely confused about where this conversation and her mind are going.

"Yeah, like put a big piece of wood across." She spreads her arms wide, showing the size of the wood she's talking about, I suppose. "And nail it to the walls."

"You can do that." I lift a brow. "Or you can sleep at my place, and tomorrow I'll fix your door and look at your pipes."

Her eyes widen, and she starts giggling.

"What?" I ask, officially lost.

"Nothing." But she doesn't stop laughing, and I can't help but think about how oddly attractive I find it. I mentally whack myself on the back of my head.

"What's so funny?" I ask her a little too harshly, and her cheeks turn pink again.

"Nothing." She averts her eyes and taps a finger on her laptop. "Are you sure it's okay with you?"

"Yeah." I scratch my stubbled chin. "I'll be back tomorrow morning for my long weekend, so I can look at the damage at your place."

"Okay." She draws her legs toward her body. "I guess I can stay if that's alright with you."

"Alright." I nod, turning back toward my house and gesturing for Ghost to follow me.

"Wait. Where are you taking him?" There's a clamoring behind me, and I turn back. She picks herself up, dusting the nonexistent dirt off her knees, looking concerned.

I take a deep breath before speaking. Slowly. "My dog, Ghost"—I point at the furry traitor looking between us with a tilted head as if deciding who he's staying with—"usually comes on shifts with me."

"Oh." She takes her glasses off and nervously fidgets with the rims. She looks like a shy sex goddess, and for the umpteenth time, I will my dick to stay still.

"Do you want him to stay with you here?"

"Yes!" Her response is a little too fast and a bit too loud to be anything but genuine. She's scared to be alone. I sigh and look at Ghost. "What do you think, buddy? Will you stay with your new friend Alicia?"

He nuzzles my hand and trots to her without giving me a second glance. I let out another sigh and lift my head to the sky, looking for an answer to why this is happening to me. Just when I got my life together, the universe threw me a curveball. I must admit, I prefer the old bat better than this angry seductress.

"I'll unlock the back door for you," I say as I leave them, Ghost curled up between her legs.

Chapter Eight

ALICIA

To say I'm relieved at his offer would be an understatement. I've been sitting here for who knows how long, trying to find who knows who to help me fix the sink.

No one. I found no one. Every single person I called had prior arrangements.

I'm exhausted from removing all the water and wiping, wiping, and more wiping. Throw a towel and squeeze the water out and repeat. A never-ending circle.

I'm sweating, and I'm a mess. I had a few wet wipes I used as a 'local' shower, but I still feel dirty. Even Ghost preferred to stay away from me for the last couple of hours when the grossness reached its maximum.

I found a contractor who can fix the floor though, and I'm sure I'll need him. He said he'll be free in a couple of days and would come take a look. He said the price probably won't be as bad as I think, which gave me hope. He doesn't work with plumbing, so I still have to find someone for that.

To be completely honest, I hope Mark can fix the pipe, so my problem will be automatically resolved. He seems capable with his hands. My cheeks instantly heat up, remembering him in nothing but sweats. No one has any business being that manly. No one.

Suddenly I become all too aware of how cold my nose has gotten from sitting in the frosty air for too long, so I stand and grab my laptop. "Let's go, Ghost. Mama needs a shower." He trots behind me as I catch myself. Mama? Really? Because Mark is his daddy. Does that make us something? I roll my eyes at my silliness. *Seriously, Alicia? Did you really go there?*

I get back inside, collect everything I need for the night and breakfast, and make my way to Mark's house. The back door is left unlocked as promised. I lock it behind me.

The first place I go is the bathroom to wash off. It seems too intimate to run a bath in his home, so I settle on a shower, running it for a few minutes until it reaches the most perfect hell-like temperature. When the water is finally hot enough, I place my body under the warm stream and instantly appreciate that the shower was built for tall people.

I'm so used to crouching while trying to wash my hair. Even at home, everything was made for my mom's height, and she's five foot five. Everything is built so she can reach without a struggle, and the rest of us can crack a skull by just walking around.

My dad is six feet tall, yet he's been living with such a low showerhead because mom said so. How? And more importantly, why? I'm assuming the answer is simple: love. Something I'm not sure I'll ever have the pleasure of understanding.

The hot water feels so good on my aching muscles after their constant workout over the last two days. I stretch, allowing myself to feel how tired they all are, and place my hand on the wall, steadying myself.

I look at my hand and imagine Mark standing in the same place, leaning on the wall as he's washing his body. A soapy hand roams down his cut torso, then lower, over his happy trail, before going farther down. Down. And down. Down to his thick, veined cock that I imagine matches the whole big package.

My eyes suddenly burst open. I didn't even realize I closed them while daydreaming. I feel so guilty for imagining that, at his place, where he trusted me with his dog.

Damn it, Alicia!

I quickly shampoo and condition my hair before using soap. I brought my own shower gel, but Mark's soap with a strong sandalwood smell is far too tempting for me to resist, so I quickly ditch mine and use his just so I can bask in this unexpected smell of safety.

After my shower, I settle in front of the mirror to do my skincare routine. Suddenly, I feel more level than I have in days. My skincare is my constant. No matter what type of day I have, I'm somewhat sane if I finish it the right way.

That and my work. I can live so many lives through my books. I can have as many adventures as I want. I can have as many kinks as I want. I have no one to judge me there. Unfortunately, that doesn't happen in real life, especially not for me. It's why I started writing. Making money off of it was sheer luck. I grabbed it with both hands, and I'm still trying not to let go.

I put my pajamas on, consisting of long, thick pants and a long-sleeve shirt two sizes bigger than I need, and walk to the living room. I take care of Ghost's dinner, walk outside with him to the backyard, and go back to the house. By the time I'm done, it's 9:00 p.m., but I can barely stand.

I decide it's time for bed, so I go to Mark's gorgeous bedroom, admiring the handiwork again before drifting off to sleep.

Waking up drenched again is a bummer. I don't remember the dream itself, but since I woke nice and dry yesterday for the first time in years, I got my hopes up, thinking maybe something about my new situation had helped cure me. A silly presumption, I know. But after so long, it felt so nice. Descending from the clouds this morning is painful.

I look at my phone. It's six thirty in the morning. I don't know when Mark gets off his shift, but I assume it's early. I give a snoring Ghost a gentle kiss between his eyes, but he doesn't stir.

"Lazy dog." I chuckle, but he only grunts in response and wiggles himself deeper under the covers.

I brush my teeth before going to the kitchen to make breakfast. I could do it at home, but I brought enough for two people, hoping I could make breakfast for him as a little thank-you for his hospitality. I fix an omelet, bacon, and some toast, then cover it in foil and leave it on the table.

Ghost trots happily to the kitchen, his nails clicking on the hardwood floor.

"Look who's awake." I crouch next to him to pet his cute furry cheeks. "You're a good boy." His face spreads into a smile. "A very good boy." I walk him outside, where he goes about his business, not looking particularly happy to be out in the cold. I fill his dishes with food and water when we're back inside and crouch next to him again.

"I'm gonna go. Your daddy will be home soon."

If I expect him to look crestfallen, I have another thing coming. He digs into his food with gusto without giving me a second glance.

"Traitor," I accuse before walking outside through the back door.

* * *

A couple of hours later, there's a knock on my door... or what's left of it. When I open it, I find Mark standing on my doorstep with a toolbox in his hands. He's wearing a worn-out, blue-jean jacket with fur on the inside, the collar turned upward. Dark blue jeans hug his powerful thighs like a second skin. I've never liked men in tight pants, but it doesn't seem as though Mark is wearing them on purpose. His legs are just so muscular, they'd stretch any pants he'd wear.

His eyes are tired, with deep dark circles under them. I instantly feel guilty for keeping him out of his comfortable bed when he needed rest. His full shift surely didn't help either.

I open the door, welcoming him in. He steps inside and shrugs off his jacket.

"Did you find anyone to fix it?"

"No." I shake my head. "But I found a guy to fix the floor. He said he'll come in a couple of days to take a look."

He nods. "You'll probably need to replace it. You don't want mold growing under it."

"Yeah, I don't." I bite my lip, not knowing what to say. I

feel awkward because I've slept in his bed twice and used his shower only two days after meeting him.

I avert my eyes from his, looking for a distraction. I find one when my gaze meets his arms as he rolls up his sleeves, showing off his corded forearms. I'm a total sucker for good arm porn—or at least, I used to be—and his are my dreams come true. Once he's done with one sleeve, he starts rolling the other. Looking up, he notices my stare and freezes.

"What?"

"What?" I blink at him.

"Is something wrong?" He lifts his arm to find what I'm looking at.

"Oh, nothing!" I squeak. "Just spaced out, sorry!"

"Alright." He finishes his sleeve-rolling porn and opens the under-the-sink cabinet. "I bet that wasn't fun."

"What?" I blink, my mind straying.

"Cleaning all of that." He points at the kitchen floor.

"Oh, yeah, not fun." I mentally smack my forehead. I'm just a charming conversationalist today. "I figured out how to bar the door, by the way." I wince at myself.

He lets out a deep sigh. "I forgot to pick up a new lock at the hardware store."

"I did it!" I exclaim, proud of accomplishing at least something this morning.

"You did?" His brows shoot up.

"I went to buy that and a piece of metal. Like a sheet. The YouTube video I saw suggested getting it to help fix the busted door." I smile sheepishly.

"A YouTube video, huh?" His lips twitch.

"Yeah." I nod. "I got everything they mentioned. It's all over there." I walk to the window in the living room and point at the massive box I brought from the store. He follows me and digs inside.

"It was a very educational video, I see." A hint of a smile plays in his voice.

"It was," I answer proudly, knowing I covered all my bases.

"Alright. I'll start with these." He picks up the box and carries it to the door. I take a seat on the floor, leaning on the couch. From this position, I can very clearly see how precise his actions are. How his forearms flex every time he uses a screwdriver... or how his biceps bulge when he bends the metal, forcing it into his desired position. I'm fixated on each move, mentally documenting every little detail so I can use it in my books.

He's handy, because it takes him mere minutes to fix the door. Rising to his feet, he moves the box aside and walks to the kitchen. I follow him, hoping to continue the ogling, but he gives me a bizarre look and kneels by the sink. "It will take me a little time to replace it. You don't have to be here if you don't need to be."

"Oh, okay." I think I'm being dismissed, my attention not exactly appreciated. "Do you want anything? Water, maybe?"

He sticks his head inside the cabinet. "Nah, I'm good." His voice is muffled. I take it as my cue to leave.

I feel weird leaving him there, doing work for me while I lounge, so I go about cleaning what I can. God knows there's enough of it around here after recent events.

About forty-five minutes later, he comes to the living room, wiping his hands on a kitchen towel. I rise, putting aside my current task of wiping dust from the floor molding. "It's good to go. I changed the whole thing just to avoid the same in the future. I've been telling Mrs. Jenkins to fix it for a long time, but she never did."

"Thank you, Mark. I honestly don't know what I'd do

without you. There was no one available on such short notice. I'm gonna pay you!" I rush to the bedroom to get my purse, but he stops me.

"Don't."

I stop and turn around. "What?"

"Don't worry about that."

"Why? For one, I'm wasting your time, and two, you did a great job. Very professional."

He chuckles, heading back to the kitchen to pick up his toolbox. "You don't know if it was professional."

I nearly snort. "I'm sure it was. Thank you. Really. Are you sure I can't pay you?"

"I said don't worry. Thanks for looking after Ghost." He puts his jacket back on and goes to leave. For some reason, I don't want him to. I try to find an excuse to have him stick around, but I can't think of any.

"No problem," I murmur before following him outside. "Thank you again, Mark. Really."

"Take care, Alicia," he says and walks away.

I watch him until he heads up the front steps of his house. He pauses, glancing at me. Caught creeping on my neighbor, I shoot back inside the house and shut the door, feeling my cheeks flaming.

I groan loudly, hitting my forehead on the door a couple of times before collecting myself and making my way to the kitchen. Trying the sink, I mentally thank my Samaritan neighbor and start making myself a quick dinner, contemplating offering it to Mark too. Just a little thank-you. I love to cook, so it wouldn't be a bother.

Forty minutes later, I fix a generous plate of salad and mac and cheese with bacon, wrap it in foil, and walk to my door. I stop in front of my mirror, noticing the complete disaster on my head. My hair is sticking out in all possible directions, and I try to smooth it out. Spoiler alert: it doesn't work. So I try to braid it. No luck. Then comes the low bun. Horrible. I go back to a ponytail, but this time I sleek it back with hair oil.

There, that's much better.

Not knowing why I put so much care into how my hair looks, I sigh, annoyed at myself as I put my jacket on. After checking myself in the mirror one more time before I leave, I walk outside.

And freeze.

There's a car parking in Mark's driveway, right behind his truck. It's a red sedan. When the door opens, I instantly back into the shadow of my porch.

A woman with the most beautiful and shiny hair in the world looks around, shivers, and starts walking toward Mark's porch.

I swallow the acid in my throat.

The door instantly opens as she walks up the stairs to his house. She didn't even need to ring the doorbell or knock. I hear Mark's laughter followed by hers, and she walks inside.

A grim feeling spreads from my throat to my chest. Here I was having fantasies about my hot neighbor while he was someone else's reality. God, I feel horrible now. I slept in his bed. Twice. What if he didn't change the sheets? I most certainly didn't. And what if she came in yesterday while I was there? *Horrible, horrible, horrible.*

Mentally thanking my hair for keeping me in the house for an extra two minutes and saving me from the embarrassment of meeting Mark's girlfriend, I walk back inside and trash the food. It's perfectly edible, but I honestly don't think I can eat it either. All I'll be able to think about is my little fantasy burning into ashes.

* * *

A few days went by, and I haven't seen Mark or his girlfriend, but the car disappeared that same evening. Not like I was looking, but I happened to glance outside—a few times—and it wasn't there around nine.

Today the contractor finished the floor in the kitchen. I was fortunate he was able to come a day after my call. He said it would only take him two days to replace it since it's a small area. We agreed on the same hardwood that Mrs. Jenkins had, considering I didn't want to make it evident that a disaster had happened here. Plus, it's not my house and not my right to make huge alterations like changing the color of the floor.

I've been told to wait a couple of hours before I walk on it, and I've been patiently waiting.

A knock on the door startles me. *Of course.* Everything startles me when I'm in dreamland, writing a sexy scene. I'm like a doe caught in headlights. I rise from the couch, where I'm in the process of describing the duke of Hampshire's steel rod in his trousers, and walk to the door, but when I peep outside, there is no one there. Hmm. Weird.

I pause, closing the door. A knock comes again from the back. I swallow nervously and instantly lock the front door, beating myself up for opening it without checking.

I grab my cast iron pan from the cabinet on my way to the back door, raising it in the air like a weapon as I go to check. This time, I peep outside through the window first.

"Holy crap, Frank. You scared me shitless!" I drop the pan on the table and unlock the door. "How did you find me here?"

He lets out a loud snort and bumps me with his head.

Or tries to. Is it just me, or did his antlers get bigger? Instead of butting me, he nearly knocks me down, making me laugh.

"You're getting bigger, good boy," I coo and walk outside. "All the ladies of the forest are yours, I bet."

He nudges me with his nose, more carefully this time, and I pet his big head.

"Why did you leave Kayla? Did she send you here?" I ask in a baby voice. Kayla would roll her eyes at the way I speak to her moose, but she's used to him being around all the time, and I'm grateful for every interaction I have with him.

Justin had been jealous of a mysterious Frank living behind Kayla's trailer for a long time, until he saw him protecting her from some goons. I think that was when they stroked up an agreement to tolerate each other. The thing is, Frank is a total ladies' man, and if you're a dude, you pretty much don't stand a chance of befriending him. I got lucky he picked me, and therefore, Frank is here.

His big nose nudges me to the side as he peeks inside.

"I can't invite you in, big guy," I say sadly, rubbing the spot between his eyes. "Mrs. Jenkins will sniff you out a mile away."

He snorts and beats his hoof, annoyed.

A loud knock from the other side of the house makes us both freeze. "You have a friend with you?" I quirk a brow, knowing how absurd I sound. Actually, scratch that. Me talking to a moose in my kitchen sounds pretty absurd, so I wouldn't be surprised with anything at this point. "I'll be back, Frankie," I say and walk to check the door.

This time, I peep through the side window and only then I open the door just enough to peek my head through. Mark is on the other side, wearing the same unbuttoned jean jacket he wore the last time he was here. His hands are in his front pockets.

"Yes?" My voice is reserved, and his face changes instantly from concerned to confused.

"Is everything okay?" As he asks, his eyes dart behind me, and Ghost tries to sneak inside. I put my foot between the door and the frame, preventing him from entering. I feel horrible for not letting this good boy in, but Frank is notorious for not liking domestic animals, and I don't want either of them to get hurt. Mark notices my movement, and his brows draw together. His eyes dart behind my back once again before returning to my face. "You are not alone?"

"I have a friend over." I glance back, hoping Frank isn't causing a ruckus. I'm well aware that it sounds like I have a dude on my couch, but after realizing he has a girlfriend, I want to protect myself and save face. Or what's left of it. Plus, I'm mad at him for sending me mixed signals and those heated glances while having a girlfriend all this time.

"I see."

Frank chooses this moment to barrel in through the back door and loudly knock something down. The sound of shattering glass makes me roll my eyes, and I yell, "Frank! Wait for me outside!" There's commotion in the kitchen, as it's clearly being dusted to nothing, and the door clicks shut loudly. I turn toward Mark. "Sorry, I gotta go."

The last thing I see before I shut the door is his bewildered face.

* * *

It pretty much went downhill from there. The house has rioted on me. Every single day something breaks. If it's not plumbing, it's electricity. If it's not electricity, it's something else. How I manage to deal with it all without my family figuring it out is still a mystery to me.

My new neighbor and I entered a cold war.

Every time Ghost sees me outside and makes a run for me, Mark barks (ha-ha) at him to come back, and Ghost trots back to his human, sending me sad looks. Every time he drives by and sees me on my porch, he circles back around the street, waiting for me to disappear inside. I could be sitting here forever with a cup of hot tea, but the man is tired, maybe after a long shift, so when I see him avoiding me, I slip inside.

I've seen the same woman stop at his place once more—not like I was checking super thoroughly. She came in and left twenty-five minutes later. They can have a quickie if that's their thing. Twenty-five minutes is more than I have anyway. I do feel a little jealous—maybe a lot—which is probably why I let him think Frank was a person. Petty, I know, but I had to save face the only way I could.

Frank came again to visit because he loves me, and I gave him carrots like the good host I am. Maybe I left carrots in the backyard, so he could come get them whenever he wanted. No one would ever know.

As I sit here on the front porch, peeping at the neighbors—one of them—who all have interesting lives while I have none, I think about how bored I am.

I need some excitement in my life, and I might just have an idea.

Chapter Nine

MARK

"Hey, how is your new neighbor doing? Burned down any houses lately?" Austin laughs next to me as we get ready to leave the station. It's late, and there are only two of us left. He was finishing dreadful paperwork, and I had to take Ghost for a walk. We've been dealing with a flu outbreak, leading to our shifts being completely messed up and not following any real order. There are only a few of us still standing at this point.

"Not yet, but the night is still young," I answer with a shake of my head. That woman is a mess. Almost every day, she manages to get into some sort of trouble she needs saving from. A freaking princess. I feel bad for her boyfriend. Or husband. Whoever this Frank guy is. Besides him, I haven't seen anyone over, but again, I spend most of my time here at the station. And to be fair, I haven't seen him either, so who knows who the fucker is.

All I know is he's an asshole. When she was in need of a place to stay, she didn't call him. He clearly isn't reliable, or maybe he's very much disposable. Neither sits well with me.

Maybe he's just a friend and not a boyfriend. Regardless, I haven't seen much of her, just glimpses here and there. Ghost has whined a few times, trying to go to her porch, but I didn't let him, keeping him with me the whole time. Today he is hanging out with me through my shift because we're pulling one and a half.

Suddenly, I'm thinking about her again. I might have missed someone coming over. It's not like I was looking really. Only went to the window a time or two when I heard a car engine, and so far, it was only her coming and going. No other visitors. That is, when I've been home.

A knot tightens in the pit of my stomach, and I figure I might be hungry.

"Austin, want to grab a bite?" I don't want to go home yet, but my stomach has growled one too many times, and I don't feel like cooking. At first, I thought the growling was coming from Ghost.

"Nah, man. Wifey's in a good mood, so I promised to take her out for dinner." He looks at his wristwatch and whistles. "Actually, she was expecting me four hours ago, so she probably isn't in such a good mood after all." He laughs, imagining his wife. I chuckle too. I've seen them bickering; it's like an old, black-and-white comedy. "I'd take you too, but you know." He waggles his graying eyebrows. "I don't share."

"Shut up. You just can't take any competition."

He laughs. "You youngsters aren't a competition to me. You can't find the clit with a map." He snorts.

"Whatever you say, old man." I flip him off with a smile.

"Alright, kiddo. See you next shift." He gathers his stuff, pats Ghost by the door, and leaves the room.

I get my bag and walk out too, Ghost hot on my heels. No matter how long it's been since he was a K9 dog, his training is always present. Whenever people are around, even the ones he knows, he's always close by, ready to protect at a moment's notice.

I'm planning to go get a bite somewhere, but the moment my ass hits the seat of my truck, my dwindling energy leaves me hunched over the wheel. Fuck, I'm only thirty-three, but it feels like I'll need crutches soon. I decide against going out for food, hoping I can find anything at home. Literally anything. Even cereal will do.

When I pull into my driveway, my eyes dart to my neighbor's house. Are there any other cars parked? I've never seen any. Maybe she picks him up. Who knows. Who cares. Certainly not me. This Frank dude is like a ghost. My own Ghost gives me a side-eye, and I ask him, "What?"

He turns to look at the house again.

We're walking to the back door when I hear a commotion from her backyard, followed by a loud *thud* and a string of words I assume are supposed to be curses but only make me laugh. "You piece of poo, smell like poo too. Why did you do that, you stinky hairy skunk? Why did you make me turn into *that*?"

I'm curious about what the ever-loving hell is happening, so I motion to Ghost to be quiet and silently move toward the fence between our yards. It's dark outside, but the lights from the front of our houses offer some remedy for weak human eyes.

101

I peek over the fence in the direction of the expletives and nearly fall on my ass.

My neighbor is dragging something on the ground, covered in a... *rug*? It's more like something rolled into the rug, poking out one side. I swallow nervously, not liking where my thoughts are going. The rug is long. It can hide a lot, like a human body. And judging by the amount of energy she's putting into her effort, the thing inside the rug is heavy.

I swallow again, not quite believing my own eyes. Ghost must have sensed my mood because he whines quietly, and I shush him immediately, hoping she hasn't heard him. I glance toward her. She's so engorged in her activity, she hasn't heard anything and continues dragging the body—yes, I'm almost ninety-nine percent positive it's a body—through her yard toward the woods behind it.

Ghost whines again, and I put my hand around his muzzle, shushing him again. He looks at me as if I've lost my mind, but he quiets. And then all I hear is silence, utter silence besides an owl hooting somewhere. I crouch so she can't see me behind the fence, but I can still see her through the rails. I can't make out her face this far away in the dark, but I can see she dropped the dead body and has turned toward me. I can imagine her narrowing her big blue eyes in my direction, trying to figure out who is witnessing her crime.

After a few moments, when she's satisfied there is no one around, she returns to her gig.

She's mumbling something, but I can't hear her clearly, so I move along the fence carefully until I'm closer to her. When she's next to the back gate, she drops the body to open it. I crouch closer, leaning in... and then Ghost sneezes. She freezes with her hand on the flimsy lock. *Some spy dog you are,* I try to tell him telepathically as I glare at his guilty face.

"Who's there?" Her voice is high and free of guilt.

I stand from my hiding place, and her eyes go round.

"Are you spying on me?" Her voice is shrill and accusatory.

"What's in the rug?" I counter, nodding at the thing on the ground behind her.

"None of your business." She crosses her arms over her chest, pushing her breasts up. Even in her huge potato sack, I can see the size of them. I haven't been able to unsee what I saw when she was wet in her kitchen. I don't think she even knows what she's doing, but she's been gifted in that department, all right, and my eyes dip lower. Just for a second, but she notices it. "Pervert!" she exclaims and drops her arms.

"Pervert? You're calling me a pervert when you have a fuckin' body in your rug?" I motion behind her.

She quickly glances back before returning to me, her eyes narrowed even more. She ignores my last statement. "I'll ask again. Were you spying on me?"

"What if I were?" I fold my hands over my own chest, mimicking her.

"Then I stand my ground. You're a pervert!" Her cute little nostrils flare, and for a moment, I forget I'm dealing with a criminal.

"What's in the rug, Alicia?" Ghost dances next to me, sensing the uneasiness in the air. "Is it a body?"

"What if it was?" she asks, as if I'm the one at fault.

"Are you out of your mind?" I yell at her, and she flinches. Good, she should. I swallow. "Is it Frank?" I ask calmer. I didn't miss how after that loud bang in her kitchen, she winced and shut the door in my face. Maybe

103

he's a violent son of a bitch, and she did something to protect herself?

"What?" Her eyes round. "No, it's not *Frank*." She snorts and rolls her eyes.

"What's in the rug, Alicia?" My tone is firm. I'm not liking how this conversation seems funny to her. "Did you kill someone?"

The atmosphere shifts, turning darker. "What if I told you that I killed someone who's been haunting me in my nightmares for years?" Her face is solemn, and her voice lacks cadence.

I look at her one more time, trying to erase her gorgeous curvy body from my memory so I can be at least somewhat unbiased. Her shoulders are squared back, her long fingers balled into tight little fists by her side. Her head is held high, probably for the first time since I met her. Her expression doesn't hold an ounce of humor or fear, which is so often there. There is no weakness, no remorse, no hesitation. Just pure determination of a person who knows what she wants and what she *needs*.

Her mask has dropped off, and I can see the yearning for freedom from her demons. I recognize it... because I see it in the mirror every single morning.

I sigh loudly, groaning as I wipe my face with my hands. I sigh again, and she's still watching me. I don't think she's even blinked once. I look around, find nothing besides the rug, and groan again.

"Fuck." I pinch the bridge of my nose. "You don't even have a shovel. Wait here." I turn around and walk to the shed in my backyard, asking myself what the fuck I am doing.

"Where are you going?" she calls.

"To get a fucking shovel," I bark without turning.

"You're going to get a shovel?" A loud sniffle. "For me?" Another sniffle.

"Not for you. For him." I turn back toward her, pointing at the body as I question my sanity once again.

I watch her swallow as she looks at the ground. A couple of seconds pass before she looks back up. Clearing her throat, she asks, "Why would you do that for me?"

I want to joke it off but notice her eyes. There's a deep sadness in them, and I understand she's waiting for a genuine answer. Unfortunately, I haven't quite figured it out yet myself. "I don't know." I shrug. "But I sense your *need* to get rid of your demons. I know the feeling more than I'd ever like to admit," I tell her, trying to understand why I decided to go off the rails myself. I turn to keep walking when a warm hand wraps around my forearm.

"Wait."

All I want to do is keep walking. I don't *do* feelings and emotions and sharing and all the shit that comes in between.

"Wait, please."

The *please* does it. I stop but don't turn toward her.

"It's... I don't even know what to say other than thank you. But there isn't an actual body in that rug. You know, no human body."

I whip back. "What?" I ask, and she drops her hand. "What the fuck is in the rug?"

"A dummy." Her voice turns shy as she plays with her fingers in front of her, looking down. Too fuckin' late for that, princess.

"A dummy," I say back. A fuckin' dummy. She made me spill my guts for a fuckin' dummy? "What the fuck is a dummy doing in the rug?"

"I was doing research." She chews on the inside of her lower lip.

"What sort of research requires you to carry a fuckin' dummy in a fuckin' rug through your fuckin' backyard?" By the end, I'm nearly yelling. A dummy. And I opened my soul to her.

"For the book." She hides behind the few strands of hair untucked from her mane, looking as if she wants to disappear.

I do too.

"A book?" I feel like someone just whacked me on the back of my head with the shovel I was going for.

"Yeah, a book." She sniffles and wipes her nose with her hand. "I wanted to try my hand at a new genre, so I started a book where a wife kills her husband and hides his body in their backyard. I needed to know if a woman can carry a dead body rolled in a rug all the way to the backyard." She points at the rug shyly. "You know, considering his size and all that."

"Can she?" I can't help but ask.

"I mean, it seems like it, if she wants to bad enough." She shrugs, her shoulders falling down like a puppet.

"Were you planning on digging a grave too?" I ask sarcastically.

"I hadn't gotten that far before you came here," she replies cheekily, thinking I'm joking.

"Well, excuse the fuck out of me," I tell her before whistling to Ghost, who sits between us with a curious look on his face, his tongue hanging to the side. I start walking back to my house.

"Mark," she calls, but I don't turn around. "Mark, wait. Please." It won't work anymore, princess. "I really appreciate that you offered."

Well, good, at least one of us does, because I sure as hell don't. I've never been so open with anyone, and here, two

106

seconds under her spell, I spilled my guts and dropped my morals, offering to hide a goddamn body. What is wrong with me?

"Mark." Her voice is sweet and laced with guilt, and I'm done with both.

Chapter Ten

ALICIA

I offended him. I see his rigid back leaving me alone in the darkness, and I can tell. Well, I'm not alone, 'Steve' is here with me.

I turn and kick the rug with my foot. It's not like it's Steve's fault, but he's the reason why this whole thing happened. In my defense, I didn't expect him to offer to bury the body. I mean c'mon, it's been three weeks since we met. Yes, I've slept in his house... in his bed, and yes, he's helped me out a lot, but to offer to hide a body? I was too stunned to speak. If I knew he'd take it literally, I'd have chosen different words.

When it clicked that he thought I was carrying a real body, something in my brain flipped. Do I give off a killer vibe? I thought I was being insulted, which was why I snapped back.

I shake my head in bemusement once again. Who would do that for their annoying neighbor? The only person who'd do that for me is Josie, who also happens to know how to hide a body in a concrete wall. Maybe Kayla. Fine, Justin too. Jake would probably call Mom, who would get Dad, so they'd be doing it together. But not a stranger. And certainly not after giving each other the cold shoulder for the last couple of weeks.

I crouch next to Steve and pick invisible lint from the rug, not quite knowing what to do with myself after that encounter. The man is an enigma, and I was certainly wrong about him. I thought he was an uptight guy who did everything by the book, judging by how he reprimanded me for not knowing what to do with the fireplace.

Do I go after him and apologize? I glance at his house. The blinds are closed, and there's no sign of life anywhere.

* * *

I haven't seen Mark for three days. Since the night of his sweet offer, he's been avoiding me. And trust me, I've tried to pop up when he's around. I've been spying out of my window after him, but there hasn't been a peep of him or his dog.

The first day his truck was parked in the driveway, I decided to give him time to cool off, but the second day, I took action.

I know he leaves early for his shifts, so I tried to take the trash out right after six, then stuck around doing front yard things... you know the ones.

Nothing. The magician disappeared the moment I sneezed, so I missed him again.

Then the same day, I tried to stay late to see what time he comes back. Nothing. Because he didn't come.

I felt something different. Where was he? With the same woman who visited him before?

I don't know why it's so important for me to talk to him. I really don't. I mean, he's just my new neighbor who I've been obsessing over because I haven't met many people for the past couple of years. That's all. Plus, he has a girlfriend, for God's sake, and I'm doing a horrible thing by lusting after him.

But when he didn't come back home even though he's definitely off shift, acid starts eating inside my chest. What if he really went to his girlfriend's, and they both laughed at how he found me in my backyard? I mean, it's really hilarious, but I don't want him to laugh *at* me *with* her.

What did I expect really? A man like him would have a girlfriend, one who wouldn't be terrified of him touching her. Or if she touched herself. They could enjoy all those normal healthy things couples do.

Mark is the very definition of a man, the ones I describe in my books, with masculine energy, smell, and power. So yeah, he'd need an outlet for his wildness.

The sound of a car interrupts the train wreck happening in my mind. I rush to the window to check who it is.

Mark gets out of his truck and walks toward his door, with Ghost trotting next to him. I'm about to run outside to demand a talk when something in his posture stops me. His torso is bent over, his left arm protectively folded over his stomach.

When he reaches the door, he leans on the wall with his forehead, trying to get his key in. Something is wrong. Of course, he could be drunk, but something tells me he's not. I grab a jacket and run outside to him.

When Ghost notices me, he lets out a happy yap but doesn't leave his daddy's side. It's a big surprise, considering Ghost is always happy to see me. Yep, something is definitely wrong.

"Mark," I call out to him.

He glances at me. "Not now, Alicia," he warns in a gruff voice, still trying to get his key in the lock.

"Are you alright?" I try to hide the worry in my voice. I know it's not my place to worry. But I think I fail.

Mark's eyes soften. "I'm fine. Go home." He continues fidgeting with his keys, still not able to fit it into the keyhole.

"You don't look fine." I grab onto the hem of my long shirt. "Are you sure you're okay?"

"I will be. When you leave." He nods toward my house, letting me know he just wants me out of his way.

He finally wins the battle with his lock. He opens the door, walks inside, and shuts it behind him. And in my face.

I blink at the smooth burgundy surface in front of my face. Then I blink some more. Nope, still shut. In my face. I guess that's how he felt when I didn't let him inside my house. Not a nice feeling. Note to myself: never do that to people again.

I take a deep calming breath, look up at the sky, and tell myself that grown-ups aren't supposed to have tantrums, so I will not let myself kick and scream and scratch his beautiful door, even if I want to, very much so.

I've tried. The universe knows I've tried. I'm not feeling

guilty for leaving him alone with his problem anymore. I march home and slam my own door—loudly, nearly taking it off the hinges—but the anger inside me subsides.

I go about my business, fix myself a cup of tea, and sit on the couch with a laptop on my knees.

Perfection. It's quiet, peaceful, and I'm guilt-free.

But of course, five minutes later, I'm back at the window, pulling the curtain aside. I try to see if I can peep on Mark behind his closed window. To my next surprise, his lights aren't on, and his blinds aren't closed, even though it's dark outside. His windows are illuminated by the streetlight, letting me see Mark's figure moving about the house, slowly and unsure. It's so not like him. He's usually confident in his body, every movement precise, every action measured. This Mark isn't the Mark I'm used to.

Dang it!

I so don't need this right now. He didn't want to talk a moment ago, so why should I bother?

I go back to the couch and pull my laptop over my lap.

And put it right back.

Covering my face with my hands, I groan loudly, remembering his rigid, unsure posture. I'd hate myself if something was wrong with him and I never did anything to help. Even if he didn't need it. Some people get grumpy when they're sick. He's grumpy in general, so I don't expect him to be any different when he's unwell.

Plus, let's not forget about the 'dead' body in your back-yard, Alicia. You owe him.

I grab a coat, my phone, and my keys and run to his house after locking my door behind me. I'm not sure when I'm coming back. I knock on his door, and I'm met with no response, expectedly. So I knock again. I hear shuffling behind the door. And a whine. A rumble. A loud curse. Only then, the door swings open inward.

Mark stands in his doorframe looking as if he's been in a brawl with fifty men and lost. He has strands of hair popping out everywhere from his low bun, there are dark circles under his hooded eyes, and the hollows of his cheeks are more pronounced than ever, like he's been starved even though he was fine when I saw him just three days ago.

"Mark?" I call, half hoping he's okay and it's my imagination playing tricks.

"What do you need, Alicia?" He props himself on the edge of the door.

"You look really bad." I glance at his feet and back to his face. "What happened?"

"Nothing. Go home." He tries to close a door on me again, but I press my foot into it. His attention slips to my face. "Just go home. I don't have energy to fight with you right now." He tries to put more force into closing the door, but I don't think he has energy left at all. My foot barely budges.

"I'm not here for a fight. Can I come in?" I make a move to go inside but he steps forward, preventing me from moving farther. I have no idea who this brave woman is, but it's definitely not me. My body bumps into his, and my hands fly to hold onto something before falling forward. They find support on his shoulders, and he stumbles back.

His very, very hot shoulders. My hand flies to his forehead.

"You're burning up."

Now it makes sense. I firmly grab his hand and move it away from the door so I can squeeze in.

"What are you doing?" His voice sounds dry, and now I know why.

"You are sick." I finally move him out of the way and walk inside. Ghost rushes toward me, nudging my hand for attention. I give him a few rubs and walk to the kitchen. "Where's your medicine cabinet?"

"In the bathroom," he answers and slowly walks to the couch where he plants himself, leaning back and closing his eyes.

I ravage through his cabinet, find a thermometer, and run back to him. He's already asleep.

"Mark," I call with no luck. "Mark." I try again, louder. Nothing. I put my knee on the couch and lean toward him. Grabbing his jaw with one hand, I force his mouth open with the other and shove the thermometer inside. I gently help his mouth to close and keep my hand under his chin just in case. The thing starts beeping in seconds. I pull the thermometer out—104.2. *Shit!* I've never seen anyone with a fever this high.

I run back to the bathroom and scavenge through his cabinet in search of medicine. Any medicine. He has a bottle of Tylenol and a few aspirin. I grab three Tylenols, run to the kitchen to get water, and rush back to Mark.

I climb on the couch next to him and shake his shoulder. "Mark."

Nothing.

"Mark!" Again, louder. "Mark!" I yell, shaking him harder.

His swollen eyes pry open. "What?" His voice is groggy.

"You have a really high fever. You need to go to the hospital."

"No," he answers grouchily, closing his eyes. Men! Worse patients ever.

"Mark." I try again.

"Mmm."

"Mark! Open your damn eyes!" I punch his shoulder, and he groans but looks at me. I'm not sure he's present though. "Now open your mouth."

"What is it?" His words are barely comprehensible.

"It's Tylenol. Now be a good boy and open up." Something funny flashes in his eyes—or maybe I imagined it—but he obeys and opens his mouth. I shove the pills inside and bring the glass of water to his lips. "Drink."

He takes a tiny sip, but I push the glass toward him again.

"More."

"No." He tries to turn away, but I grab his chin and move it toward me.

"Drink it."

His nostrils flare, but he opens his mouth and lets me help him drink half the glass. "I really can't drink anymore," he says finally, breathing measuredly and deeply.

"Okay." I stop pushing the glass and place it on the coffee table. "Do you know what you have?"

"What?"

"The fever. Do you know what you have? Is it the flu?"

"Not the flu. I don't know." His eyes shut again, and I can tell he's coherent at this point.

I stand from the couch, run to his bedroom, and bring two pillows from his bed. Fluffing them up, I place them on the side of the couch, pushing his body down to lie on it. He helps me to move him but keeps his feet planted on the floor. I crouch in front of him, untie his shoes, and take them off. Then I lift his legs and pull them onto the couch. I swear they weigh a ton. He didn't help me an ounce because he's out like a light. I check the time on the clock on the wall and go to the kitchen. Ghost's plate is empty.

"Hey, boy, come over here. I'll feed you," I call to Ghost as he sits by his dad's side with his head on Mark's stomach.

He looks at me, his eyes sad, and lets out a long whine.

"I know, baby, I know. But he will be better. Now, come here." I pat my thigh. "C'mon."

He whines again but comes to me with his head hung low, his tail between his legs.

I fill his plate with dry food, freshen his water, and go back to Mark.

He hasn't changed his position, but his cheeks have become redder. I touch his forehead. It's clammy and still hot. I take a seat on the floor by his side and wait. After a couple of minutes, Ghost comes from the kitchen to check on things. I let him outside for a few minutes, hoping he'll let me know when he's ready to come back inside. In the meantime, I go back to guard Mark's side.

Ten more minutes, and I check his temperature. It hasn't dropped at all. Wasn't it supposed to work already? I open my phone to Google possible ways to reduce fever, pronto. Some websites suggest putting ice on his neck. I've never done it before, but I've never had a fever this high either. If it doesn't work, I'm calling 911.

Willing to give anything a try at this point, I run to the kitchen when a loud ring stops me in my tracks. It's not my phone. I head toward the sound to find Mark's phone lit up. The name Rachel appears on the screen. Fuck. It must be his girlfriend I saw here the other night. Of course it's her. She's better equipped to take care of him. I take a deep breath and press accept.

"You motherfucker better have a valid reason for not responding to my messages. Did you go to the doctor like you promised?" A female voice barrels through the phone without greeting.

"Hey." I clear my throat, realizing I sound like a man who's been smoking for two hundred years. "It's actually not Mark."

There is a long and pregnant pause on the other end. "And who is this?" she asks, sounding a little accusing. I wince, not blaming her for turning a little bitchy when she heard my voice.

"It's Alicia, his neighbor," I reply, hoping it will keep him out of trouble with her. "I think Mark is sick. I mean I know he's sick. He has a really high fever."

"How high?" she asks.

"One oh four point two. And it hasn't dropped after a dose of Tylenol."

"I'll be there in a few." The phone goes dead.

I look at it, confused as to what happened. She didn't sound like a girlfriend would, even though I wouldn't know how one might sound. Maybe they like to call each other motherfuckers. Maybe it's just some sort of foreplay.

Putting his phone on the coffee table, I wonder if I did the right thing. I mean, she clearly knew something was wrong if she asked if he went to the doctor's, right? And besides, I'd be calling 911 anyway in about thirty minutes if the pills didn't work.

I let Ghost inside, and he instantly takes a spot next to the couch. He tries to climb on top of Mark a few times, but I don't let him. He gives me a stink eye but stays on the floor.

I check Mark's temperature again, and it hasn't changed. Now I begin to really worry. Ghost picks up on my mood because he starts moving around the couch and trying to climb on top of Mark, and I send him on his merry way outside to the backyard, because quite honestly, I don't know how to deal with a worried dog atop of worrying myself.

In about twenty-two minutes—I've been checking the time nonstop—a car pulls up outside. I run to the door and open it. It's *her*. The same gorgeous woman stands before me, the porch light absolutely glowing off of her beautiful dark skin. Her shiny hair is even prettier in person. She seems to be in her early thirties. After a moment, she comes rushing in without even a second glance in my direction. She's carrying a huge bag with an unmistakable cross sign.

"Hey," I greet her, feeling super uncomfortable. What do I do? Do I go home? "He is on the couch." I point in Mark's direction and go to leave, but she stops me with a firm tone.

"Where do you think you're going?"

"Home." I point at my house. "You're here. I can go."

"Hell no," she answers as she shoves a thermometer into his mouth. "I'm not moving his huge ass alone. C'mere."

Stunned, I obey. I wouldn't want another woman with my man in the same room when I was about to take care of him. I go back to the couch and watch her, blinking. "Do you know what he's got?"

"Scared to catch it from him?"

"No. Just worried." I shrug, a little offended.

"Why are you here, by the way? This seems pretty bad." She bites her lower lip in concentration.

"It would be unfortunate if I got it, but what can we do?" I shrug again. "What was I supposed to do? Leave him here alone?"

"Yeah, his whole problem is he's alone," she mutters, and I get the feeling it was not meant for my ears.

"Alone. What do you mean?" My brows draw together.

"I mean he's got no one. That's what I mean." If I didn't

watch her face so carefully, I would miss the way her lips twitched.

"But—" I clear my throat. "He's got you."

She stands tall, hands on her hips. "Who do you think I am?"

I suddenly truly understand how a deer caught in a headlight feels. "His girlfriend?" Why did it sound a question? I let out a loud groan. Mentally.

She chuckles. "Nope, he's got no one, and I'm just his dear ol' friend." She directs her attention back to him. "Help me here."

"You know what happened to him?" I ask as I step closer to help her lift Mark up to a sitting position. He's totally out of it.

He is totally out of it.

Totally out of it.

Just like I was.

The walls begin closing in on me. I don't have air. I can't breathe. I hyperventilate. My skin goes clammy. My heartbeat skyrockets. *I'm totally out of it.*

A warm hand slips into mine. "Where did you go, honey?" a soft voice calls to me through the fog of nothingness. I try to focus on her voice and the feel of her warm hand in mine, but I can't. "Mark is here too. He needs your help."

I know Mark. Mark means safe. Mark is safe.

My breathing calms down, and I'm able to take a lungful of air.

"You alright?" the woman asks, concerned.

"Yes. Sorry." I shake my head.

"Don't you ever apologize for that." She squeezes my hand. "Now, you are good? Can you help? If not, that's totally fine. I've moved bigger guys around."

"Bigger guys?" I quirk a brow, trying to lighten the mood I've put us both in. "Those exist?"

"A fair point." She laughs. "This guy is really big."

"What do you need help with?" I manage to ask.

"I need to check his back. Can you help me?" She sizes me up, and I nearly roll my eyes. I used to be a cheerleader. The bottom of the pyramid.

"Yep." I help her to lift his torso up and am about to lean him on the back of the couch when she stops me.

"I need to check his back, so you need to hold him. Alright?"

I swallow a dry lump in my throat. "Alright."

I climb on the couch on top of his legs and try to find a good position for holding his torso.

"Jesus, woman, just saddle him."

I shoot her a glare but do as I'm told. Straddling his legs, I'm able to lean him against myself easily, just as she suggested. The woman leans toward his back and rolls his T-shirt up.

"Shit! You stubborn mule!"

"What did I do?" I ask, confused.

"Not you. Him." She groans and goes to grab her bag.

"What happened?"

"He got hurt a few days ago during his shift and promised me he'd go to see a doctor about it. But this stupid mule never did and got an infection. And on top of it, I think he also caught the flu that's been going around."

"Infection?" I strain my neck to look at his back. A nasty burn adorns his right shoulder blade. It's clearly infected, since the edges are angry red. There's a huge purplish ring around the wound. It looks raw and painful. I bring my hand to touch the skin next to the wound, and it's even hotter than his body.

My eyes move along his back, the part of it I can see from this position. It's rippled with muscles on top of muscles. But it's also covered with old scars: little round ones, reminding me of cigarette burns I've seen in movies, and long white scars. Some of them are raised more than others. What are those? I try to move a little so I can see farther down his back, but the lady speaks to unconscious Mark.

"It's gonna hurt like hell, man. Hopefully, you won't remember any of this." Then she clicks her tongue. "Or maybe you should. Will teach you to take care of yourself in the future."

She brings a bottle and a few gauze pads over to him, then wets them before she starts cleaning the wound. Mark stirs and groans, but I bring my arms around his torso, moving my body to his. His face ends up at the crook of my neck, his shoulders atop mine.

While she's doing her thing, I let myself enjoy this moment. Me hugging another person—a man, a large man. Even though he's barely conscious, I'm still me, and I'm still able to think straight. I didn't remember how it felt, and I forgot how much I missed it. How wonderful it is to be connected to someone in a simple hug.

His warmth seeps through my cold skin, enveloping my loneliness in a mighty hug.

I mentally slap myself. The man is sick, he has a crazy fever, and here I am, fantasizing about how nice his body feels against mine.

Mark groans and stirs. "The fuck?"

"And he lives." The lady snorts. "Told you to go to a doctor. Didn't I?" She dabs the wound with another gauze pad. "But no. You're a stubborn, stupid man who's scared of doctors."

"I'm 'ot 'cared of 'octors." Mark slurs, so I have to use my imagination to try to figure out what he said.

"Yes, you are. Why didn't you go when I told you to?"

"'Cause I din't have time, Rashel." His speech is funny, and I'm getting more worried. And so is Rachel. Suddenly, I remember I should have properly introduced myself when she arrived.

"Now you'll have plenty of time for plenty of visits. I'll let Austin know you'll be out for a few days."

"No!"

It came out louder than we both expected, and I share a look with Rachel. The corner of her mouth quirks up.

"I'm honna go to the shiff."

"The only place you're gonna go is your bed," she snorts. "And tomorrow I'll come back to check on you."

"I'll be fine." He rolls his eyes.

"Me here or you at the doctor's office. Your choice." Rachel presses her lips together, trying to suppress her laughter.

Another eye roll, more exaggerated this time. "Fine. You here."

"Good choice." She digs back into her bag, gets a syringe and an ampoule out, and fixes a shot. "It's an antibiotic and a fever reducer. Should be enough to bring it down for tonight, and I'll come check on him tomorrow to see if he needs more or if oral antibiotics will suffice. You're staying here, correct." She delivers the information on the same note, but at the end, she lifts a brow in question, even though she already told me what my answer is supposed to be, so I nod. It's not like I can leave him alone. "Good. Now, hold steady, this big guy is scared of needles."

The idea of Mark being scared of anything sounds

funny, but here he is, pouting like a baby at the mention of a doctor's office.

Rachel puts the syringe on the table, stands next to Mark, and is prepping his vein when he stirs.

"Your tits are so ni-i-ce." He snuggles deeper against me. "Firm but so soft. Been dreaming 'bout 'em fuckin' fo'ever."

We both pause, stunned into silence.

A loud snort followed by uncontrolled laughter makes Rachel step back in order to gain her stability back.

"Gi-i-irl, I've never seen him say anything like that. I didn't even know he could." She snickers. "Oh, Mark." She laughs again.

I'm too stunned to move. Every time someone looks at me in a sexual way, I go into the dark place in my head. And here he *said* it. And yet, all I want to do is to laugh. I mean, it's hilarious. The way he slurred his words is funny. And let's not forget the way he's clinging onto me. Or is it me clinging onto him?

The weight of his heavy body feels... safe. It's an unorthodox feeling.

When Rachel has had enough of this fun, she takes a few deep breaths and wipes the tears in her eyes with her forearm. "Alright, big guy, let's do this." She cleans the area on his arm again and quickly pinches the skin, shooting the medicine in. She puts a Band-Aid on and stands. "You can put him back."

I try to move him backward, but he squeezes me tighter. Yeah, I'm not ready to let go yet either, but I have to, so I whisper into his ear, "I'll be back in a minute." My lips accidentally touch his earlobe, and he shudders. "I promise."

Only then does he relax and let go of me. I help him lie back down and throw a cover on top of him. I'm trying to fix the pillows under his head when I feel a gaze on me.

"How do you two know each other?" She crosses her arms, observing us on the couch.

"We're neighbors." I try to sound calm and collected.

"Oh, you rented Mrs. Jenkins's place?" An understanding passes over her eyes.

"Yeah." I fidget with another pillow I'm trying to stick under his head. I feel like the one pillow he has is not enough.

"Well, Mark's lucky you were here." She collects everything into her bag. "I'll come to check on him tomorrow."

"Won't he need to go to a hospital?"

"Let's hope not. It wasn't as bad as it could be, but he should have taken care of it right when it happened so he wouldn't have to deal with it now." She's done packing up and takes a seat on the chair. "I'll wait until his fever is down."

"Yeah, a good idea. Do you want anything? I mean, I know where the water is." I stop myself before I reveal too much. For example, that I've spent two nights here. "Or I can go and grab something for you from my place."

"Nah, you chill." She waves me off. "I have a hot meal waiting for me at home. My hubby will have a fit if I eat somewhere else when he cooked dinner for us." She looks at her wristwatch. "Though, I'll be late."

Interesting. So it's not like something is going on between her and Mark. Even though she mentioned that he's got no one, she's too... I don't know, caring. Plus, I don't feel jealousy from her. I'd be super jealous if I found another woman in my man's bed. Or on his couch. Semantics.

I take the other chair and ask her, "How did he get hurt?"

"We went to this huge-ass fire in Copeland."

"Why? It's like twenty minutes away. Don't they have their own units?"

"The fire was huge," she tells me. "We get called sometimes here and there if they need our help. Small towns." She shrugs. "We were called to this fire, and Mark got stuck in the building." Her eyes cloud at the memory, and I sense genuine worry toward Mark. They might be close, probably even good friends. I've heard people at the station are like family. I mean, it makes sense. They must trust each other to stay safe, so no wonder they grow close.

"How did he get stuck in there?" I try to imagine a person stuck in a fire with no escape. It must be terrifying.

"We got info that two kids were on the third floor, and he was the last to leave the building, so he went back." She says it with such affection, for a moment I again wonder if she doesn't harbor any *extra* feelings toward him. At the mention of him running into a burning building to save kids, even my frozen heart gives an extra beat, and I'm pretty sure my ovaries just ovulated.

"Are the kids—" I'm scared to finish.

"They're fine." Her face lights up with a huge smile. "Back with their family, thanks to Mark."

"But he got burned." I look at the real-life hero currently lying on the couch, nearly delirious.

"But he got burned." She confirms with a nod. "I told him the burn was nasty."

"How did he get burned on his back?" I ask.

"Took off his coat to wrap the kiddos in it." She delivers this piece of information like it's nothing. I switch my attention back from Mark to her and see a devious smile on her face. She's up to no good. She's painting him as a hero, which he is. No doubt. But she's loving what she's doing.

How do I tell her it's all wasted on me? "Plus, this flu

the whole station has?" She forcefully blows air out her mouth. "Yeah, it's nasty. I had it too and was out of commission for a week, I swear." A light shudder runs through her body at the memory. "So yeah, I don't think it's helping the infection either."

"Poor thing." I look at Mark, my head tilted.

"You have no idea," she replies quietly, and I look up. Rachel's face instantly changes, and she smacks her knees with her open palms. "Alright. Time for a check, because this mama is hungry." She grabs the thermometer from the table and shoves it into Mark's mouth. It beeps a few seconds later. "One oh one. Good." She puts it back on the table and grabs her bag. "It will go down more. He'll be sweating like a pig, but he should be fine. Tomorrow, I'll give him another set of antibiotics. Just clean the wound." She must have seen my face because she adds with a chuckle, "If you can, before me. Use this ointment"—she points a finger at the little tube she left on the table—"when the wound is dry. Call me if you need me."

"I don't have your phone number."

"Right. Give me your phone."

I pass her my phone, and she puts her digits in and returns it.

"Call me day or night. Got it?"

I nod.

"Good. I'll let Austin know he'll be out for a few days."

I nod again. I don't know why. I'm just his neighbor. Why is she giving me all this information? "Can you stay for tonight maybe?"

"Why?" She quirks a brow.

"Because, I mean..." I look around. "I'm his neighbor. I'm not even supposed to be here."

Her eyes narrow. "Are you?" She looks around. "Where is Ghost, by the way?"

"I sent him outside right before you came." I nod toward the back door. "Probably anxious to return, but he was everywhere, and I needed a break."

"Are you having problems with him?" A worried wrinkle appears between her brows.

"No. Why?"

"Because he's a vicious little asshole and doesn't like anyone?" She cackles.

"No, he's a sweetheart." I feel a little offended she thinks of Ghost this way. He's the cutest fur-baby on the planet.

Her brows rise and disappear into her hairline. "Alright then. Gotta go. Call me." And she leaves me alone with Mark.

I go to the back door and open it, expecting Ghost to barrel in, knocking me down. But the dog surprises me by taking a careful step inside and sniffing the air. A low growl comes from his chest, and he lowers himself closer to the floor.

"Are you growling at me?" I pop a hip, but he runs past me to the entrance door and growls again. "Oh, I see. You aren't friends, huh."

He growls again and goes to lick Mark's fingers.

Another groan comes from the couch. Mark's this time.

"Was it Rachel?" His voice sounds more confident.

"Yeah, she gave you a shot because your fever wasn't going down." I walk toward him and stop a couple of feet from the couch, not knowing what to do. "She said to stay here with you since it can come back."

"You don't have to," he croaks.

"I don't mind." I lock my hands behind my back,

fidgeting with my fingers. I'm completely uncomfortable with the situation, not knowing what to do and not knowing if he remembers what he said.

"Tha—" He starts coughing. "Thank you for your help."

"No problem."

He coughs again, and I rush to the kitchen to get him some water. I pass the full glass to him and accidentally touch his fingers. A zip goes through my body, and I nearly drop the cup.

"Can I ask you a favor?" His voice is still coarse, but at least the coughing subsided.

"Sure." I pause my nervous fidgeting. "What's up?"

"I'm drenched." He coughs. "Can you get me a shirt from my bedroom?"

"Yeah, sure." I'm about to run to his bedroom but pause, since I don't know where I'm going. "Where can I find it?"

A loud sniffle. "The left bottom drawer."

"Any preference?"

"A dry one." He cracks a pained smile.

"Okay." I chuckle and go to his bedroom to retrieve a shirt. When I pull the drawer open, I find everything is in perfect order. I've never had my closet so organized. I grab a white T-shirt and go back to him.

And stop dead in my tracks.

Because he took off his wet shirt and is sitting on the couch shirtless. His wide shoulders are now on full display and seem so huge and powerful. Larger than I remember. His elbows rest on his knees, and his biceps bulge at this angle. The veins pop from his arms, hanging between his legs. His torso holds so much restrained power, I stop breathing, waiting for a wave of horror to wash over me. But it never does. Instead, another thing washes over me.

129

Between my legs. Completely inappropriate timing. Warm shame rises up my neck.

I swallow, trying to moisten my suddenly dry throat.

He notices my presence and lifts his face. "Look, I'm really grateful for you coming here. I know you didn't have to, and I was an asshole, but thank you. I owe you one."

I shake my head. "We're even. You saved me a bunch of times. And if we're keeping the score, I still owe you."

"We don't." He cracks a tired smile.

I get myself together and walk over to him to pass him the shirt. He takes it with a quiet 'thanks' and puts it on. While he's doing that, my hungry eyes follow him like the little perverts they are. His every movement causes his muscles to swell and snake under his glistening skin. Glistening skin. *The man is sick, you pervert.* I smack myself, forcing myself to stop thirsting after him. Mentally.

He saves my sanity by putting the shirt on, and I can think straight again. "Do you want something? Rachel said the fever will go down soon. Maybe you want some broth?" I half turn toward the kitchen. "I can make it."

"You can make it?" His glistening forehead wrinkles.

"Yes."

"For me?" The wrinkles become deeper.

"Well, ye-e-eah." I look around pointedly. "Do you see anyone else here?" He's watching me without blinking, so I raise my voice. "Mark! Wake up. Do you want some food?"

He finally blinks and nods slowly.

"Alright. I'm gonna go check what you have in the fridge. Any preferences?"

He blinks again, like it's a foreign thing for him to do, and shakes his head. "Anything."

"Alright. Don't complain if you don't like the food I make," I say as I walk to the kitchen.

"I won't," he barely whispers, causing me to turn around and look at him again, a little closer this time. He's watching me with open wonder. I don't know why, but something in his eyes makes this big man look like a little kid.

I turn away, uncomfortable with this new discovery. In the kitchen, I dig into his fridge. I find chicken and a few sad-looking veggies. Probably enough for minestrone, but on the other hand, I don't think a guy like Mark will be satisfied with a barely existing amount of protein in a veggie soup, so I prep the chicken. I throw half of it into the pan for the broth and marinade the rest to fry later. Then I rush to the door.

"I'll be right back," I say as I pull my sweater on.

"Where are you going?" he rasps.

"I need to get some stuff from my place. Be back in a minute."

I'm nearly out the door when I hear him quietly talking to Ghost. "Go with her."

I hear claws clacking on the hardwood floor and wait for him outside without turning around. I don't want Mark to see how misty my eyes are. A little nudge to the back of my thigh tells me he's ready to go. I automatically pat his head and walk to my place, slower than I intended to. The water must be boiling soon, and the weather isn't good enough for a leisurely stroll in a thin sweater, but I need a moment to collect myself.

These tiny, sweet gestures break my heart. Sending Ghost with me outside when it's so late was intentional. He must have sensed me being jumpy, or he's just a nice guy who would do it for any woman who happens to be at his house late at night.

And that was the wrong topic. Now all I can think

about is other women in his house. I comb my memory, trying to remember if I ever saw anyone else besides Rachel coming or leaving. Nothing comes to mind. Maybe they are super sneaky? Because there is no way a man like that doesn't have needs. He oozes unrestrained, raw testosterone, and I'm sure if another alpha man would show up in the same room, there would be a fight. And I'd bet my money on Mark.

So how come I haven't seen anyone?

It's a good thing.

I think.

Chapter Eleven

MARK

I fucked up.

Well, I've fucked up far too many times in my life, but this is the ultimate fuckup. How else would you call me developing *feelings* for someone after they offered to make me food? Talk about kids not being loved enough by their families—yeah, that's me. I bet you'll find my picture under the description if you Google it.

I lean back on the couch, patiently waiting for her to be back from her place and wishing I'd gone to a doctor as Rachel instructed, but I didn't think the burn was this bad. I bet catching this nasty flu didn't help either. I've never had such a high fever, especially not to the point of delirium. And did I really tell Alicia she's got nice tits? I cover my face with my hands and groan. I hope she didn't hear me. And Rachel too. God, I hope she didn't. The woman is a shark. Once she sniffs blood, she'll never let it go. My interest in my new neighbor was a little too obvious.

Thank fuck my dick stayed put. I was coherent enough to remember the hug... and how her soft body fit with mine, her perfect curves along my ridges. How wonderful she felt to be next to me. How good she smelled. How her strands of soft hair tickled my nose. I had to bury my face deeper.

I press the heels of my palms against my eye sockets, hoping to erase all those little moments from my memory. They're no good. I can't afford to entangle myself with her now, and 'entangle' is all I can offer. Of course, I'm sure the sex would be amazing. It always is when you have even an ounce of chemistry. But she doesn't seem like the type of person who would enjoy a casual, one-time fuck. Plus, the darkness around her... She might not be up for the beast she could face.

I didn't miss the way her eyes roamed over my body while I was changing my shirt though. So different from the first time she saw me... her little nose all scrunched with clear disgust. This time was different. This time I saw obvious interest, but she wasn't planning on sharing details, judging by the blush marking her cheeks.

I instantly feel better. Of course, it might be the drugs talking, but my spirit is higher.

And I smell horrible. I've been sweating like a pig for the past hour and don't even remember when the last time I showered was. I try to stand, and it works on the second attempt. The fever must have gone down, but so has my energy level. When I manage to walk to the bathroom, I hear the entrance door opening. A second later, the bathroom door bursts open.

"What do you think you are doing?" The blonde Valkyrie shoots daggers at me, her hand on her hip, strands of hair sticking out every direction from her ponytail.

"I stink."

"And?" Her nostrils flare, and her gorgeous lips thin. "You decided to take a shower with an open wound on your back?"

"Rachel patched it up," I protest weakly, knowing she's right.

"Yeah, with *dry* dressings so you can, you know"—she points at her own back—"*heal*."

"Man, I need a shower. I haven't taken one for a couple of days; the shift was crazy." Between the huge fire, saving those little people, and being short on staff, I barely had time to drink, let alone to take care of personal hygiene.

She lets out the cutest sound I've ever heard—one that reminds me of a Chihuahua growling—and walks inside the bathroom. The space turns tiny in an instant. I mean, the bathroom is small, and when it's just me here, I have enough space to comfortably move around, but with her here, it's not enough.

"Take your shirt off," she orders as she dives under the sink. She feels awfully comfortable around here for a guest, and oddly enough, I don't mind it one bit.

I obey like the good boy I am—even if it causes me pain to do as I'm told—and stand in front of her in nothing but my sweats, praying nothing should *arise*. It would be on full display in these.

While I'm struggling with my internal turmoil, she runs some water, wets the washcloth, and offers it to me with her outstretched arm. "Here, you can use this."

"For what?" I blink at the tiny cloth.

"For cleaning yourself." She shakes it.

"How can I clean myself with this thing?"

She rolls her eyes and presses the cloth to my chest.

And freezes. I do too. I don't think either of us expected the gesture.

I can feel her hand pressed to my skin even through the wet material. My eyes dip to her face, then lower. Her slender throat bobs in a rough swallow. She wets her lips, and I take a deep breath, calling for the pain in my back to prevent me from showing what she does to me. I behave like a wild animal around her, with no self-control whatsoever.

She clears her throat. "You can wipe yourself in certain places." She moves the cloth around, grazing the tips of her fingers along my skin. "Like that." She presses the material to my chest, and I cover her hand with mine, thinking she wants me to take over.

She freezes again. A spark of fear in her eyes makes my heart sink to my stomach. I release her hand immediately, and she takes a step back.

"Sorry," I mumble and lean for the dropped cloth. The unexpected move stretches the skin around my wound, making me groan.

"Are you okay?" She steps forward, residual fear still in her eyes.

"Yeah." I cough, trying to mask another groan. "I'm fine."

Her eyes soften, and she stretches her open palm toward me. "Give it to me."

"Nah, I'm good." I attempt to put on my best brave face, hoping it screams "stay away, I'm strong and capable."

"Mark," she says gently, and it breaks me. I pass the cloth to her with a sigh.

A small smile plays on her lips as she wets it again and goes around to my back. She presses the warm material to my skin and cleans it in gentle circles. After a moment, she wets the material and repeats. Her movements are so careful around the wound, a huge lump forms in my throat. I try to swallow it but can't. It gets so big, it presses on the insides of my eyes, and I blink rapidly, trying to erase this weird, abnormal feeling.

I don't remember when anyone was so gentle with me or wanted to take care of me like this. The women I've been with in the past wanted a fast and wild ride, and I was okay with it. I gave the same in return, never asking or offering more. Growing up with no affection, I didn't even know it was an option. And here she is, a woman who doesn't even really know me, taking care of me, asking for nothing in return.

I grab the sink, steading myself.

"Are you okay?" her soft voice asks from behind me, dripping with concern. It just about does me in.

"Yeah," I croak. "I'm okay."

"Your back is done. I can help you with the front too if you want?" It sounds like a question, so I nod, not trusting my voice.

She moves in front of me, wets the cloth, and cleans my chest. Her eyes are trained on her task, and mine are trained on her in the mirror.

The fear of my dick getting hard from her touch is gone. Her gesture is so tender and foreign, I'm drowning in it. I'm so focused on trying to swallow the emotions rising in my chest so I don't embarrass myself by bawling like a baby.

Her movements don't feel sexual even once. It's sweet, tender, and caring. A solicitous gesture I'm careful not to blow up.

And I'm dying on the inside. I'm only now under-standing how much I've been missing all my life.

She moves to my neck, wiping it clean before dropping the cloth into the sink.

"I did as much as I could. The rest..." She quickly glances at my pants as her cheeks pinken a little, then back at my face. "You'll have to do on your own."

"Thank you." My voice is raspy with emotion, and I hope she doesn't notice.

"No problem. See you in a minute." She smiles sweetly.

When she leaves, I grab the sink with both hands and look in the mirror. A sad-looking fuck stares back at me. Am I that fucked up? Is my sister fucked up the same way? We've never had a parent to comfort us. We never had hugs. We never had kisses. And for us, it was normal. But is it normal for everyone? Before this moment, I didn't know what I was missing. Before this moment, I didn't even know I was missing something. I thought my life was in a good place. I got out of the trailer park. I stopped my old business I had to have in order to make money to feed my sister. I bought this house in a good neighborhood, and I thought I had it all figured out. I was wrong.

Now, I'm yearning for something I've never had. And I absolutely do not know how to deal with it.

After I clean myself like she did before, I walk—or more like crawl—outside, and the most delicious smell assaults my nose. My mouth waters. Only now do I remember I haven't eaten in ages.

Alicia is standing in my kitchen, barefoot—thank God I have heated floors, or her cute little feet with painted-red toenails would be frozen—and stirring something in a sizzling pan. She's singing something under her breath completely out of tune. It would annoy me in regular circumstances, but I find it oddly adorable. I inwardly grown. How can I find anything she does adorable?

"Oh, you're here." She notices me. "I was about to go and get you. Thought you may have decided to go against your amazing," she smirks as she points at her face, "nurse's order and drowned in the shower. But your dog wasn't worried, so I figured you were probably okay."

"That dog?" I point at Ghost as he eats something from his bowl without giving me even a glance. His ears perk up, but his focus on his food never wavers.

"Fair point." She laughs.

"I wasn't even in there for long."

"You were. Twenty minutes." She points at the clock on the wall. "The food is almost done."

"Really?" I walk over, pretending to ignore her first point, and peek in the pan.

"Yeah." She laughs again. "Take a seat, and I'll fix you a plate in a few." She glances at me. "I see you're feeling better."

"I am. I guess whatever Rachel did is working." I scratch the back of my neck. I put my hair in a bun since it's not really clean, and it's itchy now. No matter how hard I tried, I couldn't find a good position to wash my hair without wetting the bandages.

"She's coming tomorrow to check on you and give you more medicine," Alicia says as she cuts veggies that I definitely didn't have in my fridge. I nod, not knowing what else to say.

A few moments later, I have a bowl of steaming soup in front of me that smells absolutely heavenly. I eat it so fast, I don't think I'm even chewing. Alicia places another plate in front of me, filled with homemade chicken and rice.

"When did you make all of this?" I look at her, my eyes full of wonder.

"You took a really long time, plus, the chicken thawed while I was out. And I had cooked rice at home." She shrugs like it's not a big deal that she prepared so much food for me. I usually only get this many options when I go out to eat.

My plate is empty in minutes, and she offers me more. Despite how much I'd love to have it, I don't think it's a good idea to stuff my stomach when I'm this sick. I don't want to vomit all this glory.

I offer to help clean, but she waves me off, so I go to the couch with my traitor dog on my heels. I turn the TV on. Some scary show pops onto the screen, and I think it's fitting since Halloween is around the corner. Alicia makes herself comfy on the chair, her feet up.

"What are you doing?" I ask, dumbfounded.

"Watching TV. Do you mind?" She cocks a brow.

I feel my cheeks getting hot, and I look away. "That's not what I meant. I wanted to say you don't have to stay here. You can go back to your place. I appreciate your help, but you can go." *Because you're making me want something I can't have,* I add silently.

"I'd rather stay. To watch over you while you're not well, you know," she replies shyly, and suddenly her tone and her words... They make me see red.

"I don't need someone to watch over me. I've been living on my own just fine my entire life. It's not my first battle scar, and it's not gonna be my last, so don't worry, princess." I know I'm behaving like a total ass, but she scares me. So instinct takes over.

Her eyes widen, and she looks down at her hands. She's

clearly hurt. "I just wanted to help. To repay you for all those times you helped me."

I gather my remaining energy and laugh at her. "I don't need your help, princess. I don't need anyone's help. It's you who needs help, always getting into trouble." I let out another mocking laugh, hoping she won't detect the fakeness of it. "I have to come and save your ass every time. I haven't had a good night's sleep since you moved in." I force my face to smirk, hoping she'll leave now. "You're the only one here who needs saving."

She jumps up from her chair, her eyes ablaze. "I don't need anyone watching after me," she growls and walks to the door. She touches the handle and turns toward me. "I've had enough people in my life telling me how incapable I am of living on my own. I refuse to let another person"—she points her finger at me —"join the party." She flips the same finger toward her chest. "I can do it. I can do everything I set my mind to! And I don't need you near to *save* me." Her lips thin, and her nostrils flare as she tries to put her shoes on, but her laces refuse to listen to her.

I want to stand and help her, to say how sorry I am for the words I've said, but it's better this way. Stirring those feelings in me isn't a good thing. She's the first person to do that, and I'm afraid I'll get too attached and won't be able to let her go.

Because she will. Go, I mean. She's clearly destined for bigger things than living in our small town with an insignificant person like me.

She opens the door and leaves, her ponytail flying behind her back. Her hips sway with her fast, angry walk. She left her jacket on the bench by the door, but I don't think she cares. Her blood was so heated, she probably doesn't need it.

Talk about heat and blood. I groan as I look down at my hard cock tenting my sweats. If I thought shy Alicia was hot, I don't have a name for angry Alicia either—a goddess of war and sex combined in one hot-as-fuck package. And I know everything she was saying was heartfelt, I know. I know she was offended when I started patronizing her, but the way she made me feel was dangerous. I didn't want to upset her, but I needed her to go.

* * *

A couple of days pass, and I haven't seen her. I've been sneaking around my windows, trying to get a glimpse of her. No cars have arrived or left other than two delivery trucks dropping off some big boxes by her front door. I wanted to go help her carry them inside, but by the time I put my boots on and went outside, there were no boxes in sight.

At some point, I even 'accidentally' let Ghost out, sending him her way. He returned after sitting on her front porch for an hour. If that didn't work, I don't think anything will.

Chapter Twelve

MARK

Today is my first day of my forty-eight. Life at the station is getting back to normal. Almost everyone is back after the flu struck, so we're steadily getting our missing hours back. This morning I dragged the new rocking chair I made outside to sit, covering myself in a blanket like a grandpa. The mug in my hands is full of hot coffee, I have my loyal sidekick by my feet, and I feel good as I rock back and forth. And I don't need anyone caring or feeling pity for me. I'm just fine.

And that's when I see her for the first time since I was a dick to her.

I almost convince myself not to talk to her, but I can't,

especially seeing her lock her front door behind her, a bunch of crap in her arms.

"Where are you going with all that stuff?" I call, maybe a bit too loud. She has a giant backpack slung over her shoulder, with all sorts of things sticking out the top, and there's something hanging from the bottom. It's heavy and smacks her thick thighs with every step she takes, nearly knocking her down. I look closer and notice it's a freaking tent clipped to the bottom of her bag. She's barely able to move, dragging her feet with every step under the weight of all the shit clipped to her body. She looks like a giant, pissed-off turtle, carrying her whole house on her back.

"Not your business," she snaps back and proceeds through her backyard toward the woods. She's wearing tall black hiking boots, black leggings, a long red puffy jacket, and a black beanie on her head. Her long braid is hanging over her shoulder. She most definitely looks like she's going camping. In October. In Maine... when the bears are hungry and roam the woods for food, and the ground freezes at night.

"I hope you're not going camping, because you'll sure as fuck freeze to death out there."

She doesn't turn toward me but throws up a gloved middle finger. At least she had it in her to dress appropriately.

"Alright, boy. I've tried," I say to Ghost as I relax back into the chair. He doesn't even look up from the ground as he cleans his junk. *Did I say 'a loyal friend'?*

I need groceries, because some of us have real-time responsibilities rather than camping in October, so when my coffee is done, I go inside, grab my keys, and walk to the truck, whistling for Ghost to follow.

Groceries in my truck, a few things for my wood-carving hobby, and one unpleasant encounter with Justin Attleborough later, we go back home.

By the time I'm done with my chores and start making linner—lunch and dinner, as I always told my sister—it's past 4:00 p.m. I glance outside. It's getting dark, but there's no light coming from the front of the house next to mine. She usually turns the light on early, way before it's dark. I peer into her windows—nothing. A weird feeling sets in the pit of my stomach. Where the hell is she? Still out there? Did she really decide to stay there for the night? Even for an experienced camper, winter camping is possible but not pleasant. But something tells me she's not exactly an experienced camper.

I fry my ground beef and boil the pasta, mix them together, and make myself a hefty plate. But I can't eat. The feeling in my stomach has intensified ten times since I looked out the window. I'm sure it's the remnants of my job talking, caring about other people.

Ghost lets out a pitiful whine. "I know, boy. I know," I say with a heavy exhale.

I know there is no way I'll let her stay there alone, so I go to the garage, grab my rescue backpack I got a long time ago, when I had to be ready to stay alive in the wilderness for days, and go back to the kitchen to put the food into a thermos. I fill another one with hot coffee, pull out a few bottles of water, and stack it all into the bottomless pit of my backpack. Then I think and grab my thermal sleeping bag. It's not winterproof per se, but it's October, and the weather shouldn't be too bad.

Ghost is dancing around me, pushing me with his muzzle toward the door. Damn me, the bastard wants to go after her. There is no other explanation. The moment I open the door, he sprints into the woods. Who's dog is he?

I lock the door, zip up my jacket, and follow him.

It doesn't take me long to find her, maybe an hour. I don't think it was in her plan to disappear completely. She just wanted some space from humanity, perhaps. Sometimes I hike the same path when I have a heavy day and I need to check out from the rest of the world. I'm not stupid enough to stay out here for the night though. This road leads up the hill into the pine forest. It's not a high altitude, so the temperature doesn't fluctuate much, but bears sure love this path because of the hikers and the food they're making with their fires.

I step into the opening among the pines and find her sitting on a log by the dying fire with a mug in her hands, staring ahead of her. There's a tent lying on the ground in a messy pile, her backpack by her legs, half open with everything inside spilling out of it.

"Hey," I say quietly, hovering at the edge of her little camp, trying not to scare her.

She blinks a few times, clearing the fog she is in. The absence of emotions scares me a little, if I'm honest.

"Hey." Her answer is barely audible.

"Can I join you?"

A short, silent nod is her only response, so I move toward her. Ghost is hesitant by my side, and it scares me even more. He follows my footsteps, not rushing forward, like he sees more than I do. Or less.

I sit on the log next to her. There is a foot of space between us, but she scoots over, making it one and a half. I imagine half of her butt is suspended in the air, and I'm about to stand when she brings her hand to mine and covers it.

"Stay." She sighs when Ghost comes to sit next to her. Seems like my dog has some cosmic connection with the woman. "Sorry, I don't do well with people when no one else is around."

I pause for a moment, looking down at my hands. "With people... or with men?"

The silence that follows is deafening. I give up on the idea of ever getting my answer when she surprises me with a quiet 'men' and goes to rub Ghost's ears, who closes his eyes and leans into her touch, relaxing her a little.

A wave of rage rises in my chest, traveling like acid up my throat and burning me from the inside out. I try to swallow it, but it remains, bubbling near the surface. "Did someone hurt you, Alicia?" I'm aware my voice comes out as a growl, but I can't change it. Not now. Not when I can rip whoever hurt her with my bare hands. Limb to limb. My rage is already palpable. I can see it in front of me, a red fog clouding my vision.

She blinks slowly, her throat bobbing. "It was a long time ago." Her voice is void of emotion. She's like a robot sitting here, next to me. Her body is present, but her mind's gone somewhere else. I've noticed her doing that a lot.

"That doesn't make it okay." I'm breathing like an enraged bull, but she doesn't grant me a response. Not that I deserve one. Not when I act like a Neanderthal.

"I'm scared to be alone." Her voice is a whisper, and the words she's saying seem so heavy, I hold my breath, fearing scaring her off. "And I'm scared to be around people. I'm just scared all the time." She swallows loudly and continues. "I moved here because I wanted to move on, but I can't. I came here..." She presses her finger to the log we're sitting on. "Because I wanted to overcome this... irrational fear of being alone. I'm always scared I'll get attacked, and no one will be there to save me. Always scared." She gulps and looks up. "I thought I could do it, but I can't. I mean, look at this." She points at the tent on the ground. "I couldn't even set this thing up, and I had clear instructions." She pulls a paper from her pocket and shakes it in front of my face. "See, *instructions*."

I take the paper from her and frown. "These are shitty instructions."

She looks at my grimace, and a beautiful, shy smile breaks through the dark clouds on her face. "You think so?"

"Oh, for sure. I mean, look at this." I show her the paper, flipping it upside down. "Who can read that?"

"Right." She giggles and scrunches her nose. "No one."

"Told you." I click my tongue. "Good thing I used to be a pro at setting up tents, and I still remember." I wink at her and rise to my feet.

"What are you doing?" Her eyes widen, and she sits up straighter, gripping the log with both hands.

"Helping you set up this tent. Is it weatherproof?" I nod toward the disaster on the ground.

"Yeah, it had four point eight stars on Amazon." She wipes her nose with her gloved hand.

I stop moving and turn toward her. "Why not five?"

Her face looks horrified. "You think I should have gotten another one?"

I crack, doubling over with laughter. "Relax, princess. This one is good enough," I say when I can breathe again.

"Even when it's cold?"

"Let's hope it is." It's so fucking cold, my ass is completely frozen, but if she wants this—*needs* this—we will stay on this fucking frozen ground in this freezing air with our frozen asses.

But she will overcome her fear today.

Well, at least one of them, and I'll be damned if I leave her to do it here on her own. I've been facing my fears alone all my life, and I don't want anyone to go through the same, especially not her. "But camping in the cold is fun. You'll see," I say, walking to the tent. After digging through it, I can tell she spent a small fortune on it, and it will hold just fine even if the snow hits at night.

"Have you been camping a lot?" she asks as she makes her way to me.

"I wouldn't call it camping." I move the tent to the side and see if the spot it's in is any good. "Do you want it here?" I nod at my feet, and she shrugs in return. "Alright, we'll move it that way then." I point toward the young, thick pine trees that make a natural wall against the wind.

I gather all the stuff so I can move it fifteen feet to the left, and she comes to help.

"What would you call it?" she asks after a pause.

"Surviving, I guess." I shrug and start cleaning the area of cones and twigs.

"Did you grow up in the woods or something?" The way she asks it might sound snobbish to someone who doesn't know her, but to my utter surprise, I understand what she means.

"I wish I did. It probably would have been better that way." I lay down the footprint for the base. "Grab those corners so we can stretch them." I point at the two corners opposite me. She helps to spread the base on the tarp, and I drive the stakes into the ground. Then I go to deal with the poles.

The tent is basic but good quality, and it takes me about five minutes to finish inserting the poles and build the tent to its full glory.

"Wow," she says in awe.

"We're not done yet." I glance at her gleaming face.

"It looks so cool already."

"Yep." I check around the perimeter, securing the poles and hooks. "See how you did this time." I stop by her side and motion toward our creation. I briefly look at her.

I wish I never did. Her face has changed, radiating pure joy. She has a bright smile across her face, her eyes big and happy. All that from a freaking tent.

I feel unexpected emotions rising, and I swallow them down. They're new to me, but somehow already familiar. I felt it in my shower when she was helping me clean up.

"Thank you," she says quietly, clearly fighting the urge to cry.

"Yeah." I look around uncomfortably. "Do you have anything for the inside?"

"Yes, it's over there." She clears her throat and points at her backpack.

I march over and find so many things in this bottomless bag. I pull another tarp out, a thermal one, thin and light. Then comes an air mattress with a manual pump. I have more and more questions with every object I pull out. She might have spent a *small* fortune on her adventure.

Finally, I pull out a heavy duty, super warm sleeping bag before a bunch of other stuff.

I turn toward her. "How did you carry all of this here?"

She shrugs. "I had a goal." Her smile is sheepish, and I can't help but smile back.

I carry everything inside with her hot on my heels. The tent is huge. I can easily sit without touching the ceiling, which is rare, considering I'm six foot five. She slips in behind me. We spread the tarp and the mattress across the floor together. While I work the pump, inflating the mattress, she moves to the corner and folds her legs under her butt.

"Thank you for your help, Mark."

"Sure." I shrug it off.

There's a pause. "Why are you here?" she asks suddenly, and my heart skips a beat.

I switch my attention from the pump to her. I have two options here: I can make up some shit and laugh it off, or I can tell the truth. "I wanted to make sure you're alright," I tell her after a moment.

"Your profession talking?" Her voice waivers a little as she asks.

"I guess." I finish pumping the air in, not knowing how to interpret the change in her tone. The bed is a twin, raised about ten inches above the ground. "All done." I pat the velvety surface. "Looks comfy."

"Thank you for the help, again." She fidgets with her shoes.

I nod and head outside. Ghost is lying on the ground by the fire, gently snoring. I guess no predators are around if our guard dog is so chill.

Wait a minute. *Our?* Our as in fellow campers. That's it.

I go back to the log and pull the food from my backpack. Shit, I forgot plates.

"Do you have plates?" I call out to her.

"Yeah, one. Why?"

"I brought us some food, but it's in a very narrow thermos." I shake it in the air. "Fuck, I don't have any utensils either."

"I got it!" Her face brightens before dimming in an instant. "But only one spoon."

"Yeah, I don't know what I was thinking when I was getting ready." I scratch the back of my head.

"Probably how to save your stupid neighbor." She winks.

"Probably. C'mere." I gesture for her to come closer. "I'll get you dinner."

She digs into her bottomless bag and takes out a bowl. I pile up a huge portion of the steaming pasta and pass it to her. She sits next to me—half a foot closer this time—and takes a bite. I start getting mine ready when I'm stopped by her loud moan. She throws her head back with closed eyes. Holy motherfucking shit, if it's not the ultimate trial of my willpower, I don't know what is.

"It's so ho-o-od!" she mumbles, trying to open her mouth so the hot food won't burn it. "Like so fleakin' hod!"

Her mumbling is adorable, and I can't help but laugh. "That's just the fresh air talking. You worked up an appetite."

"Nah." She shoves another spoonful into her mouth. "It's really good."

Ghost lazily lifts his head and looks at miserable old me, suffering the consequences of her moan, before he rolls his eyes and puts his head back on his outstretched paws.

"Wait." She swallows the food she's been chewing. "We have only one spoon and only one plate." She offers me her spoon with a small smile. "I don't have cooties."

I used to eat after my sister when she was little, but that was a long time ago. Since then, I've never shared my food or plate or spoon with anyone. Even hated drinking water from the same bottle after my girlfriends. I'm okay with licking a pussy, but sharing a spoon? No, thank you. And here, I find myself grabbing the spoon that had just been in her mouth and digging it into the pasta, then bringing it to my own lips.

My taste buds instantly explode with different flavors: beef, tomatoes, spice, and I swear I get a hint of vanilla. I glance at Alicia. Her eyes are trained on my lips as I slowly chew. I swallow and lick my lips clean. Her throat works in a rough swallow of her own, and her eyes dart up to mine. Her pupils widen and her eyes dart around as if she's been caught doing something naughty. I feel a smile tugging on my lips.

"It's really alright." My smile spreads when I fail to contain my entertainment.

"What about Ghost?"

"He ate before we left. I packed him a puppy snack in the bag for before bed so he's good until tomorrow morning."

"The bed."

"Yeah. He likes to chew his doggy bone before he goes to sleep."

"You're staying here?" She looks shocked.

Now I'm shocked. "Did you really think I was gonna leave you here alone with the bears?"

Her eyes fill with horror as I watch her. "Bears?"

"Yeah. Are you not from Maine?"

"I am." Her tone is a bit hesitant, and I remember I know nothing about her.

"Then you know all about bears." I shrug and shove another spoonful in my mouth.

"Where will you sleep?" She looks around as if seeing the space for the first time. "Do you have a tent with you?"

"No, I don't have one handy at my house." I shrug it off.

"But you're still here?"

"Because you needed to stay here." I look straight into her eyes, probably for the first time, silently communicating that I *understand*.

"Where will you sleep then?" Her eyes dart around in pure horror, and I have to remind myself that it's nothing against me. She doesn't know I've been considered trailer trash all my life... that I've been looked upon by the people of Little Hope with judgment for years. She's been through some traumatic event in her past. She doesn't intend to be mean.

"Here, by the fire." I nod at Ghost, snuggled up by the dancing flames. I'm a little worried the dummy will burn his fur, but hey, he's a big boy, and if he loses his lashes, it's on him.

"You'll get cold!" she exclaims, and for a second I think I hear sincere worry in her voice.

"I have a sleeping bag." I motion to my backpack. "I'll be fine."

"You'll freeze to death here at night. The temperature will drop." She's fidgeting with her hands. "You should go home."

"Not a chance." I shake my head. "Not leaving you here."

She nervously bites at her lower lip to the point I fear it will bleed soon as she looks between me and the tent.

"Hey," I call, but she doesn't hear. "Alicia." I put more force behind my voice, and she finally turns toward me. When I know I have her full attention, I continue. "You don't have to invite me inside. I'm a big boy, and me and Ghost will be fine." When I see she isn't convinced, I say, "I promise. I've slept out in the cold before."

"You were camping?" Her eyes are too innocent to hear my horror stories.

"Yeah, something like that." I try to make my chuckle less dark, but judging from her narrowed eyes, I think I failed. "Anyway, get some water." I dig into my bag and pass her a bottle. "You need to stay hydrated at night when it's cold. Drink at least half of it before bed."

She eyes the bottle questionably. "That's a lot."

"Yep, and it's good for you."

"Alright. I guess I'm gonna go." She half turns, motioning toward the tent.

"Yeah, a smart idea. Good night," I say as I give her a weak wave.

Chapter Thirteen

ALICIA

You're a selfish person, Alicia!

I think to myself as I climb into the tent. It's so windy outside, and so nice in here. It's not warm per se, but there is no biting cold or wind. How is he going to sleep there? Sure, he can snuggle with Ghost, who is basically a furry heater, but he'll be sleeping on the frozen ground. Is his sleeping bag warm enough?

I shake my head, hating myself for my inability to invite him to sleep inside where the cold can't reach him. The guy came here to make sure I'm okay alone in the wilderness, and now he's forced to freeze his butt out there.

I move the bed around the tent, attempting to find the

perfect spot for it in the middle, and take a seat on it. I imagine him walking—more like crawling, considering his height—inside my temporary home, and fearful goose bumps tingle my body. No, I'm not ready to share my space with anyone yet. I don't know if I'll ever be ready, but definitely not today. It's one thing to be in a close space in his bathroom where we could at least stand, but here... It's too confined.

I pull my puffy jacket off, spread the sleeping bag on the bed, and zip it on the side so I can just climb in and go to bed. I take my shoes off and leave my warm fuzzy socks on.

Suddenly I hear a whine from outside and then Mark's muffled voice.

"Scoot over, I can't let you in. No, Ghost." Then more whining. "No, dude. You're too big for this sack."

I freeze on the bed. I really can't do this to them. They're here because of me, and I'm forcing them to stay in the cold.

I take a deep, tranquilizing breath and close my eyes, imagining once again someone in my space, close to me, when there is no one around to help me. And just as I predicted, a wave of nausea follows. Fuck this, I'm broken. I try to swallow the acidic taste in my mouth, but it doesn't go away as I imagine *someone* in the tent with me.

But then the *someone* morphs into that big body, and my nausea gets better. And when *someone's* face changes into Mark's, covered in his day-five beard, it completely goes away. I can breathe again.

I can imagine him here, in my tent, with me, the door closed—well, zipped—and it doesn't scare me anymore. Another human, a man, in my space doesn't cause shivers of fear down my back and tingling inside my skull. It doesn't scare me. Mark doesn't scare me.

I let myself breathe again and smile before carefully climbing out of my sleeping bag to poke my head outside. Mark is shoving Ghost's nose out from under his head, where he's currently trying to sneak in despite their sizes.

"Hey," I call, and Mark instantly jumps, sitting up.

"Are you okay?"

"Yeah." I smile at his worried face. "I'm just wondering if you maybe want to... you know..." And suddenly I feel awkward. "Like sleep in here."

"Inside with you?" His brows shoot up.

"Yeah." I give him a small smile.

He inhales loudly, looking around him. "Alicia, I'll be fine here. Really. Don't worry."

"Of course you will be, but it's comfy in here, and there's enough space for the both of us."

Ghost whines, looking up at his dad with the biggest, saddest, most pleading eyes.

"Three of us." I smile at the dog, and he instantly jumps up, runs past me, and disappears inside the tent. I look at Mark. "I guess you're outnumbered."

"I guess so." He smiles sheepishly before sobering up. "I don't think it's a good idea. You know—" He motions toward me, leaving the unspoken in the air.

Something cold and wet falls onto my nose, and I look up—the first snow picked the perfect time to happen.

I smile. It seems as if the sky has spoken. "I think it's a very good idea. I'll be waiting for you inside." I disappear back into the tent, where Ghost has already found his spot in the corner. He spent no time getting to work cleaning his junk. "Gross, no kisses for you."

He lets out a loud fart and looks up at me as if surprised before returning to his previous activity. A loud laugh comes from outside.

"It wasn't me!" I cry out, and the laughter grows louder.

The tent opens, and Mark stands at the entrance, holding the door panel to the side. "We'll need some fresh air. That dude is straight-up toxic after ground beef."

I scrunch my nose. "Tell me about it." I hurry outside. "Let me out." I squeal as I push him aside, running past him without even putting my shoes on.

Mark's laughter is so deep and contagious, I can't help myself but join. A minute later, the cold creeps into my bones, and I shiver.

He notices. "I think it's safe to go in now."

"You sure?"

"Yeah." He chuckles and motions for me to go first then and follows me.

Once we're inside, it's awkward again. The bed takes almost the whole floor besides the little spot we're crouched in. There is no way such a big man can fit on the side along the bed.

"Where is your sleeping bag?" I ask.

"Here." He shows me the balled-up material.

I take it and notice how thin it is. He was planning to sleep outside in this the whole night? This thing barely holds any warmth.

I shake my head and move to the bed. Unzipping his bag, I spread it on the bed like a second mattress. The bed will help for sure, but it's filled with cold air, and it's cold by itself, so this should help. Then I unzip my bag and lay it out on top like a cover. I take my puffy jacket and make a double pillow before stepping back to admire my creation. I feel pride, like one of my werewolf characters whenever they're nesting, minus the sexy moves happening.

I switch my attention to him—he's crouching,

supporting his weight with a hand on the floor. His lips are pursed, like he doesn't understand what I'm doing.

"All done."

"What's done? You stole the last barrier between me and pneumonia." A hint of humor is in his voice.

"No, we'll share the bed," I announce proudly, waving a hand over my creation.

His face turns ashen. It's so not the response I was expecting. "Share the bed? Together?" Now he looks outright terrified. "Like this tiny bed?"

"C'mon!" I roll my eyes. "I don't have cooties."

"That's not it—" He cuts himself off before he has the chance to declare how sorry he feels for me, apparently. "I mean, after everything—" He sighs deeply. "I'm not sure it's a good idea, Alicia. I'm really not sure. I don't want to trigger something."

I sigh. "You won't. I'm offering."

I'm done with this latent argument, so I climb into the bed and place my bottle of water by my side. "I hope you don't snore."

"I don't." His reply is robotic.

Once I'm good and cozy, I lift my upper body and lean on my elbows. "What are you waiting for? Ghost is about to take your place." At the mention of his name, the dog lets out a lazy half bark and leans his chin on his paws.

Mark is still frozen by the entrance. After a moment, he finally blinks and turns to the door to secure it. I scoot over to the side, freeing space for his enormous frame. I hear him shuffling around with his jacket and shoes, and the bed dips. "Will it hold us both?"

"It said six hundred pounds. I don't think you weigh more than two thirty."

"Two sixty," he says and presses his open palm to the mattress, testing it. "Alicia, are you sure about that?"

In response, I pat the bed and scoot over a tiny bit more.

"Alright. Wake me up if you feel uncomfortable," he says with a yawn.

"Will do," I say, swallowing a knot of nerves.

I will be fine. I will be fine.

There's a dip in the bed as he stretches his body. His weight is much more than mine, so I accidentally half roll onto him.

"Sorry," I mumble, trying to move back, but the dip is too big, and every time, I end up rolling back. He sighs and scoots closer to the middle, and I still end up half rolling, but this time I'm more stable with my own body.

Lying on his back, he brings his hands under his head, and my right side ends up pressed to him.

"Is this alright?" he asks in a gruff voice.

"Mhmm." My answer is barely coherent because I'm experiencing so many thoughts, feelings, and sensations at once.

I haven't touched a man in more than eight years. Like a full-body touch, I mean. Other than my brothers and my father. I couldn't even stand when someone touched me passing by at the grocery store. I'm not talking about a hug or a handshake; I mean any sort of contact.

I remember the way my body tingled when my fingers accidentally brushed his skin when I was helping him in the bathroom. It was just a tip-of-the-finger contact, but I was shocked. And now, my whole side is pressed to this living, breathing man. His body radiates heat, warming my frozen bones. We're both wearing long-sleeve sweaters and pants, but I still feel the warmth from him. It's warming something besides my frozen bones. It goes deeper.

Melting icebergs of forgotten emotions and sensations. Of feelings I dreaded.

But now, I'm not scared, no. Now, I'm *aware*. Aware of someone being next to me. No, not someone. Mark. When I feel safe, the person who makes me feel that way always has a name, always. Even if I'm not prepared, my body is ready to come out of its slumber.

Fuck. I want it to be Mark. I so want it to be. But a man like him would never waste his time waiting for damaged goods like me. No one—myself included—knows how long it will take for me to be fully ready for something physical. What can I promise him? Nothing. I can't promise anything to anyone.

Mark oozes sex through his pores, filling the little tent with palpable testosterone. I can tell he's a sexual being and probably needs a lot of sex. He doesn't need just kisses on the cheek from time to time. Who am I kidding? I can't even offer that.

My body must have moved backward on its own accord, because a big arm sneaks under my neck and settles against my shoulders, snuggling me closer.

I freeze.

He does too.

"Shit, sorry. I didn't think." His voice is full of melancholy, and his body goes tense. "Shit, Alicia, sorry." He tries to pull his arm away, but my hand shoots up on its own accord and grabs his, holding it in place.

"Leave it." I swallow, embarrassed. "It feels good."

His body relaxes. I feel him settling back down on the bed, and my body rolls *closer* into him.

I lie still, taking in the warmth surrounding me as I stare at a black dot on the ceiling of the tent. A gentle snoring comes from the corner.

A nice woodsy smell tickles my nose, and I inhale deeply.

"You okay?" His voice sounds scratchy, like he wants to cough but is scared to move.

"I am. I'm more than okay," I tell him. My voice is no more than a whisper.

His chest puffs out, and I want to smile. "Tell me if it's too much."

"Okay."

His bicep under my head is hard as stone, but it's better than any pillow I could have imagined. I get a little braver and turn my head toward him and take a deep breath, inhaling his scent.

A low rumble comes from his chest. "Are you sniffing me?"

"Sue me," I answer and inhale again. "You smell like wood."

He chokes and starts laughing. Our whole bed shakes. "I actually might have some."

There, just for a second, my gaze dips down his body, and I see he might be right. There is some nice wood in the house. Like quite a lot. His pants are thick, but they can't contain whatever is happening, and a big bulge has formed. How big is he? With a man of his size, he must have a whole weapon in his pants, like a police baton.

I close my eyes, expecting to freak myself out and him along with me, but instead, a steady warmth spreads across my chest, and I feel my cheeks turning hot.

He clears his throat. "Sorry, bad joke."

"A good one, actually." I chuckle and completely move my body to lie on my side, growing braver by the second. He's safe. He's made me feel safe. The front of my body is flush against his side, my head resting on his bicep.

His body goes iron stiff, and he's not breathing. He takes a deep, trembling breath, and wraps his arm around my shoulders, pressing me to himself.

A comfortable silence settles around us as I snuggle closer and bring my arm around his torso.

I'm about to cuddle against him more when he ruins everything with question. "Where is he, Alicia?"

My body goes rigid, and the coziness evaporates along with the calmness.

"I know you don't want to talk about him, but I have to know." There's a pause. "Please."

"Why? Why do you need to know?" I push myself away from him, but his grip is firm on my back, and my attempt turns fruitless. In any other situation, I'd be a crying, wiggling mess, but his insanely strong hands holding me firmly to his body don't freak me out.

"I have to, Alicia." His voice turns grave. "I have to."

My breathing is quick and shallow. I want to punch him in his handsome face and scratch his wide chest with my nails. My eyes are full of unshed tears, and I want to punish him for causing them. Haven't I had enough? But instead of ruining him, I find myself speaking. "I don't know where they are. I don't even know who they are."

"*They?*" His words thunder through our close quarters, causing Ghost to jump up and growl. He probably caused an avalanche somewhere farther in the mountains, I'm sure. "How many of them were there, Alicia?"

My body catches up to my brain, and I begin shaking. Trying to remove myself from his grip, I try to push away, and this time he lets me. In the process of pulling away, I land on the floor on my ass. Ghost is with me in a second, poking his wet nose to my cheek.

Mark sits up and tries to scoot away, moving the light

bed in the process. But he really can't. There's not enough space for the two of us on the floor since the bed is taking up almost the entire tent. "Fuck, Alicia. I'm sorry. I know I can't yell, but I just fucking can't."

He gets off the bed, barely fitting in the narrow space, puts his boots on, and climbs out of the tent. Ghost whines, looking after his dad, but stays with me. He lies on the floor next to me, his head on my lap. I rub his ears, hoping to calm myself down.

For a second there, I thought I was cured. Ha. A joke.

A few minutes later, Mark climbs back inside. His hair is covered in snow, his cheeks are red, and his eyes are crazed. He's still breathing like an enraged bull. In fact, I can see puffs of air coming out of his nose and mouth. It's that cold. He stormed out without a jacket, and I bet he's cold. I focus on his red cheeks instead of his eyes. I'm scared of the things I can read in there. I've seen enough pity to last me a lifetime.

He crouches next to me, brings his finger under my chin, and lifts it up. "We need to talk about this, Alicia. Please."

"I can't," I tell him. "I haven't talked about it with anyone."

"No one?"

I shake my head.

"What about your family?"

Another shake.

"Cops?"

I shake my head more violently this time.

He inhales loudly through his nose and wipes his face with his hands. "So, they're free?"

I nod.

"Alright." His jaw clenches, the muscles working like

166

they're on a mission to grind his teeth into dust. He's thinking—hard—while unconsciously making small circles on my chin with his callused thumb. And I like it. I like the feeling of his roughness. In fact, I'm almost high on this sensation.

My body is starved for it, and I lean into the feeling. I don't even think he knows what he's doing—his mind is far, far away—until Ghost nudges him with his nose. "Hey, boy. You're being a good guard dog?" Mark gives his ear a scratch and pulls away from me.

Before I can back down, I decide to ask him the question I find myself most scared of. "Are you leaving?"

His head whips toward me, his eyes searching for something in mine. He looks genuinely confused. "Why?"

I shrug. "I dunno."

"No," he answers with a sigh. "I'm not going anywhere." He climbs on the bed and pats the spot beside him. "Come on, we need to get some sleep."

I give Ghost a kiss on the forehead and get on the bed. I'm hesitant to move closer to Mark, but he presses his hand to the mattress, forcing me to roll onto him. I settle in the same position as before, but this time I put a leg over his lap, carefully listening to my body. It's quiet and at peace.

We don't say a word for a while, and I drift away to sleep.

Chapter Fourteen

MARK

Quiet sobbing, followed by someone punching me in my side, wakes me from my heavy sleep. I open my eyes to Alicia shaking, her body pressed to mine. Her little fists punch my chest, but it doesn't hurt. Silent sobs come from her open mouth.

"Alicia," I call, but she's asleep, trapped deep in her nightmare. "Alicia, it's just a dream. Wake up." I shake her carefully, but she doesn't wake up. I call louder. "Alicia!"

Her eyes fly open, lost in time and space. She's still there, whenever she was trapped, and I have a pretty fucking good idea which moment she was reliving.

"Alicia, it's me." I repeat myself, hoping she'll hear me. "Your friendly neighborhood firefighter." That seems to bring her back, and her eyes finally focus on my face.

"Sorry," she says, her voice gruff as she wipes sweat away from her forehead. "I'm sorry. I hate when that happens."

"Does it happen a lot?" My own voice comes out as a groan, and I fear she'll get scared again, but it doesn't happen. Instead, she presses her body to mine, looking for warmth and nearness.

"Less and less." She sniffles. "Thanks, I don't remember the last time I wasn't alone in that."

I don't want to respond. What can I say? I'd only get angry. At the assholes who did that. At her family who can't help her, leaving her alone with her demons. At everyone.

"Thank you, Mark."

"Do you want to talk about it?" I bring my arm around her shoulders and pull her closer. It seems like her demons checked out for a moment. She doesn't jump back in fear when I touch her. And God knows I need to touch her right now, to make sure she's okay. Somehow, I feel like I'm the one reliving her nightmares.

"No." She shakes her head against my side. "I just want to lie here. With you, if it's okay."

"It's okay." I tug her closer to me, enjoying the feel of her soft body next to mine. I just wish we didn't have these itchy clothes between us.

I mentally smack myself for being a creep. But to be fair, the clothes we wear so we don't freeze to death *are* itchy.

Her labored breathing slows down eventually, and I think she fell asleep when her quiet voice startles me.

"I haven't kissed anyone in years, and I mean it—*years*." She stresses the word as my breath hitches. *Did I just hear her right?* "I couldn't. I didn't want to." I hear her rough swallow. "Do you think you could kiss me?"

My throat goes dry, and I can barely force out a single word. "Alicia" is all I can manage.

"Sorry! Gosh, I'm so sorry." She scatters away from me, and I don't stop her. "I'm sorry, Mark. I didn't mean to make you uncomfortable, and yet here I am, draped all over you. You probably have a girlfriend, and I don't even know." She hides her face in her hands. "Gosh, it's embarrassing," she muffles into her palms.

I take a second to collect my thoughts. "Alicia," I whisper gently, but when she doesn't react, I speak a little firmer. "Alicia."

"What?" She still hasn't removed her hands from her face.

"Look at me."

"No." Her voice is muffled.

"Look at me." It comes out as an order, and I'm surprised she listens. She lifts her guarded eyes toward me, her cheeks pink with embarrassment. "I don't have a girlfriend."

"No?"

"No." I shake my head.

"Okay."

"Okay." I don't know how to proceed. How do I tell her I want to kiss her more than anything in my life? But I'm afraid I won't be able to stop at that. That I'll want to touch her in places she's probably not ready to be touched. What if I scare her, and she'll never look at me again without being horrified? How do I tell her all of that?

She bites her thumbnail. "Then you don't think I'm attractive?"

"What?" I bark out a laugh. "Why do you say that?"

"I mean you looked so repulsed at the idea of kissing me, I figured you don't want anything to do with me." She shrugs a shoulder like it's no big deal, but I know better. I see the hurt in her eyes. She took my shock as something against her, when in reality, I am shocked no one has snatched her up. Yes, she's got an attitude on her, but it's damn attractive. She isn't some doormat and doesn't let people walk all over her.

I used to date a lot. Well, not date, but hook up, and rich town girls liked to chase the high with a trash townie like myself, so they didn't make me work for it either. I used to enjoy it, but not anymore.

At one point, one of them accused me of raping her when in reality she begged for my cock while her boyfriend was downstairs getting shitfaced. The encounter was a disaster, ending with me getting beaten to a pulp. I deserved it, so I didn't throw a punch back. Not even one. I mean, the dude was in the Navy, for fuck's sake, while I was here fucking his girlfriend. I deserved to get my nose broken. But I didn't appreciate being accused of rape. I'd never force myself on a woman. Never.

Throughout my life, living in the piece-of-shit place I used to live, I stopped rapes from happening a few times, nearly killing the motherfuckers. To this day, I regret not ending them, fearing they might go do it again.

And now all I can think is what if any of those fuckers were the ones who hurt Alicia, making me responsible for her horrors.

Alicia is beautiful as fuck and sexy as a siren, no matter what she wears. She's like a mystery you want to solve, and you know the reward will be worth it all. But she's been through hell. I don't need to hear her story to know she's never recovered. The last thing she needs is a beast like me coming at her, because once I unleash myself, it's done.

It's why those girls were all over me—their stuck-up boyfriends couldn't deliver the wild I could. She needs the gentle, and I don't know how to do that. For fuck's sake, I've never once in my life had gentle sex. Even my first time was violent, with a woman older than me. I didn't have a say in it, but honestly, I didn't fight it much either. I guess it paved the road for my future escapades, and now I like it rough and dirty.

I'm exactly the opposite of what she needs, and I'm afraid I'd never be able to deliver it.

"See—that look on your face." She flinches, thinking she's the one who brought a sour grimace to my face.

"That's not it—" I cut myself off before I spurt some more nonsense. "It's just, are you sure? I mean look at me." I spread my arms wide, and her eyes widen.

"What do you mean look at you?" She sounds confused. Just how I feel.

"Why would you be interested in kissing someone like me? After all that time."

"Someone like you?" she asks slowly, still not getting it.

"Yeah, a dirty redneck." I'm aware I sound petty, but that's how I see myself. It's how I was forced to see myself.

Her face turns angry, her little nose scrunches, and her brows draw together. "Don't say that about yourself. And besides, what if I like dirty rednecks? They're quite capable of doing things those idiot Wall Street boys can't."

My stomach drops, and familiar lead settles in. "I see. You just want some thrill with trailer trash."

"What?" She shakes her head, looking shocked. "What's up with you people calling yourself that?" She practically whispers, clearly annoyed. I don't think it was meant for my ears. She sighs and says louder, "I asked you because you're the first man I've felt safe with since... yeah, well, since then."

My stomach drops again but for a different reason. I'm fucking petty. "I'm sorry, Alicia." I wipe my face with my hand. "I guess I'm kind of fucked up."

She's watching me without a response.

"Do you still want to try it?"

"Try what?" She looks down at her hands.

"A kiss."

Her eyes darken as she swallows roughly.

"It's okay if you changed your mind," I assure her.

"I didn't!" It comes out a little too loud, and judging by the way her cheeks grow an even darker shade of pink, it embarrasses her.

"Alright. Come here." I pat the space on the bed in front of me, and she eyes it warily.

"Like right now?" Her voice drops an octave, and that deep siren's tone tickles my lower belly, stirring my dick. *Down, boy. Not now.*

"Did you want to make an appointment?" I quirk a brow, and she giggles, shaking her head. "Then come here." I pat the bed again, calling my willpower to help me stay fuckin' still.

She looks at Ghost, snoring in the corner without a care in the world, and slowly moves to the bed. I sit on the side, my legs spread wide, and she sits next to me, her legs tucked under her. There's a half foot between us, but it feels like we're on separate continents. My hands itch to move her closer, but I give her the reins. No matter what I want, I don't know how to do gentle, so I'll let her lead the way.

"What do I do?" she asks, biting her lower lip and driving me insane.

"Whatever you want." My voice is coarse, and my dick is hard just from her proximity to me. I wish it would calm the fuck down, but the fucker stays up and alert. I mentally smack my forehead on the wall.

She brings her thumb to her mouth and bites it, causing a sound to escape deep from my throat, and her eyes dart up. "Are you okay?"

My chuckle is full of pain. If her biting her damn thumb causes such a reaction in my body, I have no idea what will happen when her lips touch mine. "Yeah," I answer after clearing my throat.

"Okay." She licks her lips again, and they shine with moisture. I've never fucking paid attention to the saliva on a woman's lips. What the hell is wrong with me?

Her hand comes up to my shoulder, touching it ever so slightly. She's scared to move forward, so I bring my hand on top of hers, keeping her in place. So much for giving her free rein.

Her gaze meets mine, and a shy smile brightens her face. She brings her other hand to my other shoulder and licks her lips again. How long will she torture me? At this point, my dick is pressing against the fly of my thermal jeans, threatening to escape its prison. I'm so happy I didn't put my sweats on, or I'd be sporting a huge tent.

What the fuck am I thinking about?

She fumbles, moving closer on her knees and stopping right in front of me.

"Can you do it?" she asks, her voice hesitant.

"Do what?" I don't recognize my own voice. It's close to a growl.

175

"Kiss me." Her eyes are fixated on my lips.

I don't need another invitation.

I place my hands on her lower back and bring her body to mine. It's a little awkward since we're sitting side by side. When she's close enough, I touch her lips to mine. I don't force my tongue in her mouth like an animal—even though I wish to—but carefully press my lips to hers. I have no idea where I got this self-control and ability to be patient. But she stills. Completely stills. Her body goes rigid, and she starts pulling away. I let her and jump backward, nearly landing on the floor. By some miracle, I'm still on the bed.

"I'm sorry. I guess it's not what you were asking for." I'm ashamed of myself. I shouldn't have pulled her like that. That's not what she needed.

"No, no!" She vigorously shakes her hands. "It's me who's sorry. I'm just broken. I'm sorry!"

A big fat tear falls down her pale cheek. It follows the soft slope of her face and disappears under her chin. I follow it with my eyes, hating that I'm the one who caused it.

"What the fuck are you talking about?" It comes out like an angry snarl, but I can't help myself. "You're not broken, Alicia. You're the perfect human. *Perfect*. You feel, and that's normal. *Whatever* you feel is *normal*. It's all my fault." I shake my head in disgust.

"No!" She jumps a little, frantically looking into my eyes.

Ghost stirs in his sleep, lifting his head up to look at us. I give him a quick nod, and he goes back to sleep, knowing everything is all right. But it's not.

"It's not you. It's me, I promise." She wipes her nose. "Can we do it again?"

"I don't think it's a good idea." I grind my molars, trying to calm my raging emotions and dick at the same time.

"Please." It's said in such a painful voice, I can't say no.

Taking a deep breath, I move to her this time. Bringing her face into my hands, I wipe her tears away with my thumbs. She's not a petite woman, just the perfect size, but in my behemoth hands, her face looks tiny. Another tear escapes her eyes, and I follow its trail with my thumb, wiping it away. I move my face closer and kiss her cheek, right where I erased her tear moments ago. Her breath hitches, and I move to her other cheek, kissing away every single tear.

Her hands come to my forearms, clutching them as she looks up at me, her eyes wild. I try to move away, thinking I freaked her out, but she keeps me in place. It's the only encouragement I need.

I trace her jaw with my lips, leaving tiny kisses behind. When I get to her lips, she draws in a breath, parting them. I use the opportunity and dip the tip of my tongue in, just a bit. I retract it right away, not willing to scare her off but willing to dare her.

The quick dip is enough to make her curious, and her little hot tongue peeks out, searching for mine. I smile into the kiss and pull away, but she lets go of my forearms and moves her grip to my shoulders, keeping them in place.

Feeding off her desire to be braver, I press my lips harder to hers and lick them with my tongue. A gasp escapes her, and I fear I scared her again, but her hands move to the back of my neck, angling it the way she wants it. I don't complain and follow her lead.

Her tongue meets mine halfway, shyly exploring and tasting. My dick is so fucking hard, I can split wood without a fucking axe.

As if she heard me complain, she scoots closer, pressing the front of her body to mine, and a loud growl escapes my throat. I angle my body by turning toward her so I can feel more of her.

I'm becoming the animal I know I am, and I worry I'm about to scare her shitless if she rubs against me more. I go still.

She starts moving her body, pushing against mine. Every time she does, she comes in contact with my dick, and I feel just about ready to explode. Quite literally. I'm about to come in my pants, which won't be fun out here, at night, when I don't have a spare pair of pants. It'll only get messier out in the cold.

I'm so focused on not coming in my jeans that I forget to respond to the kiss, because she stops suddenly, looking up at me. "Am I doing something wrong?"

I try to laugh but can't. The only thing I can manage is a weird choking sound. "No," I rasp. "I just got a little overexcited."

"Oh," she answers and looks down. Of course, the moment she does, the fucker twitches, nearly breaking the zipper. "Oh!" Her eyes dart up, and I'm worried I'll see fear in her eyes.

But I don't see any. Instead, I see her gorgeous, pink cheeks redden even more, the sweat on her forehead despite the cold temperature, and her enlarged pupils.

"We should stop then." Her eyes dart downstairs again.

"Yeah," I rasp.

"We should." She bites her goddamn lip again.

And I nod in response, unable to form words. What this woman has done to me is scary. I'm the one who should be running for the hills.

"Alright then." Her voice sounds lower, raspy even. Just like mine.

"Alright." I nod.

And she throws herself at me.

I catch her halfway and hug her to me, covering her mouth with mine. All finesse and gentleness are gone. I can't stop myself anymore. I devour her mouth, diving in with my tongue. A moan escapes her lips right before she wraps her hands around my neck, hanging to me for dear life.

I force my hands to stay on her lower back, but they don't listen. They grab her ass on their own accord, moving her flush against me.

She gasps again, and I stop the kiss. I look at her, making sure it's not too much. Her beautiful face is flushed and doesn't hold any fear, her lips are swollen. I resume kissing her, lifting her from the bed and setting her on my lap, her legs on either side of me. This way, her hot little pussy is right over my aching cock. I know it will only torture me more, but I'll take anything she can give me. Anything.

She begins a little dance on my lap. Her hips move forward and backward. Forward and backward. Slow at first. Her lips are on mine, and mine on hers. She's getting braver, exploring more of my mouth. My hands are firmly on her ass, helping her move along the length of my dick. It's aching and weeping for more. Begging for me to take it out and let her slide over it without a barrier.

I've never been this hard in my life. I swear. I'm holding on for dear life here, trying not to come in my pants or throw her on the bed, shooting cum all over her beautiful tits currently pressed to me. It's so damn hard. I'm so damn hard. There is no blood left in my brain. None. All I think about is her taste on my tongue and her soft body under my hands. The way she clings to me like she needs me more than air. Like she wants *me*.

Her pace speeds up, and her mouth opens. I follow her lead, helping her move faster. Little sexy moans escape her, and I swallow every one of them. The kiss gets rougher, more my speed. She digs her fingers into my shoulders, moving herself faster. Her breathing is shallow. She forgets the kiss after a moment and presses her forehead to mine. Her breath fans my face. It's sweet, and I try to steal a few kisses before she comes. I don't know if this will ever happen again.

When I can feel her nearing the end, I grab her ass rougher and press it against my dick harder, helping her get more of the delicious friction she needs. We need. But it's not about me now.

She moves her hands around my shoulders, burying her face in the crook of my neck, placing my own face into the crook of hers. She smells so damn amazing. It's dangerous and maddening. I'm so close to losing my shit and just throwing her on the bed. Sheer willpower is the only thing holding me back.

"Mark," she breathes out, and I nearly come. No one has ever fucking said my name when they rode me. No one. "Oh fuck, Mark," she says as she shudders over me. She jerks her hips, and I can't do it anymore. I shoot my load into my pants in a few hot spurts. She keeps moving over me, and I keep coming.

"Alicia," I breathe out and go still. I just said her name during my own orgasm. I've never fucking said anyone's name during sex. It's not me. I'm not a monster who likes to fuck faceless women, no, but I don't call their names out when I'm in ecstasy. I prefer to ride alone.

Her shudders subside, but she stays on top of me, her face buried in my neck. Her body goes lax, and she wiggles.

"Alicia."

"Mhmm." She sounds sleepy.

"Alicia," I say again. "Are you okay?"

"'M 'kay."

I'm not sure I understand, but her body goes heavy, and her arms drop.

"Alicia," I say again, worried. I try to move her, but she snuggles deeper against me. She's asleep.

I carefully move her so she's lying down and feel eyes on me. Ghost. His glare is accusing.

What do you want? I glare back.

Pervert, he replies before going back to cleaning his balls.

Who's the pervert now?

But he's already turned away.

I carefully get off the bed and go for my backpack, hoping I have wipes or tissues—anything—so I can clean this mess in my pants. It's not fun to walk around in the cold with fresh cum stuck to your undies.

I find a pack of tissues and thank myself for being a man and thinking ahead. Always come prepared for the worst, I always say. I turn away from her, attempting to keep some of my modesty intact, and clean myself the best I can. Ghost keeps throwing nasty looks my way, but I'm sure he's just jealous he can't use wipes and instead has to constantly lick his asshole to keep it clean.

Alicia begins moving around, her brows pinched together.

"Sh-h-h," I say as I settle next to her. Once she finds my body with her hands, she inhales loudly and tucks herself under my arm—*while sleeping*—and finally settles in and stops moving.

A feeling larger than life blooms in my chest. The feeling of being needed just because I'm *me*. She's looking for me unconsciously, seeking my presence. Right now, she doesn't need my dick. She's not thinking about all the naughty things I can do to her body. She doesn't want to keep me as her dirty little secret. In her sleep, she's seeking a safe place, and I'm *that* for her.

Chapter Fifteen

ALICIA

I wake up feeling sweet, long-forgotten peace in my mind and satisfaction in my body. I give myself a good lazy stretch and bump into someone. A body. Next to me.

I cry out in horror and jump back, landing on my ass on the floor. On someone's limb, apparently, because a loud whine followed by a loud bark thunders through the tent. I try to move but bump into a furry body, another growl erupting from them.

"What the fuck?" A familiar male voice comes from the bed, and my eyes go round. Mark. How the hell did I forget that we fell asleep together? The events of the previous evening come rushing in, burning my cheeks.

I rubbed over him like a starved animal. I ground on his lap, searching for a release I haven't felt in so long. I could feel him through all the layers separating us.

I feel my cheeks grow even hotter, and the heat creeps farther down my neck. *So embarrassing.* I acted like a hussy. Like a whore. Ashley, Justin's ex-girlfriend who knows about that night, had called me that before. Like I didn't have a care in the world. Maybe I acted like that that night, sending mixed signals to everyone around. Maybe it really was my fault.

"Are you okay?"

I blink at Mark. He's lying on his side, his arm folded under his head. His muscles bulge, stretching the beige sweater he's wearing and drawing my attention from my self-deprecating slump.

"Yeah." It comes out as a squeak, so I clear my throat and repeat it in a more confident voice. "Yeah, I'm fine."

"What are you doing on the floor?" His morning voice is raspy and sexy.

I take a moment. In the last twenty-four hours, I changed from a person who was scared to be touched and hadn't had an orgasm—even a self-inflicted one—in years to suddenly a sex-starved hussy lusting after her neighbor.

"I fell," I answer honestly.

"You fell?" He raises a brow, humor in his voice.

"Yeah." I try to stand gracefully but forget the tent is short, bumping my head on the ceiling. Mark watches my movements, biting his lip as he tries hard not to laugh. "You took the whole bed!" I accuse him once I get a hold of myself.

"You were sleeping on top of me." His lips stretch into a smile.

"I was not!" My mouth falls open in shock, even though

I know he's right.

"Were too." He smiles wider. "Did you sleep well?"

"I've slept better," I say, throwing my braid over my shoulder. I probably look like a complete mess! I'm puffy in the morning on a good day, so I probably look like I drank ten gallons of tequila this morning. I groan inwardly, wishing I could hide my face in my hands.

"Sure, you have." He smirks and closes his eyes. "Come back to bed. It's too early." A moment later, his breathing evens out. Is he asleep already?

I lean over him. Yep, he's out. I reach for my phone to check the time. It's five thirty. I never wake up this early, but I'm feeling well rested, and there's no way I'll fall back asleep, especially not next to him when my memories are so fresh.

I want to pull my jacket from under his head, but he's sleeping so soundly, so I put on my boots and hat and try his jacket on. It's huge but wearable. I fold the sleeves and zip it up. Once I do, the warm scent of burnt wood and male musk envelopes me into a strong hug. I breathe in the powerful aroma, basking in the memories of yesterday once more.

As I take a breath, I become all too aware of someone staring at me. *What?* I glare back at Ghost, watching me from under his heavy brows. I stick my tongue out at him, and he puts his head on the ground, trying to cover his eyes with his paws. *Drama queen.* I roll my eyes and step out of the tent. Ghost follows, and I close the door right behind him. I don't want Mark getting cold while he sleeps. He deserves some rest after saving so many people all the time, and I don't imagine gusts of cold wind being relaxing.

Once I'm outside, I look around. The first snow came while we slept. A couple inches cover the ground as far as I can see. White covers the trees, heavy on their bare twigs. There's no chirping, and the sun isn't even up yet.

It's peaceful out here. Quiet. I take in a lungful of pure air and nearly get dizzy. Ghost trots to a tree and lifts his leg, marking the territory. When he's done, he moves to another tree. And then another. I go to the firepit and clear the area. We have a few tiny twigs left, but it's not enough to keep the fire going, so I walk deeper into the woods to collect some more. Ghost follows me, happily trotting by my side. Surprisingly, I share his chirpy mood.

I collect wood while he goes about his business, and we return to camp. Mark is still asleep, and I start the fire. I clean the log we used for a bench and cover it with my scarf.

Ghost stretches on the snow by the fire while I boil water for coffee. I brought a few packets of instant coffee and a normal one—meaning the one I'll have to cook—with me. I read a lot of romance novels, and in Wild West romances, they always make coffee on the fire. I need to know if that actually works so I can write about it too. I brought a thermos with a fine sieve in it so I can pour the good stuff into mugs once I'm done.

I check my water supplies and see I don't have much left. There is definitely no room for mistakes, so it either has to be perfect from the first try or we will have to melt snow. The latter is out of the equation because with only two inches, there is a high chance I'll be cooking soil along with the snow. My hope for an educational moment goes down the drain. Instant coffee it is.

Once the water is boiling, I pour myself a cup, already filled with two bags of instant coffee, add more sugar, and take a sip. I'm not a fan of instant coffee, but I must admit, it's not as bad as I thought it would be. Maybe fresh air does wonders, maybe my recent activities—my cheeks heat up again—awoke my appetite. Who knows? The only thing I *do* know is that I'm enjoying everything a little more than I thought I would.

I sit on the log, take another sip, and look at the sky. It's so clear. The stars twinkle at me, lifting my spirits. It's as if they know what happened last night and are shooting me little knowing winks.

I had my first orgasm in years.

Since *that* night, I haven't been attracted to any man because they scare me shitless. The presence of them, the power, the strength... I couldn't take it in real life, and it's why I wrote my first book. I created the perfect man on paper, a man who would make me feel safe. Turns out, it's what many other women wanted too, and they bought my book.

I couldn't leave my house for months after the traumatic event, so I tried to write another book. It had the same result: people loved how safe the men in my novels were. They were protectors. They were strong and passionate and loved their women more than anything. Above all, there was nothing questionable about them. They were *safe*. People kept buying them. So, I kept writing them. That's how I got sucked into the world of romance novels.

What I put onto paper is completely different from what I have going in my life. My heroines were fierce, where I was scared to sleep with an open door. They reached orgasm on command, where I couldn't reach it with my fingers, toys, or the most lascivious porn.

After so many tries, I gave up and accepted I was forever broken. My therapist suggested to give it time and wait for the right person, whoever it might be. And I've been patiently waiting for years. Men, women, I really didn't care. I just wanted someone who made me feel safe.

Until yesterday. Well, a few weeks ago, when I moved into Ms. Jenkins's house. I think it was the first time my lady parts woke up from hibernation and showed interest in anything.

After talking to Mark a couple of times, I started realizing my body wasn't screaming. I was calm. My brain wasn't telling me to leave the situation immediately. I was okay with him in my space. I felt safe. There is a deep, settled feeling inside my chest that promises everything is going to be okay.

The feeling is there because of Mark. Because of the huge man currently sleeping in my tent. A hero who came to save me from myself.

He tried to save me, but now, I'm freaking out even more. I humped the man, for God's sake. I groan quietly, but Ghost hears me and snorts. He knows exactly what we were doing. Note to myself: never do it in front of a dog.

"Oh, you shush!" I point an accusing finger at him. "Don't you dare to judge me, mister! All you do all day is lick yourself."

He opens his big mouth and yawns before flopping back on the ground.

I keep the water next to the fire so when Mark wakes up, he'll have a cup of steaming coffee. In the meantime, I sit and stare at the sky, enjoying the peace only nature can offer. I don't know if I'd be able to enjoy the peace if I didn't know Mark was asleep in the tent next to me.

About thirty minutes later, Mark emerges from the tent before doing a full-body stretch, revealing the happy trail on his navel. I instantly turn back toward the fire, as if I were caught staring.

Which I was, judging by the smirk on his face.

Chapter Sixteen

MARK

Sweet fucking torture. The whole night was torture to me. The more time I spend in Alicia's presence, the more testosterone my body produces, and the constant need to fuck itches under my skin. It's on my mind all the damn time. After what I've learned about her, I feel like a fucking pervert every time I think about her being the star of my fantasies. It's the last thing she needs, *the very last*, and yet I can't help myself.

After last night, I know with one hundred percent certainty that I need to stay the fuck away from her. My sexual appetite is not what a woman who's gone through some serious hell needs. I've had my suspicions as to why she was so jumpy around me or why she was always looking for an escape route when I entered a room with her, but it was confirmed.

She needs a gentle man, capable of love, and all I can give her is a wild, rough fuck. Even if I tried being gentle, it's only a matter of time until I snap. Her body's driven me insane ever since the moment I saw her in that wet T-shirt. The more I saw, the more I wanted. She's got such delicious curves on her, my hands and tongue itch to trace them. And now that I know what she tastes like, how it feels to squeeze her ass in my hands... I don't know how I'll be able to control myself.

What if she asks me to kiss her again? How can this be one of the things I want most and my worst nightmare at the same time? What if I won't be able to control myself once her tongue slips into my mouth? What if I'm too rough? What if I forget I'm with her and let myself do things she can't take, even just for a moment?

I take a deep breath, and *oh, fuck*. The tent smells like sex and Alicia.

A quick look around the twenty square feet of space confirms I'm alone. *Figures.* My dog is obviously with her. I wish I could accuse him of being a traitor, but I think she needs him more than I do.

I climb out of the tent and give my cramped body a full stretch. I can feel eyes on me instantly. Smirking to myself, I turn toward Alicia and catch her ogling me. Her cheeks light up the cutest shade of pink, and she averts her eyes to the fire.

Ghost jumps to his feet and runs toward me as if he hasn't seen me in ages. Jumping and delivering his sloppy kisses to my face, he finally gives me a proper welcome.

Good, because I was so close to giving up on our friendship. I scratch the place behind his ears he loves so much and give him a kiss between his eyes.

"Morning." Alicia's chirpy voice makes me do a double take. I study her for a moment, noticing how bright she looks. It's as if she's been up for hours, has had several cups of coffee, and heard her book about a wife who buried her husband in the backyard became a bestseller. I sigh.

"Morning." I walk to the fire and take a seat on the log next to her. She instantly moves to fill a mug with something that smells like coffee and offers it to me. I accept it with a nod of gratitude and take a sip. Instant coffee, yikes, but I smile at her, making sure to show how much I'm grateful for the offering.

She's watching the fire without turning toward me. "Alicia," I call quietly.

She turns quickly, most likely giving herself whiplash. "What's up?"

"You shouldn't be embarrassed." I try to reassure her, knowing it won't go well. It never does with women. For some unexplainable reason, they think they are worse than they are.

"I'm not!" she exclaims, her eyes darting away from mine. I sigh again and remind myself to be patient with her.

"You are." I look at the sky, and a snowflake lands on my nose. The snow has started again. Soon, we'll have to start packing or we'll be forced to spend another day here. She's got so much stuff here, it'll take ages to pack. "But you shouldn't be. What we did was natural." I glance at Alicia and, seeing her beautiful eyes meet mine, I begin to think that staying here another night might not be such a bad idea after all.

"Humping your leg was natural?" Her brow quirks up, and I bark a laugh.

"Well, that's not what happened, but yeah, whatever you call it was normal. Adults do it all the time. It's called passion." I run a hand through my hair, wishing I grabbed my hat from the tent. It would be better if I could just reach out and tug her to my body. The moment the thought crosses my mind, I'm instantly warm.

"That's not normal for me. I don't do that." Her face turns grim, and I'm not quite sure if she's slut-shaming herself or what, but regardless, I don't like where it's going.

"Alicia." I sigh and palm my face with my hand. "I'm sorry."

"For what?" She looks at me, confusion written on her face.

"For acting the way I did." I feel shame for being unable to control my urges, especially around her.

She grabs my forearm, nearly knocking the mug out of my hands, and squeezes it with all her might. "Don't apologize for—" she stops, looking for the right words, "the intimacy. It's something I forgot but very much needed. It's me who needs to apologize for putting you in this awkward position." She looks down at her hands again, kicking a small twig in the snow. "You know, for asking you to kiss me and all that."

"It was anything but awkward." I cackle. "In fact, I was very much comfortable."

A smile spreads across her face. It's shy but confident. Somehow, she looks different than yesterday. *Feels* different too. I want to ask so many questions about the disturbing information I found out yesterday, but I keep my mouth shut, trying not to destroy this quiet peace by saying something I might regret. We stay sitting on this fallen log in comfortable silence for ages, watching as the snow slowly falls around us. The morning hours are chilly, but with a steaming cup of this brown mud and her presence, it doesn't seem so cold anymore.

I don't want to ask the wrong questions, but I want to hear her voice, so I suddenly find myself sharing pieces of information I've never shared with anyone.

"I grew up with an abusive father."

Alicia's face whips toward me as she draws in a loud breath.

"He was an asshole, you know. Always trying to get a rise out of me by nagging at my little sister."

"You have a sister?"

"I do." I nod. "She's in college in California."

"How old is she?" she asks, gripping her own cup so tight, her knuckles turn white. I want to touch her hand so she'll relax, but I'm scared to feel her skin on mine now. I don't want to break down in front of this woman. She unravels me with every breath she takes, and I've known her for only a few weeks. I'd think it's desire and blue balls talking, but it's not. It's something more.

And it scares me.

"Twenty. My mother left us when I was probably about five and came back for a short time, had my sister, and disappeared again."

Her eyes turn sad and *understanding*, so I look away and keep talking. "So yeah, our house wasn't full of love and laughter, so I don't know how to do this... thing."

"This thing?" Her forehead wrinkles.

"Yeah, this thing." I circle the space between us. "Whatever it is. Whatever is happening, I can't be the only one who feels it, right?" My voice is shamefully hopeful.

She lifts her eyes toward mine. "No, you are not."

I let out an embarrassing sigh of relief. "Don't expect too

193

much from me, Alicia." I swallow roughly. "Because I just can't give it."

"I didn't expect anything, Mark," she whispers back. "The kiss idea came on a whim."

"And it was the best fucking kiss I've ever had." And that's the honest truth. She doesn't need to be ashamed of her own desires.

She snorts loudly through her nose and instantly covers her mouth with her hands, her eyes widening in embarrassment. "Sorry!"

"Don't be. It was cute." I chuckle. Everything she does is cute.

She pulls her knees together. "I've been out of practice for a long time."

"Could have fooled me."

Her face brightens with a smile, and she stares at the fire. "Where is your father now?"

"Where I left him." My voice is firm, and she raises a questioning brow. "He's alive. I just don't care about him anymore."

"You don't keep contact with him?"

Compulsion to flee nearly wins over before I get ahold of myself. I started this conversation. I should be able to finish it. "I don't. But I send him money from time to time."

"You do?"

"He kept us together. Me and my sister. Didn't drop us at some gas station like our mother did. So yeah, I send him something from time to time." No one knows about that. No one. Even him. And I sure hope she keeps my secret. I don't want any contact with him, but I can't forget that he let us live in his place and didn't send us to foster care. I don't know where we both would have ended up if he hadn't.

"The scars on your back..." She trails off. "Are they from him?"

I don't have the mental capacity to go into details, so I just nod.

"I think you're a bigger person than any of us are, Mark. And you are capable of so much more than you think you are." I open my mouth to argue, but she grabs my hand and interlocks our fingers. "Just shut up and take it."

"Yes, ma'am." I laugh, giving her fingers a gentle squeeze.

After a while, Alicia digs into her backpack and produces a few protein bars. Offering them to me, she takes a chocolate one for herself. "You know..." She pauses for a second, studying a snowflake that landed on her knee. "I grew up in such a great household, full of love and laughter, and look at me now, a broken, ugly mess, not capable of loving."

I look at her face—and I mean *look* at it. She's wallowing in so much unwarranted self-hatred that she doesn't even see herself for who she is.

"We are all a little broken, and we are all a little messy, but I don't see you as ugly, Alicia." My voice is firm. I want her to understand that I mean every word. "Everything you do is beautiful. Everything. You bring so much light. Sometimes, it's very inconvenient." I chuckle at the memories. "But it's a light regardless."

She looks up at me. "You really think so?"

"You brought light to *my* life." I shrug.

"Along with a lot of *mess*." She smiles.

"Along with that. But I wouldn't have it any other way, to be honest. I thought I wanted quiet, but turns out, I wanted this mess to wake me the fuck up." I gently place

195

my hand on her knee, and she doesn't jerk away from the touch.

"Does this mean we're friends?"

"I guess it does." I wink at her, and she beams at me.

"Does it make you a little messy too? You know, for liking me?" She blinks.

Warmth spreads throughout my chest. "I guess it does. We can be a mess together."

"And create chaos?"

I let out a loud laugh. "Yeah, I guess so." I sober up. "But friends is all I can offer you, Alicia. I'm not—" I swallow. "Built for something else."

"That's alright." Her smile is accepting. "Because I'm too broken for something else."

My heart sinks toward my stomach at her declaration. She thinks of herself that way, but I can't find the right words. Not when I think the same of myself.

All I want is to find those bastards who made her feel this way. Right here, right now, no matter what happens between us and how long it will take me, I vow to myself to find those monsters and punish them. It may be too late for the law, but they'll get my punishment. And besides, the lawful way would be too easy on them.

I'm not good with words or emotions, but I'm good with actions, and I'll make sure Alicia is avenged.

Chapter Seventeen

ALICIA

I'm pacing my living room. This crazy idea took up permanent residence in my head since the first moment I felt tingles in the bathroom, imagining Mark's large body. With every time we meet, it only takes up more and more real estate in my brain. And now it's overwhelming. This urge to run to him and see how far I can go when I finally reach him, it's driving me absolutely bananas.

Back in the tent, in the wilderness, when there was no one around, I was so comfortable with him, as if he were my lifeline. Well, besides the tiny episode of me freaking out. And then we had a deep, soul-to-soul conversation. All that pain he hides so well. It woke some deep urge to comfort him, to make him feel better, no matter what it takes. But what if it would also make me feel better?

Despite my messed-up mind, my body completely relaxes in his presence. His touch doesn't freak me out—quite the opposite, actually. It's comforting. And sometimes exciting. I didn't even know how much I starved for this feeling of connection with another human being, not only sexually but simply as friends. Holding each other's hands, talking. The trust that exists between two people who intimately know each other. I want all of it. I don't even remember how it feels anymore.

Yes, I have Josie, but we've never even seen each other in real life. I don't know how it will go when we finally meet.

But Mark is right there. Twenty feet from me, one driveway away. Probably stretched out on the couch, Ghost tucked in by his feet. Looking—and feeling—cozy and inviting.

I dial Josie. "Do you think I'm capable of having sex again?" I ask the moment she picks up the phone.

Stunned silence greets me on the other side of the line. Finally, her careful voice replies, *"Even my grandma of eighty-five has sex in the nursing home. They even had a gonorrhea outbreak last year, for fuck's sake."* She makes a gagging sound. *"Trust me, I barely survived when she told me."* Another gag makes me giggle. *"So I don't see why you can't have it. The sex, not gonorrhea, I mean."*

"Alright." I let out a sigh. "Then I think so too."

"Are we talking about the hot, flannel-wearing neighbor?"

"Maybe." I giddily bite my lip.

"Go girl!" She whoops. *"Call me after!"*

I laugh it off and say my goodbyes.

Now or never, Alicia. The pep talk helps, so I take a deep breath and sprint into action.

I run to the bathroom and take a long shower, shaving everything. And I mean everything. I don't know how far I'll be willing to go, but I want to be prepared. Only one of us can be a yeti, and Mark has already established it's him. I put on the cutest matching set I have—a dusty pink lacy bra and cheeky panties—my regular oversized sweatshirt and... leggings. Yes, I want to show some ass today. A brand-new feeling for me.

I walk to Mark's place feeling extremely nervous and unsure of where the evening will go, even though I know what I hope for. As I knock on his door, I contemplate trudging back home. I'm having a little bit of cold feet over here, attempting to seduce my sexy neighbor.

No one opens it, so I think it might be the sign from the heavens that I'm being irrational.

To be sure I don't regret it in the future, I knock one more time and wait. No one.

I'm about to leave when I hear a dog's whine, and Ghost doesn't whine unless there's a reason, or he's being overdramatic. He's only dramatic when someone's around, but if someone *was* around, *that someone* would have opened the door by now.

Ghost whines once again, and I feel a chill run down my spine. What if Mark is sick again, and Ghost is trying to get my attention so I can help him? To keep my consciousness clear, I decide to investigate and to make sure nothing is wrong.

He told me while camping that he'll keep his back door unlocked for me in case of emergencies, so I run to the back-yard and turn the nob. It's unlocked. Thank God. I carefully walk inside, instantly greeted by Ghost, who runs toward me and nudges my thigh.

"I know, baby. I know. I'm here." I crouch and give him a scratch. "I'm going to check everything, alright?"

Ghost moves back and plants his butt on the floor by the wall, curiously tilting his head to the side. *Interesting.*

"Where is Mark?"

He barks loudly and sprints to the bathroom. Only now do I notice the sound of running water. Lead settles in my stomach, and the worst possible picture of Mark hitting the tiled floor and lying in a pool of his own blood invades my overstimulated mind.

"Mark!" I call. "Are you there?"

On shaky legs, I move toward the bathroom. I force myself to move faster, but my body refuses to.

When I reach the bathroom, I push the door inward, take a deep breath, and step inside.

An unexpected sort of picture greets me, completely different from what I imagined at first.

Mark's standing in the running shower, with his back turned toward me, his head hung low. He's buck naked, and the water sluices all over his huge body, tracing every popping vein and every raised ridge. He groans as if in pain, and I take a tentative step forward, quietly calling his name. Something tells me I don't want to scare him off. My brain is frozen. There are no logical thoughts left in there, and all I can do is watch his naked body under the water.

The long-healed scars on his back go all the way down to his ass—his round, firm ass. There are two deep dimples on either side of his butt cheeks, and they make my mouth water. I swallow roughly. I've never had such an intense desire to bite anyone as I do now. I want to sink my teeth into his ass and check if it's as tight as it seems.

His hair is free of his bun for the first time. It hangs in wet strands just below his shoulders, a little lighter on the ends.

His shoulders suddenly shudder, stunning me, and he finds support with his left hand on the tiled wall. His right hand is hidden behind his torso. All I can see is the rippling of his back muscles and the jerky movements of his right arm.

I take another small step forward, quietly closing the door behind me. "Mark," I whisper, but he doesn't hear me. And that's all right... I wasn't loud enough to be heard.

Another small step. His arm moves faster, and I feel my mouth falling open. My breathing quickens, and moisture forms on my forehead. My palms grow sweaty, and I wipe them on my leggings.

The hand on the wall forms a fist. His hips jerk forward. I know I'm invading his privacy, and I should turn back and walk away. I wouldn't want anyone to witness me in such a private and vulnerable moment. But a little part of my brain suggests that it wouldn't mind if Mark saw me like this.

I wipe my palms again and lick my dry lips. My whole body is on fire and in need of another shower. Right now.

Mark lets out a loud groan, and I let out an embarrassing squeak. He freezes, drops his hands, and turns around. His nostrils flare, and water droplets run down his face, gathering on his lashes. His pec muscles jerk, and his stomach ripples.

My gaze drops lower, and I'm greeted by the most gorgeous cock I've ever seen, and I've seen many in porn. For research purposes, of course. It's angry looking, probably due to my interruption. His veins are raised along its length. With an ungodly amount of restraint, I force my eyes back toward his face.

His eyes are hooded, his mouth slightly ajar. He slowly moves his hand toward his gigantic dick, watching my face and waiting for my reaction. Expecting me to bolt.

And I am. Ready to bolt.

Yet here I am, standing near the door, watching him grab his cock at the base, slowly moving his large palm toward its head, squeezing it harder, and moving his fist back down. He repeats the motion slowly again, keeping eye contact, and I give up trying to look away.

My feet move me forward on their own accord and stop only when I'm flush against the glass of the shower stall. I swallow hard and place my open palm on the glass door. I don't know what I'm doing exactly, but I know for sure I want to be close to him. He takes a step toward me at the same time and leans his forehead on the other side of the glass while jerking his cock. I lean my head on the glass too, just below his. Even though I'm a tall woman, he's still bigger, and today his physical dominance thrills me.

My eyes are focused solely on him working himself. My breathing fogs the glass, just as his does on the other side, and I wipe mine so I can see him clearly. I don't know if it's possible, but *he grows* in size, and it wasn't average to begin with. I lean closer, trying to squeeze myself through the surface, and he groans loudly. My mouth opens even more as I try to catch my breath. My chest is rising in uneven, shallow movements, and his hand quickens in pace.

"Alicia." His voice comes out as a plea. I know he's close, but I'm not sure what I should do. I don't know if I can do anything and not freak out, completely ruining the mood.

I pull the door handle, and steam rushes into the room, instantly making me wet all over. The visible places, I mean. The hidden ones have been drenched since the moment I saw his naked back. His hand drops, and he wipes water droplets from his face. I stretch my shaking hand toward him, forcing my fear away. It's Mark. I'm safe with him.

I am safe with him.

When my hand reaches his steel hard cock, he inhales sharply. His head drops low as he begins loudly breathing through his mouth. My fingers hesitate on the tip. I haven't touched a man's body in years. I don't remember what I'm supposed to do. Yesterday, in the tent, it came to me naturally, so I let nature take its course.

I brush my thumb over the slit, and the cock jerks, nearly knocking my hand off. I run the tips of my fingers over the top of his length, half expecting to start freaking out and bolt away. But I don't. Back and forth I move. And again. But fear never arrives.

I take a step inside the shower stall, instantly drenched under the downpour. His eyes are round, and he steps backward. I follow his retreat.

"Alicia." His voice is barely human anymore, and I like it. I like this little piece of power I'm holding over this big strong man.

I get braver as I wrap my hand around his cock. My fingers barely touch, and I gasp. Just from the sheer feeling of him inside my palm. I used to write monster romance and always wondered how it really feels to have something like that at your mercy, and here I am, with my own beast and with my own monster cock. I squeeze and move my hand, mimicking his actions a few moments ago. His hands drop down, his head hangs low. He takes a step toward me, backing me against the tiled wall. For a second, my hand stills. I'm back to being caged, but his soothing voice comes through the fog. "I'm here. With you."

I blink the darkness away, and he watches my face carefully, looking for any sign of discomfort. For any sign I'll bolt away. I know I can. Bolt away, I mean. He will let me. I will my mind to relax. My heartbeat slows down, and I continue moving my hand.

His hips buck forward, and his hands come to the wall beside my face, caging me. "It's me. I'm here." His voice is shaky. The muscles in his arms clench.

"I know," I finally say, and he drops his forehead to mine.

The water runs over us. My clothes cling to my hot skin. The sweet place between my thighs tingles with anticipation. It aches, and the ache is getting unbearable. I want to hump his leg, but he's so engrossed in what I'm doing, I want to give him this moment as payment for the moment of freedom he gave me.

I can feel his shaky, hot exhales on my wet skin, the raw power radiating from his coiled body. His sheer willpower is impressive, considering he hasn't flipped me over, pressed me to the wall, and had his way with me yet.

Would that be so bad though?

"Harder," he says, and I squeeze my fingers tighter as I stroke his length. "Harder, Alicia." His voice is raspy, begging even, and I obey.

I turn my face so my mouth is next to his ear, and lick the shell of it. He lets out a shaky breath, and I bite his lobe. His dick jerks in my hand, swelling more. I increase the velocity of my actions, and his hips start bucking forward. His body presses into mine, his dick squeezed between us. I alternate between biting his earlobe and licking it as I try not to lose tempo. He drops his head even lower, burying his face into my neck.

"I'm gonna fucking come," he growls against my skin, raising victorious little goose bumps all over my body.

I bring my other hand to the back of his neck, burying my nails into his skin. He lets out a loud growl and bucks his hips at me.

"Fuck." His voice is muffled.

I feel stickiness covering my fingers as he keeps shooting his release into my palm. His arms wrap me in a hug, and he presses his face deeper to the crook of my neck, as if he's trying to integrate with me. His growl is loud, and his orgasm is never-ending. I walk him through the whole thing, pumping his length in slower motions, not willing to lose a second of this moment.

Once the waves subside, I expect awkwardness, but it doesn't come. He gives my cheek a kiss and moves back under the shower.

"I'm not sure if I'm not dreaming, but thank you, even if you are a fantasy, Alicia."

"I'm real," I answer, finally feeling the awkwardness creeping up on me.

"You are not." He leans in and gives me a quick kiss on the lips. "I'm sorry about the mess. You should take it off so you can shower." He goes to unzip my hoodie, but I move backward.

"Can I do it alone?" I ask, not meeting his eyes. He hasn't seen me naked, and I know it's not fair when I just saw him in all his glory, but I'm not ready to undress in front of him completely. Not yet.

He hesitates for a moment before answering. "Yeah, sure. I'll be out of your hair in a minute."

He quickly washes off the shampoo and conditioner and steps out of the stall. Wrapping the towel around his hips, he turns toward me. "You know where the towels are."

When he's out of the room, I undress and take a quick shower, thinking about what had come over me. I'm not prude—not in my mind, at least—but I don't do those sorts of things for obvious reasons. And here I am, jerking off the gigantic dick of my neighbor whom I've known for a whole two months.

I get out of the shower and realize I have no clothes to change into, so I wrap a towel around my torso and walk out of the bathroom. Mark's making something in the kitchen, wearing gray sweatpants—help me lord—hung low on his hips, showing his pronounced sex lines. And by sex lines, I mean every single line on his body screams *raw sex*. I can imagine them flexing when he's jerking his hips on top of me. His arms on either side of my face, veins popping from the sheer strength of holding himself atop, his—

He clears his throat, and I look up, finding Mark biting the inside of his lips and trying not to laugh. My face goes hot, and I quickly turn away and find Ghost, who is doing his favorite thing, licking his balls.

"Want something to drink?" he asks and drinks half a bottle of water in one go. His eyes roam my body, stopping for longer on my bare legs.

"No." I look everywhere but him. I came here with a purpose, but now, when the idea of him is so close, I'm chickening out.

"Are you okay?" Concern laces his voice, and it kills me.

I just jerked him off, and I'm twenty-six. I'm attracted to him, and he's clearly attracted to me. So why am I scared? I take a lungful of air and blurt, "Can you have sex with me?"

Chapter Eighteen

MARK

I stop breathing for the second time in the last two minutes, I think.

The first time was when she came out of the shower, wearing only my towel and nothing else. It's the most skin I've seen on her so far. Her legs are gorgeous, shapely, and fit. Her hips are wide, perfect to grab on to. Her collarbone is so pronounced, and I've always been a sucker for those. It makes a woman fragile in my eyes. It makes me want to protect her even more. I can imagine myself leaving kisses across them.

And now, as she asks me... Did I hear her correctly?

"What did you just say?" My muscles go slack.

She inhales loudly and repeats the question. "Can you have sex with me?" She looks away from me, swallows, and says, "Please."

"Alicia," I exhale. "You don't really want that."

"I actually do."

"Look." I rake my hand through my wet hair, trying to find the right words. "I don't think it's a good idea."

"Oh." I see her closing like a shell right in front of my eyes. The light drains from her face, dissolving into her regular darkness. The blue of her eyes turns into gray, a clear indication of a mood swing toward the abyss. Her shoulders go rigid. Her lips clamp shut.

I can't stand the change, so I walk toward her, but she steps back. I stop halfway.

"Alicia. It's not like I don't want you."

She snorts.

"It's true."

She rolls her eyes.

"What? You don't think you're attractive?"

"Maybe when I lose a few pounds," she mumbles quietly.

"What the fuck are you talking about?" My genuine confusion should be a clear indication that I don't understand what she means, but it turns out it's not so clear to her, because she keeps going.

"I mean, I used to be pretty, you know." She brings her hair over her shoulder and tugs on it. "Skinny. With perfect skin and makeup and pretty clothes. But I'm not anymore." She looks uncomfortable, shifting from one foot to the other. "I guess I never thought that when I reached my goal of becoming invisible, I might actually regret it." Her chuckle is heavy. "And here I am, offering myself to a guy when I barely represent womankind anymore." She looks up, blinking away tears.

It makes me see red. I'm next to her in two jumps. Grabbing her shoulders, I pull her toward me. She's tall, but I still have to lean lower so I can reach her eyes.

"You are the most feminine woman I've ever seen. All this..." My eyes dart between hers. "It's—" I'm struggling to find the right words. "It's like you were made from all my dreams. Every piece of you." I let my face roam around hers and dip lower. "Every single piece calls out to me and makes me want things I can't want." I swallow a rough lump in my throat and continue. "You are not invisible. No matter how much you try, you just can't be. Even if you put a paper bag on. Do you understand?"

"No." She slowly shakes her head. "Why do you say it when you don't mean it?"

"Why do you think I don't mean it?"

"Because I'm here, offering a casual hookup, and you don't want it. Me." Her eyes swell with tears again, so I pull one hand away from her shoulders, grab it, and place it over my cock. It's hard, of course. It always is when she's around.

"Feel that?"

She doesn't respond, so I press her hand harder against me, and her eyes widen.

"Feel that?"

She nods.

"Yeah, I just blew my load."

Her eyes go even rounder, and I get a suspicion that this sweet girl probably likes dirty talk.

"And here I am, hard and ready again. Because of you. You make it hard. All the fucking time."

My dick twitches, and her fingers curl along its girth.

My forehead drops on hers, and I take a deep breath. She squeezes it through my pants and gives it a lazy stroke.

A few water droplets run down her temple from her wet hair, and I watch, fascinated with how they move down her round cheek and disappear under her chin. She squeezes the base of my cock, and her hands turn explorative. She moves her hand up and traces lines with her fingers across the hem of my pants. Goose bumps run down my body, and I swallow.

"So why can't we have sex?" Her voice is raspy.

"Because—" I need to clear my throat before I speak. "Because that's not what you need."

"How do you know what I need?" Her fingers keep playing with the skin above my pants, and I just want her to move lower. Right where all the blood is.

"You need someone who can go slow." My voice betrays me, going shaky at the end.

"And you can't?" The little witch dips a finger lower.

I don't have the willpower to utter another word while her fingers keep grazing my head—the lower one—a gentle scrape of her nail along the sensitive skin. I don't have any boxers on, and my dick saluted as soon as she stepped out of the bathroom. I can't believe she hadn't noticed the tent in my pants when she was saying all that nonsense about her being unattractive and unwomanly.

I was hard before, but dear lord, when I touched her soft shoulders, it was game over. All I want right now is to rub myself all over her.

"Mark?" she calls to get my attention, but I completely forgot what the question was.

"Mmm?"

"Can you go slow?" She pulls on my waistband and sneaks one finger in.

"I can't." I swallow. "I'm a rough man, Alicia. I wasn't made for sensitive things." My voice is scraping. "I told you this already. Even if I wanted to, I don't know how."

"What if I wanted you rough?"

"Not like that. No." Despite what I'm saying, my hips have their own mind and buck toward her, and she gasps. "That's why we can't do it. I really can't do slow."

She pulls her hand away from my pants and her body away from mine, and I nearly weep.

"Alright. Sorry I asked," she says, turning away.

"Alicia," I rasp. "I really want you. I so fuckin' do, but I'm not the man you need."

Her head whips back toward me. "I knew. I fucking knew it was a bad idea to overshare!"

My eyes widen. Alicia doesn't curse. Not really. "It's not that, Alicia."

"Right." She snorts. "You see me as fucking damaged goods after what I told you."

"Shut up, woman." I step closer and grab her shoulders, pulling her closer.

With her body plastered to mine, I bring my lips to hers and swallow them in a rough kiss. I'll show her a glimpse of the real me, and she'll forget this crazy idea.

I'm waiting for her to push me away when she lands her hands on my shoulders and pulls me toward herself.

I'm waiting for her to freak out when I pull on the towel, and it drops between us.

I'm expecting her to run away when I pull away to take a good long look at *her*.

She's standing naked in front of me, her gorgeous tits on full display, large and heavy. They might be too large for some idiots, but I'm a big guy, and those gorgeous things?

They're perfect for me. I itch to touch and feel their soft-ness. My mouth waters to taste them.

My gaze dips lower, to her perfect waist and wide hips. Perfect woman. I feel the pre-cum shooting from my cock and wetting my sweats. With the light gray fabric, there will be no hiding how my body reacts to her. Her eyes scan my body, taking me in. And I know she loves what she sees, because her eyes widen, and she licks her lips. Her pupils are so blown, I can hardly see the blue anymore.

My cock twitches. She notices and switches her weight from foot to foot, as if trying to scratch the sweet place between her legs.

My abs contract in anticipation, and she takes a step farther.

"Don't, Alicia." I shake my head, bringing my hand up. "If we continue, I won't be able to stop."

"You will." She takes another careful step. "But I don't think I'll need you to."

"You don't need me," I tell her. "I'm not good, baby. I'm not." I hang my head low, trying to remember every time I was rejected for someone better, richer, or more handsome. When I was rejected by my mother who deemed me too complicated and fled town. By women who'd rather accuse me of rape than announce they actually wanted to fuck me.

A woman like Alicia would never want something more than that, a fuck in the darkness. But for the first time in my life, I reject sex because I think she can hurt me more than any of them ever did. She has this power over me that I didn't know I could give away.

But when I lift my eyes and find her standing right in front of me, naked and proud, I don't see fear in them. No shame. Just pure desire. And for some reason, I believe it's me she wants. Me.

"I think you're a good guy, Mark." She cups my face in her hands. "In fact, you are too good for someone tainted like me, but I'm selfish and I want you anyway." She takes a deep breath. "Do you want to have sex with me?"

I groan and land my lips on hers. She leans into me with no fear.

I bring my hands under her plump ass and lift her, nearly impaling her on my dick through the pants. I walk to the couch and awkwardly fall backward, trying to keep her on top of me. With me leaning on the back of the couch and her body atop mine, I don't remember when I've ever felt so comfortable.

She makes cute, nearly moaning sounds into the kiss while my hands roam her body. At the same time, hers explore mine. Every time she touches me in a sensitive place—which is pretty much everywhere where she's concerned—my hips jerk, and her body slides over my over-stimulated cock.

"Are there things I shouldn't do?" I ask before I'm too lost in her. "Things that can trigger something?"

"I don't like anyone behind me." She withdraws a little, and I wish I could say I want to smack myself for bringing it up, but I don't. I must know her limits, so she won't get traumatized all over again. I want to be her peace.

"Okay," I whisper into her neck. "Come back here."

I latch onto the sensitive skin of her neck and pull on it with my teeth, and her hips buck over mine. *Oh, she loved that.* So I do it again, this time alternating with sucking. Her panting into my ear drives me absolutely insane, and I let out a growl as I grab her ass and pull it toward me.

The minx bites my shoulder, and I smack her naked ass. Everything stills. We both freeze.

"Do it again," she whispers into my ear, and I stop

213

breathing. I gently smack her again. It's so pitiful, it doesn't even make a decent sound. "Harder," she says again on a breathy exhale.

Oh, fuck me. I smack her ass harder this time, keeping my hand on the spot, trying to erase the sting. After feeling how wet my pants have gotten, I get the feeling I don't need to.

"You like that," I half ask, half confirm, stunned. "You like my big hand on your perfect ass, don't you?"

"Yeah," she breathes out, bucking again.

"What else do you like?" I trace the vein on her neck with my tongue.

"When you talk." She moves and licks the shell of my ear, sending tingles down my back.

"You like me being dirty with you?"

"Yes." One raspy word.

"And what about this?" I move to cover her tit with my hand. "Do you like this?" I massage the soft flesh while circling her nipple with my thumb.

"Yes." She swallows and drops her face to my shoulder.

"What about this?" I move the same hand lower, between her legs, and move it over the seam of her lips. Her wet and hot lips. She's so sleek and ready, and I'm so hard that I want to get inside of her and start moving, but she is not ready. "Do you like this too?"

"Yes," she breathes out.

"Good. 'Cause I like it too." I carefully dip a quarter of my middle finger in, and she gasps. I pull away, trying to see if it's from fear or pleasure, but she relaxes, and I get my answer. I start moving my finger, burying it deeper every time and pressing my thumb to her clit.

She throws her head back in pleasure, her eyes closed but mouth open as she moans. I kiss up her neck, running my tongue along her jawline as I taste her skin. Her breathing catches.

With every shove of my finger, she gasps louder. And louder. Until she comes all over me. A warm gush of liquid wets my hand and sweatpants. I try to swallow the lump in my throat, forcing my willpower to come back from its hiatus. At this point, all I have to do is to take my cock out, and it will come from touching the air.

Her body is still shaking when she lifts herself up on her knees and maneuvers the hem of my pants down so my hard cock springs free. She grabs my aching dick in her hand and brings herself over it.

I swear I stop breathing. And she stops moving.

Her eyes are shut, concentration clear on her face.

"Alicia," I call. "Alicia, look at me."

When she finally opens her eyes, there is less blunt desire in them. It's going to hurt like a fucking bitch, but I say it anyway.

"It's me. Just me." I lick my lips, and her eyes focus on the movement. "We can stop if you want. Don't force yourself. It might not be the right time. That's oka—"

She doesn't let me finish. Pressing her lips tight, she impales herself on my cock. Her eyes are wide and bright, and she freezes. I'm scared to move, because A, I'll blow my load, and B, she's probably in pain. Most likely. I have a huge dick, all right, and it usually takes time to adjust to it. I'd do things differently, but she needed to do it on her own.

"Are you okay?" I can barely speak.

"Yeah." She pauses. "It's like I'm a virgin all over again. *Fuck*."

My pulse quickens. "I like when you curse in bed."

She chuckles and leans on me, kissing my sweaty shoulder. Then she bucks her hips. And again. I grab her thighs,

215

slowing her down. "Wait. Wait," I rasp. "Give me a minute to breathe."

"Weakling." She bites the skin on my neck and gently pulls on it.

"Vixen." I grab her ass and move her up and down my length.

"Oh Lord, you are huge." She exhales loudly, and I stop.

"Does it hurt?" I try to pull away, but she plants herself so deep onto me, her ass slaps my balls, and I nearly come.

"In a good way. Now can you start moving already?" She pulls away to look at me. She's biting her swollen lips, her cheeks red and her forehead sweaty. Her long hair, in a state of artful disarrangement, covers us both like a coat.

She is gorgeous.

"Are you sure you're okay?" I'll stop even if it kills me.

"More than okay, Mark." She leans closer, a breath shy from a kiss. "I'm perfect."

I squeeze her ass and move her along me like I mean it this time. Oh, how much I want to throw her on the couch and plunge my whole length deep into her, reaching places no one ever has. But I can't. She's in control, and she is the one who leads the game. I'm here as her slave and her personal toy.

And I'm so fucking in.

After I reach the most intense orgasm I've ever had, I remember I forgot the one crucial thing I promised myself to never ever forget. A condom.

Chapter Nineteen

ALICIA

My thighs are still quivering from the real orgasm with a real man when I feel stickiness between my thighs.

And I freeze. Oh, shit. Did we forget a condom?

"Alicia." Mark's voice is strained.

I lean on his shoulders with my hands and push back. "A condom."

"Yeah." He looks pale, as if he's seen a ghost. I rush to explain.

"I'm on a birth control." I nervously bite my thumbnail, not knowing how to go about this. "But—" I bite harder. "I mean—"

"I'm clean." He interrupts my blubbering and releases my ass from his hold.

I exhale with relief. "Me too. I forgot to even think about that before we, you know." I wave my hand between us.

"No." His nostrils flare with anger toward himself. "It was my responsibility, and I failed you. I'm sorry, Alicia. I'm so sorry." He wipes his face with his hand, looking like he's going through internal hell.

"Hey." I grab his hand, attempting to stop the incoming panic attack. "Hey, stop that. I know I should be thinking about that, but I trust you. It wasn't even a question in my mind."

His face twists into an even more severe grimace. "See? You trusted me, and I fuckin' failed y—"

I don't let him finish before I cover his lips with mine. They're swollen from before, just like mine. When I pull away, his cock, still inside me, grows harder again, and I cackle. "Seriously?" I ask and look down. "Already?"

Looking sheepish, Mark gives me a quick peck on my lips and lifts me from himself. Placing me gently on the couch, he kisses my nose. "You're probably sore."

"I am." I wince, trying to shift my weight from leg to leg. "You are not exactly tiny, you know."

His lopsided grin is infectious, and now I'm biting my lips. "I know." He winks. "Now, we need another shower."

"Where's Ghost?" I look around, searching for the little pervert.

"He's in the bedroom. He escaped the moment you began humping his daddy."

"Daddy, huh?" I shamelessly walk toward the bathroom, feeling his hungry eyes on me the whole time.

I look behind me, and his eyes turn molten again.

"Don't do that again, or we'll end up exactly where we started."

"And where is that? The place where you say you won't have sex with me?" I meant for it to sound funny, but it came out anything but, judging by the cloudy look on his face.

"Yeah, I meant that, Alicia."

"Well, we did have sex, and I'm still standing." I spread my arms wide, and his eyes quickly scan my body from head to toes. His thick throat bobs when he swallows.

"That can't happen again, Alicia. I'm sorry."

"Why?" I shift my weight to one side, popping my hip as I cross my arms over my chest. His eyes take me in. For some absolutely unknown reason, this gorgeous, hot man finds my love handles sexy. And for some absolutely unknown reason, I'm not ashamed to show them to him.

And also, to my surprise, I'm relaxed enough that I don't feel the need to hide under a pile of covers. In fact, I *want* him to see me. I want to swing my hips as I leave the room, knowing he'll be watching them. Knowing that the second his eyes land on my body, all he'll want to do is take me.

I glance at his cock, and of course, it's there, at full mast. I've never felt more like a woman than I do now. Two months ago, the idea of being in a similar situation would terrify the hell out of me, sending me running and hiding in my room for years, but now? Not if the man is Mark. If he's in the room, I feel safe. His face represents safety. His body, protection. I can't believe I've known the man for just a few weeks, and he's become a part of me so fast.

"Because I'm not good for you."

I roll my eyes. "Let me decide that. I'll be back in a minute." I leave him nude in the living room. I know if I invite him to shower with me again, there's no way I'm ignoring the huge thing between his legs, and I'm too sore for it. Maybe the idea of impaling myself so fast wasn't the smartest. I wince, a little shameful.

I snort as I turn the water on. I nearly freaked out and ran away, so instead, I ripped the bandage off in one go. I quietly chuckle as I remember his face when I did, his eyes full of shock and wonder and his mouth slightly ajar. It was a good look on him.

Talk about looks. While the water heats up, I look in the mirror. I have beard burns all over my face, and two hickeys are on proud display on my neck where he latched onto my skin. My belly clenches at the memory. I take a step closer to the mirror. My lips are so swollen and red, my eyes half closed and crazed. Damn, but it's a good look on me too.

Feeling lighter than I have in years, I jump in the water and take another quick shower. After I'm done, I keep the water running so Mark doesn't have to warm the water up again. I wrap another towel around my body and walk outside. "It's all yours."

He solemnly nods and disappears inside with a soft click of the door. I roll my eyes again, understanding the battle I'm about to face to convince him that *he's* too good for *me* and not the other way around.

By the time he's back, I'm waiting for him in the kitchen with two sandwiches. For some reason, every time I make something for him, he melts, and I'm not above using all my dirty little cards right now.

"Here." I push the plate toward him.

As I predicted, his eyes soften, and he sits at the table, taking the sandwich. "Thank you."

"Sure." I prop my elbows on the table and lean toward him. "So?"

He starts chewing slower and quirks a brow.

"Can we do it again?"

He chokes on the poor sandwich and coughs. I walk to him and helpfully give him a few not-so-gentle pats on the back. "Better?" I ask when he's finally done coughing and looks up at me.

"Again?" His brows draw together.

"Yes."

"Why would you want to do it again? With me?" He blinks.

I blink back. I hate that he thinks so poorly of himself. "Who wouldn't want to do it again?"

"Alicia." He clears his throat. "I'm not a good match for you."

"Who said anything about a match?" I curl my toes, losing patience. He doesn't notice. "I haven't had sex in years, and I feel safe with you. In fact, I didn't even want to have sex, you know."

"Sex and masturbation are different."

"They are and they're not." I prop myself on his knees, and he stills. His arms hang awkwardly at his sides. "To tell you the truth, I haven't touched myself since that night."

"Never?" His brows shoot upward.

"Never. In fact, last night's orgasm was the first for me. I honestly gave up ever having one again, and here you are."

"Why me?" He breathes the question out, and I feel the *weight* of it. He really needs the answer. *Needs* it.

I twist my body to fully face him. "Because you are the most gorgeous man I've ever seen. Because you're the most reliable. You're strong." I bring my hands behind his neck. "You make me feel safe. And more than that, I know you can keep me safe." Then I say with a shrug, "I just trust you."

His arms shoot up and wrap around my body. He brings

his forehead to mine. "You make me feel like fuckin' Superman." He swallows roughly. "Like some sort of a hero."

"Because you are." I gently massage his neck with my fingers. "You save people for a living." My voice turns into a whisper. "You saved me."

"Fuck, baby." He covers my lips with his in a quick but deep kiss. After only a moment, he pulls away. "We can do that again, right?" he asks hopefully, making me laugh.

"Yes. We can do it casually."

His arms around me turn to steel. "What do you mean casually?"

"I've never had casual before, so it'd be fun to try." I shrug shyly.

"The fuck you will." His nostrils flare as his eyes narrow at me. "If we do this, we are exclusive. Do you understand?"

I've never heard him talk to me like this, and I expect fear to strike me. But instead, heat pools between my legs. "You don't share?"

"I do." His curt response turns my insides into acid. "But I'm not sharing you." He presses his lips tightly, and I breathe a sigh of relief.

"Alright." I wiggle. "But I'm not sharing you either."

"You won't have to." He responds a little offensively, like the idea of him having someone else during our arrangement offends him.

"Deal." I nod.

"Deal." He smacks my ass and pushes me away from his lap. "Let me finish my food, woman, or we're gonna fuck like rabbits again if you keep wiggling your sweet ass."

My eyes widen as I hear him speak like that. I was never into dirty talk, but turns out, maybe I am. Character development?

While we finish our food, I fix Mark another sandwich,

and Ghost trudges into the kitchen. He loudly sniffs the air and sneezes, making us laugh. He sure doesn't like the smell of his daddy making love.

Two hours later, we're chilling on the couch and watching TV. It's some mystery show, which I would absolutely love if not for the hard cock under my cheek. I'm lying on Mark's lap, and his dick is literally poking into my cheek. I pull up and shoot him a glare.

"Is it always like this?" I ask, sarcasm dripping from my voice. Unfortunately, it doesn't seem like sarcasm is a language he's fluent in, because he swallows and looks away in shame. "Mark."

He keeps watching the wall.

"Mark!" I bark louder and grab his chin, turning his face toward me. "What just happened?" The skin above his beard is pink. It would be adorable if I didn't know that he's really ashamed. "What happened, babe?"

I momentarily stun myself by using a pet name.

"I have a problem, Alicia," he answers with a sigh. "I have a high libido and too much fuckin' testosterone."

"A problem?" I blink, not understanding.

"I'm always fuckin' hard. That's the problem." He nods at his lap. "Especially when you're around."

I laugh hysterically. Even my eyes water. He thinks he's scaring me off, when in reality, he's giving me a compliment. Silly man. When I'm finally done, I face his stone-cold eyes. I sober up and wipe my tears away. "I'm sorry, but I don't see how it's a problem."

"Here." He points at his dick. "You're lying next to me, we're watching a movie, and I'm hard. All I can think about is fucking you. All the time. Does it still not sound like a problem to you?"

"Hmm. Let me think." I dramatically tap my finger on my chin before replying. "No."

"Right." He snorts and pulls a pillow over his lap. "You just had sex for the first time in forever. You are sore, so nothing else is happening." He points at his lap. "It's painful." His anger deflates, but not his cock.

"You do know there are other ways, right?" A note of interest flickers in his eyes. "I've done so-o-o much research while writing my books."

"What kind of books are you writing?" His brows shoot upward.

"The interesting kind." I wink playfully. "So anyway, I've done so much research that I'd like to put it to good use." I grab the pillow from his lap.

"What kinds of things are we talking about?" he asks, licking his lips. His eyelids turn heavy.

I look up and meet his gaze. "I want to watch you do it to yourself."

"You do?" He swallows.

"Yes." I nod and scoot away from him to the side of the couch.

He watches me for a few heartbeats, lifts his butt up, and pulls his pants halfway down to his thighs. I never thought a man with his pants down like this could look so freaking sexy. His cock is fully erect, veins wreathe his impressive length. He slowly wraps his long fingers around it, giving himself a couple of lazy pulls before bringing his hand back to the base. Another pull and back again. A squeeze.

The head turns a darker shade, and he tugs on it. Hard. I nervously lick my lips and snake my hand under Mark's T-shirt I'm wearing. Finding the wet, aching spot between my legs, I begin rubbing it in gentle circles. Mark's eyes dart down, and he tugs on his cock harder. Squeezes the base stronger. Moves his hand faster.

I move my hand faster too. My breathing turns labored, and I gasp. His powerful chest expands with every breath. His arm flexes with every move. The head of his engorged cock begins glistening, and he speeds up the tempo. I match my movements to his.

"Fuck, Alicia," he groans as he shoots thick white strands all over his stomach and chest. With every spurt I see, I press my finger harder and rub faster. A few breaths after, I follow him with his name on my lips.

I think I just discovered my new favorite activity.

* * *

We fall into the comfortable routine of two people who have been in a relationship for two hundred years.

Every night, we sleep at Mark's place. He leaves Ghost with me when he leaves for his shift, and I write steamy novels about hot couples pleasuring each other in his rocking chair. My upcoming book will have a lot of *watching* involved. I wonder why.

Now I know it's him who made all the beautiful furniture in his house, and my chest fills with pride every time I look at it. His hands are masterful. And they're mine.

Sometimes I bake something and drive it to the station, where everyone showers me with gratitude as they fight over the goods. But the only approval I truly seek is *his*, and every time his eyes close with pleasure after a bite, I'm left filled with happiness.

The first time I went there was weird. I was scared and felt out of place, but when Rachel saw me, she came and gave me a warm hug, as if I were her long-lost relative. She then introduced me as Mark's girlfriend. I remember how scared I was to look at Mark after she said it, but he just came over and gave me a quick kiss. Since then, I was 'one of them.'

Every single time he comes back home from a shift, I have a dinner waiting for him. When I told Josie about it on the phone—her project got postponed, and so did her trip to Maine—she laughed and lovingly called me 'a housewife from the sixties.' I laughed with her but didn't stop doing it. Seeing Mark's face light up after a long shift when he finds Ghost and me—wearing fuzzy socks and a big sweater—in the kitchen cooking for him, makes up for all the trouble.

He's been missing the feel of home all along, and I'm ready to give it to him. No matter how cliché it sounds, I found my own home with this man and his furry baby. I bought the latter a doggy toothbrush, because really, he's constantly at his jewels.

The few times Mark went to the Cat and Stallion, a local bar, to meet with his friends, he invited me to go too, but I wasn't ready to bump shoulders with strangers. Yes, I'm better now, but with Mark. Well, mostly. I'm okay going to the station when he's around. Plus, no one touches me there. I still don't like it.

I went with him once. It was the first and last time. Buddies from his team were getting together for drinks, and he invited me out with him. Everyone brought their significant others, and it was pretty fun. No one tried to involve me in their conversations, something I was terrified of, or question me like most boyfriend's friends would do. Instead, they shared silly jokes and old stories. It was cool. Until someone bumped into me from behind, and I freaked the fuck out.

Spilling my Coke all over myself and Mark, I jumped

up with wild eyes and ruined the fun for everyone else. They don't know my story, but they've seen a lot of bad things happen to other people, so I'm sure they could figure out something was wrong with me. Mark was trying to convince me that nobody paid attention to the little 'situation,' and to be fair, even now when I go to the station, nobody looks at me any differently, so he might be right. But it doesn't cancel out the fact I'm not ready to socialize like that. Not yet.

I talk with my mom every single day on the phone and even visited them a couple of times while Mark was out, but I haven't invited anyone to my house yet. Especially since I'm never even there. I've just seemingly found myself, and our relationship is so new that I'm scared to mess it up by introducing it to someone.

Jake took a long leave and decided to stay longer at rehab before taking a few weeks to travel 'to find himself.' He certainly needs it, considering the man is *now* hated by a few (many) locals. To explain the extent of Jake's situation better... I'll just say that even my mom is ashamed of him, and she's never ashamed of her kids.

I have no idea how he was able to get such a long 'vacation' with his boss, the sheriff, but he didn't tell anyone when he's coming back.

A huge improvement happened with Justin. He's calling me every *other* day instead of twice a day, and it makes me feel like he believes I'm getting better. If he thinks so, then I probably am.

Though to be completely honest, I still don't like anyone being behind me. We've tried to have sex that way once, but I totally freaked out, and it took Mark a hot minute to calm me down. Mark always makes me so hot and bothered, and I was sure I wouldn't be scared if *he* was the one behind me. Turns out, I was. And it took me a few days to stop hating myself for ruining the moment.

Today is the day I ask Mark if he wants to go to Thanksgiving dinner with my family. Mom was being Mom, and she figured I might have someone new in my life. It wasn't too difficult to figure out since I've been all bubbly and happy these days.

I asked Mark a couple of days ago if his sister is coming to spend the holiday with him, and he said she's going to her friend's house in Los Angeles for the holidays, which leaves him by himself. He mentioned that he's picked up Thanksgiving shifts at the station a couple of years in a row, since he didn't have anyone to celebrate it with. I want this year to be different for him. If he doesn't feel comfortable coming to my parents' house, I'll just stay with him here, in his cozy place.

When the doorknob turns, I rush to the door and jump into his arms. He grabs me by the ass and hauls me up, swallowing my lips in a hungry kiss.

"I've missed you so much," he growls into my mouth. Fresh out of the shower, he envelopes me in his pure masculine scent I love so much.

"I've missed you too." I squeeze my legs around him and wrap my arms around his neck. "Dinner is ready."

"I want the dessert first today." He carries me to the bedroom and drops me on the bed. "Oh, Alicia. I've missed you so fuckin' much."

I love when he comes home like this, all hungry and riled up. I like him *feeling*, like he's finally allowing himself to be happy. Just like I am.

I smile and crook my finger, inviting him to play.

* * *

Later, after dinner—I figured it's better to ask Mark about anything after food is served—we chill on the couch. My feet are on his lap, and he's massaging my toes.

He's full, happy, and relaxed. Now is the time.

"Mark, do you want to come with me to my family's Thanksgiving dinner?"

Chapter Twenty

MARK

Ever since she invited me over to her family's house for Thanksgiving, uneasiness has settled over me. When she moved in next door, at first I thought she was a city girl, looking for a thrill and a new adventure. I thought she wouldn't last a month. But she stuck around, making my grumpy dog fall in love with her. Making my team fall in love with her. Making Rachel, a mother hen extraordinaire, fall in love with her.

Then she cracked my steel armor with her constant care, not asking for anything in return.

She became something more than a neighbor. Something *other*.

And now, three weeks since we started our little arrangement, which has clearly *already* grown into something else in a short period of time, I'm driving to her family's house for Thanksgiving dinner, and I have a really bad feeling about it.

I mean, she's got a family here, right? A family we've never talked about. Every time I've tried to bring them up, she says that they're 'always around' and diverts the attention to mine. Since I have nothing good to say about mine, the topic gets shut down. The one time I shared glimpses of my childhood was painful enough to never repeat it again.

"Turn left here," she says from the passenger seat of my truck. I swallow and do as she says. We turn onto the 'rich' streets—meaning the streets of people I try to avoid.

"So who lives here?" I ask casually as I grip the steering wheel tighter. The lack of air is getting to my brain.

"My family," she answers, typing something on her phone. She's probably talking to her friend Josie, considering it's the only real name I've heard her mention.

"Right." I clear my throat. "Who exactly?"

"Oh, my mom and dad and brother."

I feel like my life is about to turn upside down, and I take a deep breath before asking my next question, knowing deep in my bones that it'll knock me down. "What did you say your last name was, Alicia?"

"What?" Her laugh is nervous and too forced. "Alicia Jericho."

I humorlessly shake my head and glance at her. "Are you sure?"

She gulps loudly. "Well, it's my middle name." Another forced laugh. "I use it as a pen name, so yeah, I use that as a last name too."

I grip the steering wheel tighter, not liking where this is going.

"I mean, it wasn't a lie." Her voice flutters.

This time I turn to look at her. "But it wasn't the truth either."

Her throat bobs as she swallows. "Not entirely."

"Why?" I want to hear her answer, hoping to God it's not some sick game.

She turns away, hiding her hands under her thighs. "Because I wanted you to treat me like... well, *me*, not related to anyone. My brother's shenanigans didn't exactly make our family popular."

Her brother. Her brother?

It would make sense if I wasn't pissed right now. All I want to do is drop her off right here, turn around, and get the fuck out of here, but it's Alicia, and I promised her I'd be here. Even when she lied.

"Alicia."

She keeps looking outside so I call again.

"Alicia, look at me." I put my hand on her knee, and she tenses under my touch, but I keep my hand firm, ready to bolt any moment if she freaks out. There is always a thin line with her when touches are involved, and for the thousandth time, I want to hunt down the motherfuckers who hurt her and kill them. She eventually turns toward me, and I keep alternating between looking at her and the road. "Because I didn't want you to think of me like you did at first. Alright? You know, all judgmental."

"I did n—"

She stops me with a slightly raised voice. "Please, don't insult my intelligence. You thought I was a spoiled city girl at first, and I'm not." Then her brows furrow. "I suppose I was a spoiled kid at some point, but not anymore. So yeah,

Jake is not a popular person nowadays, and I figured if you knew he was my brother and all that, you'd look at me even worse." Her leg tenses under my touch. "Turn right there and park on the side by the blue house." She points at the huge-ass house, and lead settles in my stomach.

"What's your last name, Alicia?" I repeat the question as I park next to this gorgeous home I could only dream of owning one day.

Unfortunately, I already know the answer.

She turns toward me with a tight smile. "It's Attleborough. Alicia Attleborough. Nice to officially meet you." She offers me her hand for a shake, but I'm frozen. I can't breathe.

I should have known it was too good to be true. I had been having this feeling since the night in the mountains that the second shoe would drop anytime now. She was too perfect to be mine. I gave myself hope when I agreed to her proposal, but now I'm so deep, I can't climb out.

And I was right. About all of it. She's Justin Attleborough's sister, the asshole who beat the shit out of me that night. The asshole I let do that to me.

About eight years ago, we had a nasty fight when I slept with his girlfriend, and he went to jail. He thought Kayla, his now fiancé, had something to do with it, and he had been bullying her for years for it. How she forgave him is still a mystery to me, but she never told me what exactly happened between them and how it all turned out. The only thing I know is that night I let him beat the living shit out of me because I felt fuckin' guilty. The dude was in the Navy while I was shagging his girl, so yeah, he deserved to throw a punch.

But it never stopped there. Something escalated in his life after that night, and I don't think it had anything to do

234

with prison where he spent a couple of years, I think. He brought that on himself when he beat the cop who arrested him. The man has some serious anger issues. Regardless of what's been happening in his life, everywhere our lives overlap, we fight, quite literally. We've had a few nice brawls over the years, and every time I wanted a fight, I made sure to stick around the places I knew he'd be. Me and him in one room is a sure recipe for disaster.

And now, she tells me she is his sister—the sister I saw in passing when she was a kid at school. I don't even remember her because I was a few grades older. I didn't even know her name since I wasn't interested.

Justin and I were never in the same circles, so I knew nothing about him. I've never even seen Alicia around town before, which makes sense now, since I know what happened to her. Otherwise, I'd never miss her. She's the most gorgeous woman I've ever seen. The woman of my dreams. You know when you're a teenager, you have this crush on someone and then you grow up just wanting the person? She was always that, the dream in my mind. And when I saw her, she turned into reality. My dream had a body and face that belonged to a goddess.

And the goddess has a dickbag brother.

Fuck my life.

"Mark. Mark, are you okay?" I finally notice Alicia calling out to me.

I try to focus on her and blink. Her hand isn't outstretched anymore, her face is full of concern.

"What happened, Mark?"

"Nothing," I lie through a forced smile. "Are you sure you want me in there?" I nod toward the house. "It looks fancy, and I'm anything but," I ask jokingly. Partially.

"What are you talking about?" Her brows draw together in genuine confusion.

I let out a long sigh. She's really so far from what I thought of her at first—too pure for her own good—and I want to punch my own face in for judging her too soon. Plus, she clearly doesn't know our history, or I wouldn't be parked next to her parents' house. What does she know about me besides those few glimpses of the old me I've shown her? She knows me as a firefighter who saves lives. *Now.* She doesn't know where I came from and what I did when I was younger. Not entirely.

"Just joking. C'mere." I take her hand and pull her to me. My gut tells me it might be our last kiss, and she'll hate me later once her brother tells her all about me.

"It's my parents' house." She giggles but lets me pull her.

"It's alright. They can't see us from there." I place my hand on the back of her neck and angle her head for the kiss. I brush my lips across hers, and she whimpers.

"You know what this butterfly kiss does to me, and you still do it before family dinner?" she murmurs against my mouth.

"Yeah," I breathe out and swipe my tongue across her lower lip. "You'll be wet, and I'll know it."

I press my lips harder and slide my tongue in. She meets me with the shy swipe of hers. The tip of her tongue gently pokes at mine, and I dive in deeper. I wrap my other hand around her back and pull her closer. Her back arches, and she lets out a loud gasp. I can almost smell her wetness in the air. It makes my dick harder than steel, and it presses on the zipper, nearly ripping it apart. It weeps, remembering how good she feels. How right it feels to be inside her. How amazing it is to make her forget. How victorious.

And how it'll all be gone in a moment.

"*Khe-khe.*" Someone's clearing their throat outside, and I pull away from the kiss with regret.

Once Alicia straightens in her seat with the cutest blush of her cheeks, Justin comes into view. He's standing on the passenger side of the truck, and he doesn't know it's me. This is a new vehicle I purchased a couple of weeks ago and still haven't driven around town much.

I see the exact moment he realizes it's me. His eyes widen, his jaw sets, and his shoulders square back. He's about to open his mouth and rip me a new one when Alicia smiles at him.

"Hey, Justin. This is Mark, my friend." She's trying to hide her blushing face, but there is no need. His focus is solely on me. "And this is Justin, my big brother." She moves to open the door, but Justin doesn't move. "Hey, moose, move away so I can get out."

That snaps him out of his staring, and he steps back. Alicia jumps out of the car and gives him a side hug. Then she turns toward me and gestures for me to follow. How she doesn't pick up on the atmosphere is a miracle to me.

I slowly get out of the truck, feeling his eyes on me the whole time. Yeah, I bet he wants to put me in the ground right now, and I don't blame him. I mean, I slept with his ex and now I'm sleeping with his sister. That goes against any bro code. He might think I've used it as a revenge on him by using his sister.

I didn't.

But I'll never be able to prove it to him.

"Is this like a staring contest between two alpha dudes or something?" Alicia laughs nervously, and I try to relax for her sake.

"Nah, just flexing muscles." I wink at her and hear a loud air intake from her brother. *Yeah, fuck you too, Justin.*

"What is he doing here?" Justin growls.

"Be nice." She gently smacks him on the chest. "Mark's my neighbor and the only reason I survived on my own." She smiles at me, but it's forced. She feels something's going on.

"Do you even know who he is?" His voice raises, and my fists automatically ball. She doesn't like loud voices, and he should know it.

"Yep." She pops the *p*. "A firefighter and my friend. So chill with your brotherly thing you're doing right now." She circles a finger in the air around his face.

Justin's face turns concerned, and he swallows loudly. He turns toward Alicia and watches her carefully. Almost too carefully. With every passing moment, his face turns grimmer. When he finally switches his intense attention back to me, his jaw grinds so hard, I can almost hear his teeth cracking.

He turns toward Alicia, smiling. "The food's ready. Mom doesn't let us touch 'cause she doesn't want to ruin the *aesthetics*." He accentuates the last word and pointedly looks at me.

"Great!" Alicia claps her hands and starts walking toward the house but stops when she doesn't find us following her. "Are you guys coming?"

"Yeah, in a minute. We'll just have a quick chat." Justin waves her off.

Her eyes dart from her brother to me, and I give her a reassuring nod. She smiles weakly and leaves, clear concern in her eyes.

When she disappears in the house, Justin turns into the real Attleborough I know and grabs the front of my shirt.

"The fuck is your game here?"

"Take your hands off me." I grind my teeth, pointedly looking down.

"Or what?" His fist squeezes the material harder.

It takes all my willpower not to put him on the ground.

"Or you're gonna end up with a few broken bones." I meet his eyes.

"Bring it on, trailer boy."

"Hands off, Justin, or I won't care that your family is right there."

The mention of his family brings him back to reality, and the muscles in his jaw slow their chaotic movements. He lets go of my shirt and steps back. "I don't know what your game is here, but you need to turn around and get the fuck outta here."

"Trust me, there is nothing more I want to do than to get *the fuck outta here*," I say, mimicking his tone, "but I came here with Alicia, and I'm not leaving her alone."

"She's with her family, you asshole." He pushes my chest. "She's not alone."

I clench my jaw, trying to refrain from a lot I want to say about his family and him, but Alicia is a part of it, so I'm trying to be good.

"Get out." He points at the way we came.

The temptation is strong. I longingly look at my truck, and I'm about to make a move toward it when the entrance door bursts open, and a firm "Justin" snaps me back. Alicia's standing at the threshold. She took off her coat and is left wearing black leggings and a huge, fluffy sweater. She looks cozy, and my chest begins to ache.

"Are you—" Justin clears his throat. "Are you wearing leggings?" His voice is weirdly raspy, and I give him a second glance.

239

"Well, yeah." Alicia shrugs one shoulder and fixes her loose hair behind her ear.

"And your hair's down," he declares, and I turn to look at him. What's up with these weird questions?

"Yeah," she says, a little shy, and my head snaps toward her. Alicia's cheeks pinken, probably because of the cold, and she looks even more beautiful than I thought possible. A dull ache in my chest intensifies with every blink of her eyes, and I bring my hand to rub on it.

"Alright. We're coming." Justin plants his palm on my shoulder, nearly knocking me down—and I'm no small boy —and pushes me forward, his intentions clear. I throw him a questioning look, but he stares ahead. I swallow the dry lump in my throat and start walking toward the door.

Alicia folds her arms across her chest and uncomfortably wobbles from foot to foot. At the steps, Justin moves past me, grabs Alicia in a side hug, and walks inside, leaving the door open. Thank fuck. I don't remember when I felt so unwelcome before but still stuck around. Should have taken Ghost with me so he could bite his ass, and I could blame all of it on him being 'just a dog and doing doggy things.'

Chapter Twenty-One

MARK

As I walk inside the house, a shorter version of Alicia flies out from the kitchen. She's like a foot shorter, but her face resembles Alicia's so much. But that's where the similarities end. Where Alicia is guarded and reserved, her mother is bubbly and extraverted.

"Hey there!" She wipes her hand on her apron and offers it to me. "I'm Mary, Alicia's mom. And this..." She points at the tall, balding man who just walked in from another room. "Is George, her father. Well, and you met Justin." She waves at the stoic figure by the door.

I shake her hand and move to her father, who's hesitant to offer his. I find his eyes and stretch my hand, mentally praying he doesn't start anything right now. Clearly, he heard about my 'disagreements' with his son, and he is not happy to see me in his house. I can't even blame him. If I had kids, I'd be on their side no matter what. I bet he wants to throw me out, but he doesn't want to look like an evil bastard in front of his wife and daughter, judging by the looks he throws them every other second.

When he finally grabs my hand to shake, he gives it an extra-hard squeeze, and I let him. My palm is twice his size, and I could easily crush his hand in mine, but he's Alicia's father, and no matter how tempting, I choose to behave and be an adult. I've never met anyone's parents before, but I want Alicia's to like me—even though I have a strong suspicion it will be the first and the last time I'm in this house.

"George." His voice is clipped.

"Mark," I manage to say.

"I know," he answers quietly and lets go of my hand.

I step back and nod in acknowledgment of the situation that's escalating with every second.

"You didn't tell me he's so handsome!" Mrs. Attleborough whispers so loud, people in the trailer park on the other side of town can hear her. I feel my cheeks heat up and then I hear a snort. A moment later, Justin walks by me, knocking into my shoulder. I'm taller and bulkier, and he almost managed to move me half an inch. Such determination.

"The table is set!" Mrs. Attleborough says and claps her hands, clearly not reading the room. "We're not at a full set today."

Thank fuck for that.

"Jakey is... away."

Well, that's a nice way to put that the asshole is away in rehab, as rumors have it. *Jakey* is a tool, and I hope he'll be fired from the police because he doesn't deserve to be one. Since Kenneth became sheriff, life became somewhat bearable—until Jake was hired as an *officer of the law*.

"It's the first Thanksgiving he'll be away, but it's good for him, you know?" She's watching me with hopeful eyes, and I nod to make her feel better.

But I don't agree with her. The asshole deserves to lose everything for using his position of power. And him being related to Alicia? Well, she's right. If I knew it from the beginning, I'd be biased as hell, and there's no way our relationship would have gotten anywhere. I'd be avoiding her like the plague.

I feel curious eyes on me and find Alicia's baby blues trained on my face.

"Are you okay?" she asks quietly.

"Yeah."

"Alright." She clearly doesn't believe me and takes my hand. "You're not mad at me for not telling you my full name, are you?"

I sigh. "I am, Alicia. I'm really upset about that."

"It doesn't change anything though, right?" she asks hopefully.

I smile sadly. "It changes everything."

"But why?" Her brows furrow in confusion.

Her mom saves me from answering when she calls her from the living room. "Alicia Jericho Attenborough! Get yourself and your friend over here! The turkey is getting cold!"

Alicia gives me another long look and whispers, "We'll talk later," before dragging me behind her.

When I walk into the dining room, I feel like I stepped into the pages of a design magazine. I've never seen so many matching cushions and drapes and dishware in my life.

"Mark?" a surprised but very familiar voice says. "What are you doing here?"

Of course Kayla would be here. And of course she knew Alicia was Justin's sister. And judging by the look on her face, she didn't expect to see me at the family gathering. I shoot her a glare. *The joke is on you, Kayla,* and she has the decency to look guilty.

"Was invited for dinner." I make the sarcasm drip from my voice as I take my seat to the left of Alicia and to the right of Mrs. Attleborough, who's at the head of the table on one side and George on the other. Kayla sits across from me, looking sheepish and guilty as hell, as Justin takes a seat to the left of her.

"How awesome." Kayla forces a smile as she fidgets with her fork.

"You don't say," I answer quietly, making Alicia do a double take at me and Kayla. I bet she's thinking we had something in the past, which cannot be further from the truth.

I don't belong. I see it clear as day now. Even Kayla was able to mingle with them, but I'll never be able to do the same. So yeah, this dinner is destined to be the last.

Everyone is picking on their appetizers while Kayla's happily chatting with everyone. There are no conversations happening among anyone else, but she's really trying. She gets a few grunts from George and a kiss from Justin. Mrs. Attleborough laughs at something she says, while she only gets a hot stare from Alicia. Yeah, I'll have to explain our history without giving away too much of Kayla's struggles. It's not my story to tell.

"We're so happy you're here!" Mrs. Attleborough dotes on me. I think she's the only one who's truly happy right now.

Justin lets out a loud snort, and Alicia snaps at him, "Justin!"

"What?" he replies innocently.

"Stop it!"

"I didn't do anything." He dramatically throws his hands up. In that moment, I so want to paint his face blue and green and black. I've never desired violence so intensely. Yes, we've had our differences over the years, but can't he pretend to be civil for the sake of his sister? I've seen him doing a lot of nasty shit over the years, and yet I'm trying to behave like a human.

"Justin, don't." Kayla touches his shoulder and shakes her head. It seems to calm him down, because the jerkface softens as he kisses her hand.

Mrs. Attleborough returns from the kitchen with a plate of steaming mashed potatoes and makes a beeline toward me. "Mark, honey, I think I've seen you somewhere before." She places a huge spoonful of potatoes on my plate, and normally I'd be ecstatic at the sight of food, but today all I can taste is metal. Probably from biting my tongue too hard.

"It's a small town, Mrs. Attleborough. Perhaps you've seen me around." I shrug, trying not to keep attention on myself for too long.

"The station!" She places the plate on the table and claps her hands. "I've seen you at the station. You're a fire-fighter, aren't you?" Her eyes turn dreamy, and Alicia groans next to me, "Here we go," making Kayla chuckle.

"I am, ma'am." I nod, inwardly sighing. So much for diverting attention.

"Oh, you stop it with this ma'am nonsense." She play-fully smacks my shoulder, and I feel my cheeks turn pink. I'm so grateful for my beard right now, it's not even funny. "Someone who saves lives on an everyday basis is at our dinner table. So exciting!" She sits at her chair and keeps her eyes trained on me, making me uncomfortable. At her words, I can hear Justin loudly grinding his teeth together.

"He is." Alicia's voice is filled with pride. "In fact, he's saved me so many times since I've moved in next door." She places her hand on my shoulder and proceeds to tell them all the times I've come to her rescue. I know how much she didn't want to share her misfortunes with her family, but she's doing so to rectify my presence at the table.

I whisper as quietly as I can, "Alicia, you don't have to." But she continues with her story, making her mother gasp a few times, her father clench his jaw, and Justin do a double take of me. The only person who's enjoying the dinner is Kayla. She's watching Alicia with a dreamy smile on her face, sighing wistfully from time to time. Is she okay? I glance at her, and she notices it, her smile spreads so wide, I bet it hurts her cheeks.

"Why didn't you call me? I'd come and get you back home right away," Justin asks through gritted teeth, clearly unhappy that so much was happening without him knowing.

"That's why." Alicia points a finger at him. "I wanted to start living on my own. I'm twenty-six, for fuck's sake."

"Alicia, language!" Mrs. Attleborough cries out, and I agree with her. Alicia doesn't curse much, not really. And I don't expect her to start in her parents' house. She's anxious and frustrated.

"Sorry, Mom." Alicia winces and turns back toward her brother. "Really, Justin, what's wrong with you? I supported you when you messed up with Kayla. Why can't you be supportive of me?"

"It's not the same." His voice drops low. "Completely different, Alicia."

"It's really not. It's either you support my choice or not." Her voice is firm, reminding me of the one she used to explain why she had a body in her backyard.

"Alicia, you don't—"

"This is a Thanksgiving dinner that your mom spent hours making. Stuff your faces with food and keep quiet," George booms firmly.

Everyone quiets, even Justin. I look at Mr. Attleborough with newfound respect. Alicia gives me a small warm smile and finally starts eating. I inhale deeply, filling my senses with delicious smells, and dig in.

Maybe, just maybe, we will survive this dinner without bloodshed.

Chapter Twenty-Two

ALICIA

I knew from the beginning that at some point at dinner something would blow up. I expected Justin to be difficult about me bringing a man home, even if I just said we're friends, but the way he's been looking at Mark throughout the whole dinner was something... different than a brother giving his sister's boyfriend a hard time. I take a moment to thank the heavens that Jake is away. I can't imagine how bad things would be if he weren't. Two overprotective brothers at one table is two too many.

Even though we haven't put a label on our relationship, I was still excited to introduce him to everyone. At first, I thought he'd drag Mark out of the truck and punch him in the face. I'm sure he'd get punched back because Mark is bigger than Justin, but I also know my brother, and he can be vicious. In fact, I think he should be in that rehab center along with Jake. But Kayla acts as his leash, so he's been doing better.

Until he saw Mark. I'm sure he wanted to drive him off, but he seemed to change his mind when he saw me coming out of the house. The look on his face when he noticed what I was wearing was one of pure, unfiltered wonder as a million things raced through his head. The world hasn't seen my butt in anything other than super baggy pants in nearly eight years, so it's reasonable for him to be surprised... and smart enough to put two and two together and figure out that Mark was probably the catalyst for my change in wardrobe.

And now, every time Mom sings a praise to Mark or offers him something to eat, Justin squeezes his glass tighter. And even Kayla can't relax him, even though she's been trying to the whole evening. She looks like she knows more than I do though, like there's something no one is telling me. Since the moment Mark walked in, she braced herself for a fight. I noticed how her posture changed the moment he showed up. Her back straightened and her shoulders drew back as she plastered a fake smile on her face. She's been trying to lighten the atmosphere the whole evening.

To be honest, for a moment there, I thought they might have been something in the past, and that might be why Justin was acting this way. But then I quickly ditched this theory because Kayla would find a way to tell me about that at dinner. She's too much of a decent person to keep such a bombshell from me. I mean, we live in a small town, so it's expected that someone has dated someone you might know at some point, but Kayla is family now, so it would be weird for me. And for Justin too, to be fair.

"Mark, honey." My mom's hand is placed on his shoulders while she's holding a tea kettle with her famous raspberry leaves over his cup. "Would you like more tea?"

"No, I'm good, Mrs. Attleborough," he answers with a forced smile. There is a dark cloud over the table, even though my mom and dad are trying really hard to make him feel welcome. I was surprised when Dad did a one-eighty somewhere in the middle of dinner. He wasn't happy to see him at first.

"Oh, honey, you stop it. I told you to call me Mary. You'll be seeing a lot of me, I'm sure." She giggles like a schoolgirl, and Dad chokes on his dessert. We share a look with him, and I'm trying to keep myself from laughing. Mom is charmed by Mark's warm presence in the best way possible.

"Of course, Mary." He gives my mom a small smile, and she giggles again. I nearly cackle, knowing how uncomfortable he is.

"Stop, Mom. He'll be leaving soon and won't be coming back," Justin says as he leans on the back of the chair and throws his arm over Kayla's shoulder.

"Justin," she hisses and pokes his ribs. "Be nice, you behemoth."

"Why would I?" He turns toward her, not bothering to even try lowering his voice. "You know he can't be here."

"Why is that?" She pulls away from his hug.

"Because *you* out of all people know who he is."

Kayla rears back. "What's that supposed to mean?"

"C'mon, Kay baby." He lowers his voice, but we still can hear him. "You don't think he's here because of Alicia, do you?"

"I think that's exactly what he's here for." She shoots him a glare, and he laughs.

I'm scared to look at Mark because it's clear something is happening that I'm not privy to. All three of them know what it is, and I'm the only one on the sidelines who doesn't. And something tells me I won't like the truth.

I take a deep breath and turn toward Mark. His face is a mask of pure anger. His gaze is fixed on Justin, his huge hands in tight fists on his knees. I want to touch his hand, but he pulls away without looking at me.

"Mark." I know my voice is small and miserable, but I don't care what people around the table think. They've seen me at my worst. "Mark, look at me."

"He won't, Alicia. He won't look at you because he knows I'm right," Justin answers instead, his eyes locked with Mark's. The atmosphere can be cut with a dull knife.

"Shut up, Justin," I snap. "For once in your life, just shut up."

All heads whip toward me, Mark's included. None of them are used to me having outbursts like this.

"What is he talking about? Do you know?" I ask the man next to me.

Mark's jaw tenses. I can clearly see the muscles in his cheeks working. "Yes, Alicia. I know."

"What is it then?" I ask desperately.

"Part of me being trailer trash, I think," he answers without missing a beat.

I hear a loud intake of air. My mom is shocked. We don't talk about people like that.

"That's not it. And you know it." Judging by Justin's tone, he's about to lose it.

There's a long pause. "He is right." Finally—*finally*—Mark meets my eyes. "That's not it."

"What is it?" An icicle starts forming at the pit of my stomach, and the cold spreads through my whole body.

"We—" Mark swallows and keeps talking. "We don't have a good history."

"Who?"

"Your brother and me."

"Alright. A lot of people don't have a good history with Justin. He's got issues. Just ask Kayla. She's a saint, and I genuinely have no idea how she deals with him." A weird sound comes from Kayla, and I lift my eyes and find her face twisted with befuddlement. Did I step too far? I was hoping it was going to be a lighthearted joke. Kayla is usually the first one to bug Justin, but she isn't laughing this time. Her eyes are full of sorrow.

"Our issues..." He quiets as he searches for the right words. "Run deeper."

"That's alright. You can resolve it, and we can all move on with our lives, right?" I look around the table. My mom is wearing the same perplexed expression as I am, so I know she's not in the loop either. But Dad looks between Justin and Mark, scratching his chin. "Right?" I push harder, and Justin finally snaps.

"No, Alicia, this situation cannot get resolved."

"Why? You're both adults and can freaking talk it out, right? It can't be so bad that you can't do it for me, right?" I don't know who I'm trying to convince at the end. "Justin, am I right?"

"For fuck's sake, Alicia." Justin throws his hands in front of him. "This"—he circles his fingers between me, Mark, and himself—"cannot get resolved. He slept with Ashley, and we were fighting at the gas station the night you were raped, alright? He was one of the reasons why I didn't get to you on time."

A sound of glass shattering on the floor.

A loud gasp.

A soft cry.

I don't know where they all come from because I'm solely focused on what's going on in my head.

Pain. Emotional and physical.

If he slapped me with a wet towel, it would have been less painful. I rear back as my whole body freezes. My muscles go rigid, but my hands begin to shake.

"Alicia," a soft voice calls to me, but my mind is numb.

I'm back to *that* moment.

The moment I've been reliving in my nightmares for years.

"Alicia, fuck." A grunt follows. "I'm so sorry. I didn't mean it to—"

"Shut up, Justin." Someone's loud voice comes through. "Just shut up."

I hear the commotion that follows, but I'm not here. I'm back *there*. But now, instead of two scary faces, I see the face I came to love. Mark is there too. Before this evening, he has been a face of security and comfort for me, someone who wasn't connected to that night. Now he's in the same nightmare that's been haunting me for years. He's watching.

He's watching me be humiliated and violated. And his face is emotionless. He will never look at me the same way. Never.

And I will never look at him the same way.

"Alicia, honey." A warm voice comes through. My mom. It's her. Her voice has been here even before I knew what her voice meant. Childhood. Safety. A gentle hand touches my shoulder. "Are you alright?" The worry in her voice snaps me back from my nightmare. "Do you want them to leave?"

I swallow a dry lump in my throat. "No, Mom." My own voice sounds too coarse for my own ears. "*I* need to leave." I stand from my place, ready to leave, when Mark's voice stops me.

"Alicia."

I turn my attention to him. "Did you know?"

He shakes his head, his misty eyes fixated on mine. "I didn't even know you're his sister until we came here." He swallows, pausing. "Believe me, I didn't."

"It doesn't really matter," I whisper. "It's broken now."

"What's broken?" His voice is rough. Red rims his eyes.

"This. Everything." I sniffle loudly. "I'll never be able to look at you without remembering... everything. You were a safe haven. But not anymore." I dwell in palpable sorrow.

"Yeah, it's better this way." Justin stands from his chair, but I stop him.

"And you." I point my finger at him. "Do not talk to me ever again. I never blamed you for that night nor will I ever, but I blame you for this. This was my chance, and you threw it out of the window."

I march out without looking at a single person.

Utter humiliation threatens to swallow me, and I'm trying to reach my bedroom so no one will see me being devoured by it.

When I open the door, a familiar smell reaches my nose, and it triggers something in my brain. A wild spirit possesses my body, and I jump to my desk and swipe everything away. Then I move to the floating shelves on the wall and swipe everything away there too. I grip the shelf with all my might and try to rip it off the wall, but it's anchored so thoroughly, and I'm only able to rip it away just a bit.

Leaving the shelf hanging by its last breath, I move to the standing shelves. My childhood photos from 'before' are thrown on the floor, but they are still looking at me, mocking me for not being able to laugh like I used to. I stomp on it. Again. And again. And again.

The door opens, and large hands pull me from behind. I hate being hugged or touched from behind, but this time, I don't even flinch. Instead, I turn around and start punching the wide chest. I punch until my fists start to hurt and all the fight leaves my exhausted body, and I sag against the man who's holding me.

My sobs come in waves. At first, they move my whole body, and I feel a sense of coldness envelope me in its freezing hug. The second one releases the pent-up fear I've been holding onto for so long. And after, I'm a blubbering, sniffling mess.

My nose is pressed against the warmness of the body I grew to love. His smell is tingling my nose, calming my hysteria. His large hands make circles on my back as I cling to him.

I hear the door opening and closing again, but no steps follow. Someone decided to retreat. *Good, I'm not up for visitors.*

When I'm finally relatively calm, I relax into his arms, knowing I will never *feel* him like this again.

"I'm sorry." His voice is raw with unsaid emotions. It's rough and full of pain.

"Me too," I answer as I burrow deeper into his embrace.

"I love you, Alicia." His words, raspy and heartbroken, are shredding my heart to pieces. "I will do anything to make you happy. Anything." His arms pull me tighter. "Even if it kills me."

I close my eyes, knowing I'll be back at that night and hoping I won't see his face.

But I see it.

Again, on the sideline. Quietly watching. Not participating... but watching. I furiously squeeze my eyes shut, trying to erase his face from the most painful memory of my life. But he is still there.

My eyes fill with tears as I come to understand what this means.

I won't be able to be with this man even if I love him with every fiber of my soul.

He pulls away as if sensing my turmoil. When I let him go, he brings his large hands to my cheeks and lifts my face toward him. When I meet his eyes, I find unshed tears in them, and my own eyes tear once more.

"I don't want to cause you pain. Ever." His wet lips gently touch mine. He moves them along mine. His teasing touch is butterfly-like. He tastes like salt and sorrow.

He softly moves his lips along mine one more time and pulls away.

Then he stands and leaves me in my solitude, surrounded by people.

But still lonely.

Chapter Twenty-Three

MARK

I wipe away the tears. I should be embarrassed about them, but I'm not. Walking out of her room—away from her—was one of the worst pains I've ever experienced.

The asshole is standing in the hallway next to her room. Her mom, dad, and Kayla are there too, but my sole focus is on him.

"I hope you are happy with your accomplishment," I tell him, standing as close as I can, hoping he feels as small as he really is.

He has the decency to look ashamed.

"Mark, he didn't mean to—"

"Stop right there, Kayla." I raise my hand. "You knew.

You were probably the only one who knew who we were to each other."

"I did!" she exclaims. "And what? I saw two people who were perfect for each other."

"Really?" I ask sarcastically. "How perfect are we now, huh?"

She deflates. "It was never supposed to end like this. You were supposed to fall in love with each other and not be sidetracked by anything else."

"Yeah." My chuckle is dark. "On our own terms, maybe." I shift my attention to Justin. I take pleasure in the fact that he looks like a truck just ran over him, but even that's not nearly bad enough for what I want to do to him right now.

But I have no anger left. My life is falling apart as we speak, and the only reason I ever wanted something bigger, something *more* for myself, stayed in that room, crying on the floor. And I left my heart bleeding on the same floor with her.

"Fuck, man," Justin says as he covers his face with his hands. "Is she okay?"

"No, but she will be. Because she's so fuckin' strong, and she doesn't need you to treat her like an incapable infant." I look at all of them. "None of you."

Everyone looks at the ground, ashamed, even her parents. Her mother sniffles, bringing her hand to her chest. I want to say more, but I decide I better not start something that might worsen the already-shitty situation, so I walk toward the exit.

I knew this day would be a major clusterfuck from the moment I woke up. I'm not a good fit to bring to a family dinner, not a polished version of a perfect boyfriend. I'm a barely civilized guy you fuck in the darkness and don't tell anyone. I'm still in awe about how a woman like Alicia could find me interesting. I guess I'll never know now.

I'm out the door when Justin catches up to me. He jumps in front of me and stops me with his raised hand. "We need to talk."

"Not now. For fuck's sake, not now, Justin," I growl, and his eyes widen. We are not on a first-name basis, and I can't even remember calling Justin his name to his face.

"Look, I know I fucked up. I didn't want to say anything about the rape. Alright?" He places his hands on the back of his head and pulls his hair. "I got overheated when I saw you being so fuckin' cozy with my family. With my sister. You clearly fucked her, and I just fuckin' snapped."

I clench my jaw, trying not to say anything back and make the evening even more horrid. Instead, I'm trying to focus on the rim of my truck, which needs a scrubbing.

"Please, tell me you really didn't know she was my sister." His voice takes a pleading tone, and I switch my attention to him.

"I didn't." I take a step toward him, and he doesn't back down. "Alicia is the best thing to ever happen in my fucking life, but now, you took that away from me. Why did you push me inside the house if you thought I was here just to taunt you, huh?"

His anger dissolves as he responds. "She's been wearing those humongous sweats and shirts for eight years. And I haven't seen her hair down for about the same time. And here she was, standing right there"—he points at the door—"in leggings with her hair down. Smiling. I don't remember her smiling. I mean, she smiled, but it never reached her eyes, but when she saw you, she was almost fuckin' shining. So I guess I wanted to see her like that for a bit, maybe." He shrugs, and fuck me, but I understand him. I understand because I have a little sister too. And I would kill anyone if they meant her harm. "Did I really fuck it up that bad?" Uncertainty is clear in his voice.

"If you told me about that first, I could have thought of how to present that information to her, but not now. The damage is done." I shake my head and step around him, ready to leave.

"I thought you were just trying to fuck me over."

"Justin, I didn't even know your sister went through that." I stop and turn toward him. "Shit, I didn't even remember you had a sister. My life doesn't revolve around you, for fuck's sake."

"Alright." He looks distraught. "We can explain it to her. *I* can explain it to her."

I look at him like at an idiot. "You truly don't understand, do you?"

He clenches his jaw but doesn't say a word, so I walk back to him and get in his face.

"Just to make it clear for you. Every time I touch her, she'll remember that night. Every time I kiss her, she'll remember that night. Every fucking time we do more than just kiss, she'll be remembering that fucking night," I nearly yell. "Every. Fucking. Time. Because I was *safe* for her. Someone not connected to the nightmare she went through. But now, you took it away from her. You took it away from me. She will never look at me the same. Never." I take a deep breath. "And I love her too fucking much to force her to live through it every single day," I say as the last nail in the coffin and walk away, leaving him standing in the front yard of the perfect house of his perfect parents with my perfect woman inside.

The woman I'll never get to touch again.

Chapter Twenty-Four

ALICIA

He walked away, taking my heart with him. I hear muffled voices in the hallway behind the door, but none of them come in. At some point at night, Mom's head pokes inside, but when she sees my face, she closes my door with tears in her eyes. I want to be alone.

But I cause pain for everyone I love.

Closer to morning, when I have no tears left and my face looks like it was stung by a whole hive of bees, I get to work. I go downstairs, where it's quiet and empty, to grab a few garbage bags and run back to my room. I try to be stealthy and not wake my parents up.

I clean my room from the disaster I caused. It takes me a

good three hours, but I don't stop at the damage I caused. No, I trash the remnants of my old life.

Of eight years being stuck.

Of years being fake before that.

I only keep a few pictures from when I was a baby, but my school years are gone. School years when I was too focused on how I looked and not how I felt. That one college year when I was obsessed with what other people thought of me. All gone.

I take my mom's car and drive to the store and buy new paint. Ignoring everyone in the house, I walk to my room and paint it the new color. I ignore the knocks on my door, the phone calls, and the voices. I'm trying to erase everything that makes me hurt again. But no matter what I do, it still hurts. I still see them, and I still see Mark, and they are still in the same room. No matter how much I'm forcing myself to divert my mind somewhere else, they always keep coming back to the same place.

And I hate it. It makes me mad! I don't want to associate him with the most painful period of my life, but I do it anyway. I can't help it.

I moved almost everything to Mrs. Jenkins's house, and now I have to find time to go and bring it back. When Mark won't be around. Or will be. I don't know which scenario I yearn for the most.

The next morning, the door opens without a knock. I'm sitting on the bed with big headphones over my ears.

"Alicia," Justin calls, and I ignore him. "Alicia, talk to me. Please." The mattress dips under his weight as he sits at my feet. "I'm sorry."

I keep ignoring him and scroll through my phone faster. Maybe if I do it long enough, he'll disappear.

"I'm sorry for what happened." His voice cracks. "I didn't know you loved him."

"Loved him?" I put my phone down. "Loved him?" My voice raising. "It's not just love, Justin. Because the feeling I have for him is different. He's like oxygen. It's a *need*. I need him. But after what you said... I can't look at him without thinking about that. Do you understand? About seeing him as a part of that night?" I smack the pillow in unrestrained anger.

"I'm sorry, Alicia. I truly am sorry." His forehead is wrinkled. There are dark circles under his eyes.

"When you fucked up with Kayla, I was on your side and thought you made a mistake. You know, it happens. You'll learn your lesson and get better. But you didn't. You are the same jerk." I grab my phone again and hide behind the screen, wishing this interaction to be over.

"I know I shouldn't have said that, but it doesn't change the truth, you know. A fact is a fact. He was there." There's less remorse in his voice this time, and it pisses me off even more.

"I didn't know that, Justin!" I throw my phone away in rage. "I was fine before I knew it. *Fine*. Finally. Do you understand? I was *fine!*"

He looks around, avoiding my eyes. "Maybe you can go back to him if you love him so much. If you call him, you know, I'm sure he'll be here at your beck and call." He chuckles at his own unfunny joke.

I lean closer to him. "He's not a dog to be on my call, Justin. He is a person. An amazing one. You'll do better to remember it."

A flicker of surprise in his eyes is instantly replaced by a hard stare. "He's not as good as you think he is, Alicia. He's done bad things in the past."

"Like what?" I tilt my head in mocking shock. "Selling weed so he can buy food and school supplies for his sister? Or so he can put money toward her college fund? Yeah, only a bad person would do that."

He looks taken aback. "He has a sister?"

"He does. But looks like he hid it well from you—a smart choice if you ask me."

His nostrils flare. I'm sure he has a lot to say, but he's interrupted by a soft knock on the door and Mom popping her head in without a reply. She's holding a tray with tons of food. "Do you want some dinner, honey?"

I'm about to refuse when I see her hopeful eyes. I've caused enough stress to my family, so I soften in an instant. "Yes, Mom. That'd be great. Thank you."

Her eyes brighten, and she hurries inside to put the tray on the nightstand.

Justin stands and goes to leave. But before he does, he grabs the edge of the door and turns toward me. "He's not the man I'd choose for my little sister, but if he's who you choose, I will not stand in your way. Doesn't mean I won't torment the shit out of him at family dinners."

My lips twitch. "I wish it was that easy, Justin." I shake my head in sorrow. "I don't think I can overcome this... knowledge this time."

"I hope you will," he replies sadly and leaves.

I hope so too, but I don't count on it.

It was too good to be true. He was too perfect, and my life is anything but. No matter how perfect my life looks from the outside, my soul is in shambles.

Chapter Twenty-Five

RCHIE. **At the same bar where the truth has a tendency to be revealed.**

This small, charming town is growing on me, I think, as I take a seat at the local bar, Cat and Stallion. A bartender with a generous bust leans on the counter, her eyes are half-hooded, her whole presence suggestive.

"Whatcha want?" she asks, her voice seductive.

"Besides a drink?" I quirk a brow, chewing on the toothpick I've had in my mouth for the past hour. It's a little habit of mine I picked up to annoy my father.

"Well, if that's what your heart desires." She smiles playfully, and I shoot her back a fake smile. We aren't talking about my heart. My heart hasn't desired anything for years. The other part of me hasn't gone on a hiatus, thank fuck.

"Bourbon. Double. Neat," I answer, and she assesses me

from head to toe. I'm sure she'd love to also look between my legs, but I'm hiding behind the bar.

"Coming right up." She walks away, swaying her hips suggestively. It might have interested me other times, but not today. Today is one of my bad days, and I just need a fucking drink.

A minute later, she places a glass in front of me. "I'm leaving at midnight. Will be happy to grab a bite together." She winks and walks away.

I wish I met her any other time. Such a pity to waste such a gorgeous woman on such a bad day. I throw the drink back and gesture for her to make me another one. Her brows go up, and she brings me another.

"Bad day?" she asks, reading my mind, and I nod. She doesn't offer anything else but leaves the bottle on the counter.

A few minutes later, someone takes a seat next to me. I'm not interested in conversations as drunk people love to do in bars, so I keep my eyes on my glass.

"Usual, Rory." Then he says with a deep sigh, "Please."

"You're getting a little *too usual* here, Mark. What about all those people you need to be sober to save?" The pretty bartender, Rory, stands in front of the new guy with her hands on her hips.

I know she's asking the man next to me, but it hits too close to home, and I flinch inwardly.

"I'm not here to be chastised, Rory." He spreads his palm on the counter. "Just please give me a drink."

"Can't do, big guy." She shrugs a little too cheerfully. "Your friend over there..." She gestures at me. "Got the last one."

"How can you be out of fucking bourbon at a bar?" he

grunts, raking his other hand through his messy hair. He looks like a clusterfuck if you ask me.

"It's Little Hope, asshole, not Chicago. Get a beer." She flips him off and walks away.

The guy groans and longingly looks at the bottle in front of me. I wasn't planning to have a conversation, but the dude looks miserable, so I move my bottle toward him without a word.

"You sure?" he asks hopefully, and I nod.

He lifts his body, leaning over the counter, then grabs a glass and pours himself a hefty drink from my bottle. Swallowing it in one gulp just like I did a moment ago, he hopefully looks at the bottle. I take it and pour him another. He nods and takes the glass, pacing this time.

We sit in a surprisingly comfortable silence until I can't take it anymore.

"So, what got your panties in a twist?"

He half turns his head toward me and lifts a brow. "Are we chitchatting now?"

"Do you have anything else to do?" I ask.

He takes a moment, the glass at his lips. "'Suppose not." He takes a sip of his drink. "A woman."

I chuckle. "Thought so."

"Got one of those yourself?"

"Got many of those." I laugh.

"So, you got no one?" His question is too... understanding, so I don't bullshit him this time.

"So, I got no one."

"I thought I wouldn't have anyone either, because a long time ago, I had many too." He looks inside his glass as he swirls the liquid. It's fascinating. As an artist, I love watching people, and I love watching people making little

269

pieces of art when they don't even know it. "But then I found someone."

"Why aren't you with her?" I'm invested at this point, so I want to know.

"Why do you think I'm not with her?"

I snort at his question, and he continues.

"Fair." The sigh that follows is painful even for my trained pity ears. "I can never be with her."

"Romeo and Juliet, are you?"

He shoots me a glance. "Sort of. Plus, being with me is painful for her."

I recoil back. "Do you abuse her?" My voice comes out as a hiss.

"Fuck no!" He rears back. "I love her, and I would never hurt her. Ever." His words are full of compassion, and I believe him. "But being with me brings bad memories to the surface. Really bad memories." He downs the rest of his drink and pours himself another one. "I can't make her go through that." He chokes on the words. "I just can't."

I choose what to say very carefully. I see a man desperate, on his last breath, and I know how it feels more than most. "Were you a reason she has these bad memories?"

He looks down at the bar, his fingers around the glass going white. "I didn't know—" He covers his face with his hand. "I didn't know, but it turns out I was one of the reasons. Yes."

Well, that's a bummer. Ignorance of the law doesn't relieve you from responsibility. "Does she blame you?"

"Not openly, no." He shakes his head. "But I saw the demons in her eyes."

At this point, I'm not sure he's sober enough to talk, because I can barely understand him anymore.

"The demons of the past, you know." He looks at me. "Those who she sees when she looks at me."

Fuck that, but do I know. I so desperately want to help him. I so desperately wanted someone to help me, but it's too late for me now. Maybe he still has time. "Tell me more."

"I can't." He shakes his head again. "It's not my story to tell."

"Tell me without the names."

He gives me a comprehensive look and bites the inside of his scruffy cheek. "Something... bad happened to her a few years ago, and I—" He cuts himself off, clearly looking for the right way to tell the story without revealing too much. "And I was a part of the reason her brother didn't get to her on time. I didn't like do *do* something to her, but I was a part of that night, you know?"

I have a bad feeling where the story's going. And I also think I know who we are talking about. The guy downs another drink, and I'm thinking of taking his keys, so he doesn't end up in a ditch to add to his current problems.

"Want more?" He takes the bottle and offers it to me.

"Nah, I'm good for tonight." That wasn't my plan, but it's changed since I met this guy. My plan is to drive his drunk ass to his house so he can go and make up with his lady.

"Your loss." He shrugs and pours the rest into his glass. "So yeah, the last time I saw her, we knew it would be the last." He slurs the words. "But at least she let it all out, you know?" He waves his hand in front of my face. "She *cleansed* her soul. It was beautiful." He swallows. "And terrifying."

"Did you talk with her after that?" At this point, I'm invested.

"No-o-o."

"Why?"

He looks at me like I'm an idiot, and the answer is obvious. Well, not to me. "Because she hurts every time she sees me."

"Did she tell you that?"

"No," he snorts. "She's too polite for that."

"I think you should talk to her."

"And I think you talk too much." He waves at Rory to come over, and she rolls her eyes.

"People who went through what she went through—"

His head snaps toward me, and he gets into my personal space. I hate it, but I decide to tolerate it from him because he isn't in the right headspace. "How do you know what she went through?"

"Figured from your story. And you need to back off before your face ends up on the floor," I warn. I fucking hate people in my space.

He pulls back, his brows furrowed. "Alright. I'll bite. Why do you think I should talk to her?"

"Because people who are considered to be victims often blame themselves for what happened to them, and they think other people see them as..." I look for the right word. "Unclean."

He recoils with a look of pure horror on his face. "That's a pile of bullshit."

"I agree, but society is not always kind to them. So, in their minds..." I watch his whole body change with my words. His shoulders drop, and he looks smaller, even though the dude is huge.

"Fuck. I didn't think about that." He scratches the back of his head. "Do you think she thinks that too?"

"I think you should talk to her." I give him a pointed

look, and just when I'm about to go into a philosophy of a victim, the pretty bartender finds the worst time possible to come check on us.

"What's up, Mark?" She looks him over, concerned. All her flirting toward me is forgotten since she's busy with Mark.

"Ca' I get anoda one?" He flutters his eyelashes at her. "Pitty please."

She snorts at his sudden inability to formulate words. "You're done for tonight, buddy." Then she grabs a huge glass and fills it with water. "Drink up, big boy."

He furrows his brows even more, and I'm afraid the crease is about to wrinkle his brain. That's how deep it looks. "You no fuun, Rory."

"I know." She sighs. "Do you want me to call Austin to come pick you up?"

"Ma boss?" He snorts. "Nah, thanks."

"Alright. I'll take you after my shift. Chill here." It's nice of her to offer. They don't seem like people who had a fling, so her behavior must be a small-town thing.

"Nah, I'll drive." He waves her off dismissively. "I'm fine."

"You're not. Sit and wait here." She points a red-tipped finger in front of him.

"I'll take him." I was already going to drive him home, but this conversation was too hilarious not to watch. This pint-sized woman ordering this big dude around was entertaining. "Give me his address."

"You sure?" Rory chews on her lips, carefully watching my face. "Do I know you enough to give you his address?"

I quirk a brow. "You knew me well enough to practically offer me *your* address." It should have thrown her off, but she just laughs.

"Fair." She walks to the left of the bar, takes a pen, and scribbles something on a napkin. Then she comes back and passes it to me. "He has a mean dog, be careful. Hope to see you soon again." She winks and walks away.

"Di' Rory hit on you?" Mark slurs from his chair.

"I guess she did," I answer as I type his address in my phone and see it's only seven minutes away. Cool, we'll take his car, and I can walk back. I could use some air to clear my head.

"She 'oes it to everyone. Sush a free 'pirit." He tries to stand but fails, so I help him.

"Let's go." We walk outside where I open my palm in front of his face. "Keys?"

"What? Don' wanna check ma pocke'?" He laughs at his own joke.

I roll my eyes.

He places the keys into my open palm, and I hit the panic button. A sound comes from two cars down the parking lot. We walk toward his truck, where he climbs in the passenger seat without a fight. Thank fuck. My mood for nice conversations is gone.

"I didn' know I can love someone like dat, ya know," he says a few minutes into the drive. "And I didn' know someone can love me. *Me*. The poor schmuck from da trailer side."

Here lies another problem, and I can't do anything to help him unless he will accept himself, so I glance at him and offer generic advice. "Understand your worth, and then you can bring something to the table. It doesn't matter how much money you make or what car you drive. How you feel yourself is what matters. And it's exactly how others will see you."

He stares ahead of himself, not indicating if he's heard me or not. But my work here is done anyway.

I park next to a well-maintained house, well loved and lived in. It obviously costs ten times less than mine, but I'd pick this one any day over my cold, soulless monstrosity. This house feels like home—another reason why it's too late for me.

He gets out of the car, and I walk with him toward the door. He takes the keys from me and unlocks it. A huge German shepherd jumps on the man, covering his face with sloppy kisses. See, I can't even get a fucking dog because I'm so fucking unreliable.

Mark turns toward me and asks. "Wanna come in?"

I snort. "I'm done with your sob story. Get your ass inside."

"Fucker." He laughs and walks into the house. His happy dog is at his feet. He sits in the chair next to the door and tries to take his shoes off. "What's your name?"

"Archie."

"Alex Crowley's friend?" His brow rises.

"Yeah. You know him?"

"Everyone knows him. He's a hero." A note of admiration in his voice makes me want to bite my tongue.

We certainly don't see ourselves as heroes, even though some people call us that, but I hear myself saying, "Yeah, he is." And he is. I think he really is. It was not his fault.

It was mine.

My mood changes drastically, and I start walking backward from his porch.

"Thanks for the advice." He sounds soberer now. "I'll work on myself before going to her."

"But do go to her." I point a finger at him.

"I will." He nods solemnly.

275

* * *

I'm walking down the road when I feel someone's presence behind me. The person is hesitant to step closer. I feel her turmoil in the air. The person needs something from me but doesn't want to be near. Interesting.

"Is he alright?" a feminine voice says from behind me.

"He will be," I answer as I keep walking.

"Why did you bring him home? Was he hurt?" The voice is to my right now, and I glance at the woman. She vaguely reminds me of someone I can't place. Throwing constant looks behind her and keeping a healthy distance between us, she keeps following me.

"Just drunk."

"He's drinking so much now." Pure sorrow laces her words. I glance at her again. Her head is bowed downward, and she's chewing on the inside of her cheek. Mark was constantly doing that too.

"Is he?"

"Yeah." She nods and glances back again, her long neck moves in a swallow. "He didn't drink so much before. I'm worried he'll get in trouble at work, and he loves it so much." The sigh that follows is super sad, and it makes me do a double take. "He's been calling out sick a ton because of, you know, being drunk the night before." Her voice shifts. "I don't know why he would do that. He loves his job so much."

"Because he doesn't have anything else to lose," I blurt before I can think.

She stops. "What?"

I stop too and face her. "He feels like he doesn't have anything else to hold on to. That's why he doesn't care anymore."

Her face pales. "He has a sister he loves very much."

"Sometimes, sibling love is not enough." I see how my words are breaking her heart, but she needs to hear it. Something tells me she's the main character from Mark's story.

"How much love is enough?"

"Are you asking me? Do I seem like a good person to give advice?" The corner of my lips lifts.

"You are the only one I got now, so yeah." She shrugs.

"Do you love him?" I watch her face. Not really knowing this woman, I don't know how deep her feelings run.

"Yes." Her whisper is loud.

"So why aren't you with him?"

She's watching my face, contemplating how much of her story she can trust me with. Then she bites her lower lip and lets out a loud exhale. "He found out something, and now I'm afraid he will never look at me the same."

"Why is that?" I narrow my eyes at her.

"Because he will see me as... a bad one." The last two words are barely audible.

"A bad one?"

"Yeah." She nods, not meeting my eyes.

"A bad one what?" I tilt my head with pure curiosity.

She swallows. "A partner."

"Are you a bad partner?"

She nods, and I keep questioning. "Why?"

"I have... issues with intimacy." The confession is not given easily, and I appreciate her willingness to get help. It's hard for people to ask for help.

"Does it bother him?"

She shakes her head.

"Did he give you any indication that he doesn't see you as equal?"

Another shake.

I push harder. "Did he ever treat you like a victim?"

At that, her eyes go round, but she shakes her pretty head again.

"Then he doesn't see you as one. And he doesn't see you as a bad partner. It's all in your head." I tap my temple with a middle finger. "Others see you how you see yourself. Embrace yourself, and others will too."

"Do you think he will embrace me after that?" Her voice is small but full of hope.

"I think he already has." I stretch my arm and gently touch her shoulder, ready to move backward at the first indication of panic. But she doesn't flinch, which is another indication that Mark is wrong about her, so I lean closer and kiss her forehead. "Go talk to your man, Justin's little sister."

"How do you know that?" Her eyes are wide with surprise.

"You look like him, but cuter." I tap her nose once and walk away, leaving her in awe on the sidewalk. It's too much happy meddling for one night for such a dark soul as mine.

Chapter Twenty-Six

ALICIA

The talk with the stranger seemed to plant a seed in my brain, and it's been growing roots ever since. I was so scared to talk to him, but I was even more scared for Mark. When I saw someone else was getting out of his driver's side door, I panicked, threw a sweater on, and ran outside. Mark was wobbly on his feet, but the man helped him to get into his house and left. By foot.

I was so nervous to face the man, but I had to do it. I needed to know what happened to Mark. To face a stranger was less scary than to face Mark.

This time, fate was on my side, because the stranger turned out to be a saint. And a really good advice-giver.

When I was seeing my therapist a year after that night eight years ago—well, way before I gave up on the idea of being cured and stopped the sessions—I used to think I'd never fall in love or even look at a man again. At some point, I was hoping I'd find out I was attracted to women, and all my problems would be resolved since women don't trigger me. No such luck. I wasn't attracted to anyone in general. And it was just my luck that when I've finally found someone who made me feel like a whole person again, the universe had to go and ruin everything by making him the bad guy in my nightmares.

To be fair, last night my usual nightmare was different. The same night, the same people, Mark there too... but this time, his eyes were burning bright, and he was repeating *"Push back. Push back. Push back."*

And I pushed. For the first time in eight years, I pushed back, and it felt good.

Maybe, it's my time. *Thank you, stranger.*

I decide to try something. I dress into my usual potato sack attire and run down the stairs.

"Be back soon!" I yell to Mom, who's cooking in the kitchen. Not waiting for her to come out and question me, I rush outside to the car. It's cold, but I don't feel it. I didn't even put a winter coat on. Just my regular dark-gray sweatsuit.

I've never been to the new PTSD center that Freya opened, but it's easy to find a huge mansion on the outskirt of the town. I didn't make an appointment, and the decision to be here is spontaneous. I fear that if I make an appointment and I have a date, I'll have too much time to overthink and change my mind.

Freya greets me at the receptionist's desk with big round eyes and an open mouth. "Alicia? Hi. Is everything okay?"

She blinks a few forceful times, possibly thinking I'll disappear.

"Hey," I reply. She doesn't know why I'm here, so she doesn't know if she should greet me as a friend or as a patient. "Sorry for coming without an appointment."

"That's totally fine." She waves me off, composing herself. "What's up?"

"I need help." I drop the mask I've been wearing for eight years. I do need help. I want to be cured.

Freya instantly looks like a woman on a mission. She walks from behind the table, hugs my shoulders and leads me to the hallway. "Whatever problem you have, it will stay absolutely confidential between you and your person. None of the people who work here check patients' files unless it's special circumstances. The people here are the best you can find."

"You mean therapists?"

"People." She gives me a side glance. "We don't use that word here. Some guests clam up when they hear it, so we use a special language here."

"Smart." After that traumatizing event in my life, I shut down every time someone mentioned seeing a therapist.

She leads me to a room with bright-pink walls, and I look around. It doesn't look like a therapist's room, nor does the center look like a PTSD facility. Not that I've ever seen one, but I don't imagine their walls painted weird colors. This place feels too homey. You know, like your crazy aunt's artful house.

A few minutes later, a well-put-together blonde lady in her thirties walks into the room. "Hey, I'm Jenna."

"Dr. Jenna?" I clarify.

"Just Jenna." She smiles and sits in the chair next to me.

Not at the table, separating us with a physical obstacle, not on the couch, but close to me.

"I'm Alicia."

"Nice to meet you, Alicia." She smiles warmly as she puts her notepad on the side table. "How may I assist you on your journey?"

I take a deep breath and tell her my story. The whole thing. Everything I haven't told anyone. I've told Mark pieces here and there, but I couldn't tell the whole thing. The pained look on his face every time I brought it up made sure I'll never speak about it again.

By the time I'm done, she lost her shoes and has climbed in the chair with her feet tucked under her.

"You do know why Mark doesn't like to hear the story, right?" She looks at me from the top of her rims.

"Because he sees me as damaged goods?" I fidget with the hem of my sweatshirt.

"No." Her response is calm, but I feel like she wants to roll her eyes, and my lips twitch. "Because he can't stand the idea of you being hurt. And I bet he wants to rip them limb from limb. I want to rip them limb to limb, and I bet my face turns feral when I'm thinking about it. And I can guarantee you with a hundred percent certainty that I don't see you as damaged goods. Does it make sense?"

"Are you even supposed to tell me things like this?" I rub the back of my neck. "You know, as a therapist?"

"We are not therapists here." She winks, grabs her notepad, and writes something in it. "I want to see you here tomorrow."

"I can't. I have... prior arrangements," I lie through my teeth.

She lifts her eyes from her notepad, pulls her glasses lower on her nose, and watches me over the rim. "I want to see you tomorrow. Ten a.m. Don't be late." She taps her lips with the pen. "Or early. I'm cranky before I get two cups of caffeine in the morning." And she walks away.

Well, that was the weirdest therapy session I've ever had, but to my surprise, I feel like I'm four hundred pounds lighter.

I'll be here at ten.

* * *

In the evening, I hear Dad's voice calling my name from downstairs. I walk down and find Alex standing in the hallway with a hat in his hands. He's raking his hand through his long-ish hair, and I feel a pang in my chest, seeing him. He reminds me so much of Mark...

"Get dressed," he orders without a normal greeting.

"What?" I cross my arms over my chest.

"We need to go."

"Where?" I narrow my eyes suspiciously. There is no way it's random after my morning visit to the center.

"It's a surprise." He narrows his eyes back, making his scar more visible.

I give him a glassy stare. "Alex."

"Alicia." He mimics my tone, and it sounds ridiculous, so I chuckle.

"Fine, you win." I walk and grab my coat from the hanger. Turning toward my father, who is highly amused, I complain, "You pick his side over your baby girl."

"No, I'm on your side, and that's why you should go."

I quirk a brow and follow Alex to his truck. When I'm inside, I finally ask, "Will you tell me what this is about?"

The side of his lips tilt up. "It's an early Christmas gift. From Freya and me."

All right. Now, I'm curious.

We drive to Copeland, and Alex stops by a red brick building in an area I've never been before.

"There. That's the gift." He takes a paper from his wallet and passes it to me.

When I open it, my eyes water. It's a gift certificate.

"Self-defense courses for women by women. Do not ever feel afraid again."

"Thank you, Alex." I try to blink away the tears, but they already started falling, and nothing can stop them now. "Will you come with me?"

"If they'll let me. Let's go." He shuts the engine and jumps out of the car. I take a deep, shuttering breath and take the first step on the road to not being afraid.

Chapter Twenty-Seven

MARK

I sit at my kitchen island, staring out the window and thinking about how I want to go about the information I have in my hands.

I found them.

Both of them.

They live the happy lives of two shitheads and have a reputation of rapists. I asked around after I knew their names, and my assumptions were correct: Alicia wasn't the first or the last.

Ghost feels my turmoil and places his head on my lap where I plant my hands, balled into fists. I keep them placed ahead of me, focusing on the pain in my knuckles and trying not to go there on my own and kill them. Oh, don't get me wrong, I want to kill the fuckers so badly, but I think someone else wants to participate too, and to my utter disgust in myself, I feel like I want to let him be there too, so I pick up the phone and call the number that has been sitting in my phone for who knows how long.

A gruff voice answers on the third ring. "Yeah?"

"Meet me at the same gas station in thirty minutes." I hang up, hoping I'm not making a mistake.

I go into the garage and think about what we might need. I throw a few items in the truck and go back into the house. Ghost's waiting for me by the door.

"No, boy, you'll have to stay here and watch the place in case our princess ever wants to come back, alright? She's gone from the house, but as far as I know, the lease is still under her name. So, let's hope, alright?" I crouch next to him and kiss him between his eyes. He whines. "I'll be back soon."

I walk outside, get in the truck, and leave.

* * *

He's already waiting for me at the gas station, leaning his back on the hood of his truck. When he sees me, he pushes away and takes his hands out of his pockets.

"Alright. Let's talk."

"I didn't call you here to talk, Justin."

"What the fuck did you call me here for? To fight? I'm up for that too." He cracks his neck and moves toward me. We've been in a few brawls, and I'm usually all in for it, but not today.

"I found them," I say calmly, making him freeze. I don't think he's even breathing.

"Them?" His voice is void of emotion, sort of like the last time we were here, in this very space.

"Yeah." I nod. "They live in Springfield, and I have their address."

Justin turns away, hiding his face, his shoulder rising rapidly. "You positive?"

"Yes. I'm leaving to go there now. You can come or not. I don't give a shit." I walk back to my car.

"Wait," he calls. "Why?"

"What why?"

"Why are you telling me this?"

"Because you're a big part of her life, and she's blaming herself for your guilt. Well-fucking deserved, by the way," I say without missing a beat.

"Did she tell you that? Does she blame me?" he asks after a rough swallow, and I take pity on him.

"She doesn't. But don't you?" I wait for his nod and continue. "I'm giving you a chance here." I point at my feet as if the chance is standing right in front of me. It sort of is. "To clean up as much of your consciousness as you can, but you will leave me... *us* alone. You give me a fair chance. Because you sure as fuck know you fucked it up for us big time. I don't even know if I can repair it, but I'm sure willing to try."

His jaw's moving. His eyes dart between mine. Then he nods and walks to his car, and I go to mine.

Right before I get into my truck, a car speeds up to the parking lot and stops with a screech in front of me. The wide frame of our dear Sheriff Kenneth Benson gets out of the driver's side and strides toward us.

I throw an accusing look at Justin. "Really? You needed backup?"

"I didn't call him." Justin looks as confused as I feel, so my anger subsides.

"Then what the fuck?" I switch my attention back to the sheriff, who looks outright pissed. Well, that makes three of us.

"Going somewhere?" he asks once he stops in front of us. I share a look with Justin, and we synchronically shake our heads, making Kenneth cackle. "Well, well, well, look at you, all teamed up and working together. Do you have matching undies too?"

"We were just leaving." Justin tries to move past Kenneth, but the sheriff stops him by grabbing his arm.

"Leaving where?" But Justin keeps staring straight ahead, neither confirming nor denying. His lying game sucks. No Oscar for this dude. Then Kenneth's attention switches to me. "Well, Mark, if Justin's leaving to clearly nowhere, where are you going?"

"I'm going about my business. If you are here to arrest me for an imaginary crime..." I meet his gaze and hold it. "Do it now or move out of the way."

The anger dissolves from his features. "I'm not here as a cop." He sighs.

I exchange a curious look with Justin, waiting for the sheriff to elaborate.

"I'm here as a friend."

I raise a brow. We've never been buddies before. Kenneth is a fair cop, but folks from my side of town are reasonably prejudiced toward law enforcement. "As Alicia's friend."

I clench my jaw, and he half smiles. "Easy there. Just a friend."

"How do you know?" Justin steps forward. His face is void of emotion.

"It's my county, Justin. I know what's happening here." He runs his hand through his hair. "I just wish you told me yourself so I could find the assholes."

"I didn't know shit—still don't." Justin's voice is full of self-loathing.

"How did you find them then?" Kenneth's eyes dart from me to Justin.

"Mark did." Justin nods toward me.

"And how did you find them?" Kenneth switches his attention back to me.

"She told me how it happened."

Justin loudly inhales.

"I sent the word out. I still have some connections. Trailer trash and all that." I shrug, not offering any other explanation.

Kenneth's watching my face for a few moments and then nods. "Let's go then."

"What?" Justin exclaims. "Dude, you are the fuckin' sheriff. What we're planning to do is not for cops' eyes."

"I'm not a sheriff today." He spreads his arms, drawing our attention to the lack of uniform.

Justin gets in his face. "Be very careful here, Benson. You know what we're planning to do, and you can lose your shiny badge if you're caught."

"Let's not get caught then. We'll take my car." He starts walking toward his car. "So you don't get linked in case of..." he throws a warning look at us, "anything."

I glance at Justin as he glances at me, and I roll my eyes. How the hell are we so attuned already? I guess nearing face-beating can do that to people. We rush to the truck, and while Kenneth slips into the driver's seat, Justin and I glare at each other at the passenger's side.

"I'm the one who knows the way." I stare Justin down.

He clenches his jaw and moves to the back seat, making Kenneth chuckle. I climb in and give the sheriff instructions.

"Are you sure, Benson?" I ask again while staring at the road ahead. I feel his eyes on me for a brief moment, then notice in my peripheral him glancing in the mirror at Justin before firmly saying, "Yes."

"Alright." I relax a little. It's one thing to call Justin. Alicia's his sister, and he is a person who was somewhat responsible for what had happened. He was going to drive to pick her up from a party that night. And there is me, who is responsible for it too. If I didn't fuck his girlfriend back then, she wouldn't have accused me of raping her, and he wouldn't have had a reason to get distracted by unfinished business. It went all downhill from there.

I wouldn't have chased him down, trying to settle the score, just so he could be stopped by a cop thirty minutes later for assault, which I sure as fuck did not file. His girlfriend back then, a problem to many, a cancer eating on a man's soul, was the one who called the cops while he was delivering punishing punches for a supposed rape that never happened. I tried to avoid her at all costs, but one time we were at the same place at the same time, and I asked her why she did it. Her answer astonished me, and I couldn't find it in me to respond. She said she'd wanted to have someone behind my back too, and she wished she'd tried harder with me. It would be a wasted task, if you ask me. I cherish loyalty above all, and she's anything but loyal. Plus, knowing she was one of the unfortunate reasons why my woman got hurt—I can't even look at her anymore.

When he came to deliver his punishment, I wasn't going to protect myself. I was getting what I deserved for sleeping with the girlfriend of a guy who left to serve our country. We were there for different reasons, but we all were to blame. All of us.

That time was the last time I touched those types of girls. I swore to myself to never go there again. It was also the last time I slept with someone else's woman.

The drive takes about thirty minutes, and besides a few two-word phrases, it's quiet. I motion for Kenneth to pull into a complex that has about twenty apartments, maybe less, and he parks down the street, three houses away.

When he turns the engine off, he looks at me with a stern look on his face. "Are you sure it's them?"

"One hundred percent positive." I feel a muscle in my cheek twitching. The anticipation rises in my chest, and I just *know* it's here. Justice is here.

"I'll ask you again, Kenneth. Are you sure? Because I know what I'm here for, and I still don't know why you're here." Justin's grim voice comes from the back seat, and I sort of agree with him.

Benson's sigh is heavy. "I'm here because a girl was raped. I wasn't the sheriff back then, but I wish I knew. I wish I knew at any point in time so I could take care of it."

"How would you? She refused the kit. She didn't even talk about it."

"There are ways," Kenneth answers, and when he notices the sardonic look Justin throws at him, he repeats himself firmly. "There are ways."

"But it wasn't my story to tell." Justin keeps insisting.

"It's your sister, Justin." Kenneth's nostrils flare. "I know you've been protecting her in your own way, but she was hurt, and no one was found responsible. No one. They're still out there, doing evil things."

"Don't you fucking dare blame Alicia for it!"

291

"I'm not blaming her for that." Kenneth shakes his head, and I feel an urge to punch him in the face.

"Sure as fuck sounds like it," I say.

"I'm not, man. I'm not. But I know there were a few group rapes happening around here, and no one has said a word. No one. I've heard rumors but never found a victim. Never." He wipes a hand over his face. "I was thinking I was fucking paranoid. And I so fucking wish I was. Better than what happened to them." He stares ahead, and I see him aging in front of my very eyes. For a moment, I look at it from his point of view.

The man swore to protect the citizens, and he couldn't. It's hard to punish someone when no crime was reported, so I do understand where he's coming from. "You know how fucked up it is that those women can't come forward? You know why they can't?" He stares at me. "Because of us. *The law.* We're supposed to protect the people." He lets out a loud exhale. "That's why I became a cop. Because I want to change the system. Step by step. I want people who get hurt to be able to come forward and be treated with respect and dignity. I don't want them to be scared of me. I want them to be able to trust me. Do you understand that?" His eyes are on fire. I see the real Sheriff Benson for the first time. I think Little Hope might actually have some hope.

And he understands it wasn't Alicia's fault. It wasn't her fault. It was not. We, large men, will never understand what it feels like to be forced by someone bigger. I fuckin' hate it for Alicia. For my sister who is far away from me. For everyone who ever has to face that. And it's why we're in the car, here to deliver punishment and maybe save someone else in the future. And it's why Kenneth sits in the driver's seat, and not Sheriff Benson. Sheriff can't do what Kenneth can. I wish Justin could see it, but he's been stuck

292

in this stage of self-loathing for too many years to see through the crimson veil over his eyes.

"Alright. What do we know?" Kenneth asks after a long silence.

"Two of them. They live on the second floor of that house." I point at the four-level, worn-down building.

"Together?" He quirks a brow.

"Roomies."

"Anyone else besides them?" Benson's tone is professional.

"One has a girlfriend most likely there too. And the other one should be alone."

"Alright. Do you know the names?"

I spit out their names, and Kenneth writes them down. "Why?" I nod at his notepad.

"I'm gonna see what I can find before we go in there."

I tense at his words.

"Chill out, we need to know if we can get them for longer than a week in a hospital."

I'm fuming, past the point of hearing him, so he places his hand on my shoulder and presses it.

"Do you feel me, Mark? I will not let you kill them." He shoots a look at Justin, fuming silently in the back. "No matter how much we all want to. Because in this case, Alicia will lose both of you. We will go about this in a smart way. Do you hear me?"

We are quiet, so he pushes harder.

"Do you hear me?"

We both grunt something in response and wait for him to make his call. Someone picks up on the second ring. His speaker is loud. The dude won't keep any secrets this way.

"'*Sup, Kenney. Long time no hear, Hung-y.*" A feminine

voice singsongs from the phone, and Justin and I stare at each other when we hear '*Kenney Hung-y.*'

"Hey, sweetness." His chuckle is supposed to be seductive, I think. Not sure though. "I need you to do me a favor. *Off* the records." He stresses his last words.

"*Oh, interesting. Who pissed in your morning coffee, darling?*"

"Is this off the record?"

"*You know me.*"

"Alright. I need you to get me any information you have on—" He looks at the paper and gives their names to the mysterious woman.

"*What are we looking for?*" Her tone turns professional.

"Anything I can put them in for a long time for."

The silence that follows is clear and crisp. "*You got it.*" And she hangs up.

Kenneth puts his phone on his knee and watches a house while we're watching him.

"Kenney?" Justin breaks down first.

"Hung-y?" I say.

"I liked you both better when you were enemies." He flips us off, looking out the window, and a chuckle comes from the back seat. The atmosphere is somehow more tolerable after the call.

We don't chat until the sheriff's phone rings a few minutes later.

"Do you have something good for me?"

"*I might.*" The lady clears her throat. "*There was a woman claiming she was attacked by them, but the story never went to trial.*"

"Why?"

"*The official version is that there not enough evidence.*"

294

"And unofficial?"

"One of them is the judge's nephew."

"Fuck."

"Fuck indeed. I'll forward everything to your email. From what I've seen, they need to be taken down. Call me if you need anything."

"Thanks, sweetness. I owe you."

"You do. See ya, Hung-y." And she hangs up.

We're all stunned into silence.

"Can we do anything here?" Justin asks as his face pokes between the seats.

"We sure as fuck can do much less now, knowing that," Kenneth responds as he flips through the insane amounts of text on his phone.

"Can we contact this person?"

He meets my eyes and says. *"I can't."*

I nod, understanding what he means.

"I need to check something in the back." He leaves his unlocked phone on the seat and gets out of the car.

I glance at Justin. His eyes are serious as he nods. I take the phone and scroll through the open texts. I take a picture of the women's names and addresses, then put the phone back. After a moment, Kenneth slowly gets back into the truck, locks the phone, and places it into the back pocket of his jeans.

"Do you know what they look like?" Kenneth asks.

"Yeah." I nod.

"I don't." Justin pipes in from the back seat, and Kenneth gets his phone back up and shows him two mug shots. From here I can hear Justin's jaw clash together, and I'm sure a tooth cracked.

Right on cue, both of the fuckers walk out of the main entrance to the building, get into a brand-new luxury SUV, and drive away. Kenneth instantly starts the truck and follows them.

I'm sure they don't expect the tail, but Benson is careful anyway. I feel like I'm in the movies, chasing the bad guy. Adrenaline is pumping through my body, but not for the usual reasons. It's not the anticipation of a fight but a feeling of delivering justice for my woman. Even if she may never belong to me, my heart is still hers.

We follow them to a club, where they get out of the car and rush inside. It's a popular joint for hooking up and getting drunk. Kenneth moves the car to a strategic place, where we can see the front of the building but we are not in the spotlight. We can also see the back exit in case they slip away. I'm not sure how we will get them, but the only thing I know is they are not walking from here on their feet.

We quietly talk until we see the back door burst open an hour later. The two boys rush through it toward the dumpster behind the building. One of them is half carrying, half walking a woman who can barely stand on her feet. Her head keeps falling on his shoulder. I grind my teeth, knowing what's happening.

Kenneth is about to get out of the truck when I stop him by grabbing his forearm.

"Wait. Stay here."

"Why the fuck would I do that?" He's pissed at my suggestion.

"Because you will lose your job if you do. You're a good cop. You can make a change. Don't risk it." I hold his eyes. "You've already done enough."

"He's right," Justin says as he jumps out of the vehicle. "We will let you know when you can come."

Kenneth groans loudly. "Fuck. Fuck! Don't do anything

stupid. We can push this case if we do it right. Do you get me?"

"Yes," Justin answers as I nod, and we both jog toward the back of the building.

I'm about to rush them, but he stops me by grabbing my shoulder. "Wait."

"What?" I bark, pumped for the fight I've been yearning for for a long time.

"His uncle is a judge. He'll make sure whatever we say will be erased."

"So what do you suggest we do?" I ask sarcastically, trying to keep my voice down.

He shudders with disgust. "I hate this is even needed, but I have a plan."

He pulls a phone from his back pocket, swipes the screen up, and motions for me to follow him quietly. At the corner, he points the camera at the group and begins filming. I want to throw up. I hate myself for staying here and letting it happen, but somewhere at the back of my head, I know he's right.

One of them is standing behind her, his hands roaming her body. Her head leans on his shoulder. She's out of it. The other one runs a hand up her skirt, and I swear I'm about to run in there to stop it when Justin's hand lands on my shoulder once again.

"What the fuck?" I hiss at him, seeing only red. I want to rip them limb from limb. The loud, booming music from the club muffles my voice.

"Not yet," he answers, signaling for me to lower my voice and reminding me that he's filming by nodding at the phone. His face is void of emotion. This is the Justin people fear.

"What do you mean not yet? They're about to fucking rape her!" I hiss back.

"Not. Yet." He gives me a stern look he might have used at the military. Or prison.

There is a struggle in the group, and the girl's voice is loud and clear. "No, don't" reaches my ears.

"Now," Justin says as he turns the camera off.

We run toward the assholes.

"What the fuck!" one of them cries just as I barrel into his side.

"Get going," the other says as he drops the girl on the asphalt.

"We were going here." Justin smiles as he swings at him, and he goes down the second Justin's fist reaches his face.

I take the first one. They can't deliver even one punch. Neither of them.

We are enraged. We are here for Alicia. And for this girl. And for all the girls who were here before.

I don't feel the pain in my hand anymore as my fist connects with the face I'll be seeing in my nightmares forever. The face of the person who stole the happiness from the girl I love. The face of the person who stole the feeling of safety and purity from her. The face of the person who made her feel at fault.

The face of the person who stole her from me.

Strong arms pull me back as I try to deliver another punch.

"Enough, Mark." His voice comes through the bloody haze I'm in, but I don't stop. Arms wrap around my shoulders and pull me back stronger. "Enough, Mark," someone hisses into my ear. "Think of Alicia."

I struggle to break free.

"Think of Alicia!" He shakes me. "Alicia, Mark."

Her name puts me firmly back on earth. I stop struggling and let Justin pull me away.

The door behind us opens, and a girl's scream pierces the air.

Justin lets go of me and turns toward her. "Those guys were trying to rape that girl. We tried to stop them. Call 911."

She's looking at him with wide eyes. She's scared out of her wits. I don't blame her. He looks wild. Blood all over his shirt.

To get her out of the stupor, he barks louder. "Call the cops. Now!"

"Okay." She grabs her phone from her purse and dials it. "Hey! There are two guys trying to rape a girl." There's a pause. "No, they were. They are on the floor now." A moment passes. "I don't know!" Then she looks at Justin and at me. "I don't know who did. They were just on the floor when I came outside to look for my friend. Can you send someone?" She mumbles the address, hangs up, and runs to the girl who's leaning on the dumpster now.

Only now do I remember there was someone who might be hurt. I go to check on her, but the girl with the phone stops me with her hand. "Go. They'll be here soon."

Justin shakes his head. "We'll stay until the cops arrive."

"And say what?" she asks. "That you did this?" She points a finger at the two beaten bodies on the ground.

"We can't leave you here alone with them." I push one of the bodies on the floor with my foot.

"Fine." I think she likes the idea, and there is no way in hell we will leave them both here. "But go and wait over there." She points at the darkness behind the next building. "So no one will see you."

I nod with gratitude and grab Justin's forearm while he's transfixed on the monsters on the floor.

"So many years they've been haunting my family. So many years. I hoped to feel something—anything—when I got my hands on him, but I don't feel anything." His nostrils flare as if he's struggling to breathe.

"I know the feeling." I place my hand on his shoulder and squeeze it—without desire to cause pain for the first time since we've known each other.

The sirens blare through the cold air, and the girl says, "Go. We'll be fine."

"We'll stay," I answer stubbornly.

"Go!" she yells, and we exchange a look with Justin.

"C'mon." He nods toward where Kenneth is parked.

"Are you sure you'll be alright?" I ask once again. She's a brave woman.

"Yeah, I'm good. Go." She finishes the conversation by turning toward her friend, who mumbles something with a smile on her face.

I nod and follow Justin. The sirens are closer, and I rush forward. "Let's go, man."

We run to the car, where Kenneth's waiting for us. The engine is on. The sirens are way too close for my comfort, and the driver's side is closer to us, so Justin rips the door open, and we both jump into the back seat. He takes off before I even have a chance to shut the door. When the patrol cars show up ahead, Kenneth pulls over to the curb and waits for them to pass like a law-abiding citizen.

"Do I wanna know?" Kenneth asks when the patrol cars drive away.

"No."

"Okay." He nods, squeezing the wheel.

He stops at a bar a few blocks away. "C'mon."

"Why?" Justin looks at me, like I figured out the enigma of Kenneth Benson. Newsflash—I haven't.

"You need an alibi, idiots."

We exchange looks and walk inside the bar, where I come face-to-face with the dude from Cat and Stallion who drove me home. He looks happy to see us as he walks toward us, leaving his table of two piss-drunk men. "Well, how long did it take you to take a piss? Did you cross swords too?" he asks way too loudly, and way too clearly, for everyone to hear.

I glance at Kenneth, who has a smile plastered on his face. He goes to Archie and smacks him on the back. "You fucker, never change."

"I don't intend to." Archie winks, smacking his butt.

I don't know what in the ever-loving hell is happening and look at Justin for clues. But he has the same look of horror and awe. I guess we're in the same boat for once in our lives.

Chapter Twenty-Eight

ALICIA

I moved home for good, along with all my belongings that I collected from Mrs. Jenkins's place when Mark was on his shift.

I painted my room and asked Kayla to help me put some art on the wall. We'd been thinking for a long time about what I should do, until the morning I saw her drawing a phoenix on her pad. She was doing a piece for one of her clients, and I just knew it was what I wanted. I wanted a phoenix on the wall. A symbol of rebirth, of coming pure out of ashes.

I wanted to be that, a phoenix.

She told me to get out of the room and not come in until she's done, so I took up residency on the couch downstairs.

When she finally called me upstairs, I cried. It is perfect. Instead of making it a red bird, she made it a blue phoenix to match my eyes. She said it's me, and she cried too. My mom came to the room and started crying as well. When my father found us like that, he just about had a heart attack, not knowing what's happening. So now, every time when I go to sleep, she's watching over me, shooshing the demons away. They still come, but less.

Mark is still there, in the same nightmares, but I came to the understanding that his presence in my nightmares is comforting. I know it's him, and it anchors me to reality. He encourages me to fight back.

Since the last time he appeared in my nightmare and told me to fight back, I started fighting. I still do. Every single time. The nightmare slowly turns into just a dream because I never let it go that far. I always fight back at Mark's encouragement. He is so good at that, my dream Mark.

Sometimes, he comes to me in sweet dreams too. That's when things get heated. One time when I woke up, I had to mentally thank my parents for giving me the farthest room from them, because the stuff he did... well, it was dirty, to say the least. I haven't had naughty dreams in eight years before Mark, and now, I'm having them nearly every single night. They sure beat the nightmares.

It's been four weeks since the last time I saw him. Well, saw him up close. I saw him a few times around town from afar, plus, that one time when the guy with black hair drove him home. For the first two weeks, I heard he was drunk a lot, and I thought it had something to do with our situation. I secretly hoped it was the reason, because my feeling toward him was—is—real. I thought it was going to get easier, but it's not. It's getting worse. Every desire to be a woman again disappeared along with him.

The past two weeks, he's been better, and I should be happy about that, but a weird feeling pings in my chest. *It took him only two weeks to get over me?* I was right, and he stopped seeing me as a woman after the bombshell Justin threw at the dinner. He probably took a deep, cleansing breath since he had a valid reason not to deal with my crazy anymore.

As for the family dynamics, I still can't stand Justin, just like he can't stand Jake, so the sibling connection is severed. And at this point in my life, I'm sad to say I'm okay with it.

Jake is traveling now. I think he chose not to be here for the holidays after all that happened with Kayla, even though it's been a while since he put his long nose where it didn't belong, I honestly think he's trying to get better so he can make amends with Justin and Kayla.

Today is Christmas Eve, and Justin is coming over with Kayla. We all love her so much, considering she changed my douchebag of a brother into something tolerable. Don't get me wrong; I absolutely love my brother, and I'll die on that hill, but I don't particularly like him now. I hope I'll outgrow it one day, but I don't see it happening anytime soon.

I know Mom invited Alex and Freya, but I don't think they're coming, since apparently Freya is working on fixing the relationship between Alex and his family. Good for them. Alex deserves all the love in the world.

Yesterday, we stayed up late with Mom, cooking and prepping for today since Christmas Eve in our house always ends up with us all in a food coma. I'm placing garlic knots in the oven when the doorbell chimes.

"George, can you open the door, please?" Mom yells at Dad, who's secretly watching Harry Potter, even though he'd never admit it.

"Sure thing, pumpkin."

They're so sweet, it's sickening. Growing up, we had high standards for family in front of us, so we would never settle for anything else. It's why I know I'll never have it. The only person I see myself spending my whole life with isn't here. Because of me and my weakness.

I lose focus for a second and burn the top of my hand on the oven.

"Motherfucker," I cry out and push my hand under the running water only to yell again. It's hot.

"Alicia!" Mom exclaims loudly. She doesn't even need to add anything else because I know she's shocked. I don't curse, especially not in front of my parents and not in their house. I respect them too much for that.

"Sorry, Mom." I feel my cheeks heat with embarrassment. She shoots me a glare that used to put me in my place —still does—and keeps cutting the salad.

Kayla comes into the kitchen, looking cozy in a big red hat with cat ears, an oversized red fuzzy sweater—a color that would look ridiculous on me but somehow works on her—and black leggings. Her feet are covered in big fluffy socks, and she's holding an insane amount of bags.

"Ho-ho-ho!" She mimics Santa and shakes the bags. "Where is the Christmas tree in this house?" Her acting game is horrible, and we all laugh.

"It might be that huge thing you had to walk around on the way over here." Mom chuckles as she points at the ten-foot monstrosity in the middle of the living room.

"You're no fun." She pouts her painted-red lips. "I'm gonna drop them off and be right back." She disappears into the hallway, and Mom's eyes follow her. A faint smile is playing on her lips, and I know it's the look of a happy mother. I smile too. I'm so grateful for Kayla.

When she comes back, she plants her butt on the stool and sighs. "It smells so good in here; I'm gaining ten pounds as we speak."

"That's garlic bread. It always makes me hungry." I go to put the kettle on. "Do you want some tea?"

"Yes, please. Or anything you'll be having."

"Mulled wine?" I ask hopefully.

"Yes, please!" Her eyes twinkle, and she rubs her hands together.

"Me too," Mom chimes in, and I laugh.

"Fine, freeloaders." I turn off the kettle and go to get ingredients. Only then I notice the absence of a certain loud voice. "Where is Justin?" I ask sourly.

Kayla exchanges a look with Mom. "He's getting the last gift."

"Where? Everything is closed already."

And I mean it. Everything in Little Hope is closed at midday on Christmas Eve.

"Dunno." She shrugs and bites a huge chunk off an apple she picked from the glass fruit vase on the table. She's chewing too aggressively, and when I ask her if she's okay, she nods and bites into the apple again, even though she hasn't swallowed the first bite. Weird, but okay.

A few minutes later, the mulled wine is poured into pretty glasses that Mom saves for special occasions, and we go to set the table in the dining room. Mom put so much work into decorating the room and picking the plates that we must set everything by the rules, meaning we have three sets of knives, spoons, forks, glasses... and the list goes on.

The table is ready, the food is ready, we are ready, and Justin is still not here.

"If the garlic knots go cold while we're waiting for him, I'm gonna riot." I sit on a chair and sulk. And I mean it. I'm always serious when it comes to my grandma's garlic knots. It's a famous family recipe.

At this moment, the door bursts open, and Justin walks in, a huge smile on his face.

But he doesn't come alone. No. Mark is hot on his feet. I stand, taking them both in, looking for signs of a fight. I mean, why else would they be here together, right? After that fateful dinner, I asked around, and turns out my brother and Mark could never spend two minutes in each other's presence without trying to murder each other. And here I thought I knew everything, living in the same *small* town. I didn't even know they were enemies.

But they don't look like they've been in a fight. In fact, Mark looks good. Very good. His beard is neatly trimmed, and his hair is gathered in a bun at the base of his head. He lost some weight, but he looks great. His ugly red sweater with a dancing green gnome makes him match the decor of the room. Even though my mom is a good decorator, she tends to go overboard when holidays are concerned.

A huge German shepherd runs in and nearly knocks me on the floor. Giving me a thousand doggy kisses, he runs around my legs like a crazy Chihuahua. I can't resist his love and crouch next to him, hugging his furry neck.

Justin walks by and takes off his winter coat. Under it, he's wearing the same sweater as Kayla. He walks to her as if they haven't seen each other for days, grabs her from the chair and gives her a deep kiss. Right here. In front of my parents and me, in their dining room.

My mom clears her throat, and Justin lets go of Kayla;

her cheeks are flushed, and she's trying to fix her sweater after Justin's wandering hands. He walks back toward Mark and puts his hand on his shoulder. I expect Mark to shrug it off, but he doesn't. Instead, he's frozen with his eyes fixed on my face. He feels out of place. I know it by the way his shoulders are squared back and how his eyes are slightly squinted, as if he's searching for an escape route. But that's not what he's looking for. He's looking for something on my face.

Justin pushes Mark farther. "This is my Christmas gift to you. Sorry I forgot to wrap it up 'cause the package is pretty fucking ugly."

"Looks good if you ask me," Mom chimes in, and my father groans.

"You'll be the death of me, woman."

Mom is known to have crushes on celebrities, and she's clearly crushing on Mark. We all chuckle.

I clear my throat. "Looks perfect to me too."

Mark's cheeks above his neat—a rarity—beard pinken, and the corner of his lips tilts up.

"What are you doing here?" I ask.

"He's my guest. So too bad if you don't want him here." Justin chuckles and goes to pick a garlic knot from the plate. He instantly gets smacked on the hand by Mom. "Ouch! I just can't win in this house," he pouts like a baby.

"I'm here to see you, if that's alright." Mark's voice is firm but careful.

"Is it alright, sis?" Justin's voice loses all playfulness. He's my big brother now, the one who's been protecting me all these years.

I nod, and he gets up from the chair.

"Cool. We're gonna go and start opening presents."

"Nonsense!" Mom cries out, offended. "Before the

dinner? I don't think so. Let's go fix some lights in the living room. I have a couple more to put on."

Everyone groans but follows Mom. She's the queen of the house, and you don't come to a queen's house with your own rules. Trust me, I learned it the hard way.

A moment later, we're alone in the room. Even Ghost trotted after everyone. Well, everyone was giving him so many hugs and kisses that he chose to follow a fun bunch. I look at Mark, and I don't think he moved at all.

"What are you doing here, Mark?"

"Justin invited me over." He puts his hands in his front pockets.

"Right." I pinch the bridge of my nose. I'm about to get a nice Christmas headache.

"He really did."

I open my eyes and notice him taking a measured step toward me.

"When did you become friends?" I ask.

"We—" His eyes dart around. "Made amends."

"Amends?"

"Yes." He takes another step.

"And what are you doing here?"

"I'm trying to see if there is anything, I mean *anything*, I can do to fix the situation between the woman I love and myself."

"The woman you love?" I snort pitifully. "I heard you forgot about said woman pretty fast."

"That's not true."

"Really?" I squint my eyes. "You know, when you flew around the town with a wide smile on your face, you didn't look all too heartbroken to me."

"Did you keep track of me?" He bites his lower lip,

trying not to smile. But he fails because the crinkles around his eyes give him away.

"No."

"Liar." His smile is full, and I forgot how blinding it can be.

I roll my lips before asking. "Why are you really here, Mark?"

"I'm here..." He takes a careful step forward. "Because I can't live without you." Another step. "I've tried"—he takes one more—"but failed. I know my presence causes pain to you, but I'm willing to try anything, I mean anything, if you want to see if it can work." He takes another step and then he stops two feet from me. "I can even wear a paper bag on my head if it will help."

I look up and see a small smile playing at his lips. "It doesn't cause me pain."

"No?" His brows shoot up.

"No." The vigorous shake of my head makes my hair fall to my chest over my shoulder. "Not anymore."

"I'm not in your nightmares anymore?" he asks hopefully.

"You are."

His face falls.

"But you're my hero now. You turn a nightmare into a dream," I explain shyly, and his face brightens in understanding.

"Does it mean we can try again?"

I give him a wicked smile because he doesn't know what I've been doing and how I was working on myself so I could take my life into my own hands. And if he didn't come here, I'd go to his place and demand we make up.

"We might."

Chapter Twenty-Nine

MARK

When she offers for me to stay in her bedroom at her parents' house, I'm not going to lie, I feel super uncomfortable. What do I do? I haven't touched her in a month, and the moment her body lies next to mine, I know I won't be able to control myself like a fucking animal. But I have to keep quiet. We both know she's anything but quiet when it comes to sex, so I think she's testing me. I can do that. I am a grown man who can control his urges.

I am a strong man. I am a grown man.

Maybe if I chant the mantra many times, I'll believe it.

"Good night!" Mrs. Attleborough yells from the kitchen as Alicia drags me upstairs by my hand. Memories from the last time I was here assault my mind, and I grind my molars, suppressing the rise of my anxiety.

When she opens the door to her room, it's different from what I remember. Obviously, it was in a state of total disarray, but even the wall color is different now. It's a soft peach. And what is that? A phoenix on the wall? It looks like Kayla's work. The phoenix is her signature tattoo. I glance at Alicia. It's *her*. My phoenix has risen to its full power, spreading her gorgeous wings and leaving the darkness behind her.

I find her watching me as I'm taking in the art on the wall. I pull her into a side hug. "Come here, my beautiful phoenix."

A shy smile appears on her face, her soft cheeks turn pink. "How did you know?"

"Did you really think I wouldn't recognize you?" I kiss her softly on the top of her head and look around. "Where will I sleep?"

She gets out of the hug and strides toward her bed, where she jumps on top and pats the space next to her. "Right here."

I nervously look back at the door. "But what about—" I let it hang in the air. I mean, I'm always hard for her, but in her parents' house, on the first day they seem to accept me? I really don't want to push my luck.

"Their room is on the other side of the house." She notices my not-very-convinced face and says with a raised brow, "On the first floor."

I visibly relax, and she cackles. "Come here." She pats the cover she's sitting on again.

I take off my sweater, staying in a T-shirt and pants, and climb next to her. Her hand stretches toward me, and I grab it and pull it down in a tight hold. "Alicia." My throat is dry.

"I remember what you told me here, in the same room. Do you remember?"

"Yes," she whispers.

"If that still is a problem, you need to tell me now. If seeing me—being with me—hurts you in any way, you need to tell me." I swallow roughly. "I need to know because if you don't tell me now, I don't think I'll be able to stay away from you if you change your mind."

Her beautiful blue eyes peer at me, unblinking.

"Do you understand, Alicia? I can't do that knowing I might lose you." I hold her stare and stress the next words. "It will be the end of me. Do you understand?"

She blinks for the first time and squeezes my hand. "I understand."

I think my soul is leaving my body when I hear the finality of her tone. I relax my fingers, releasing her from my hold, but she grabs it back. "I understand and accept it. I don't want to be without you either." She smiles shyly. "I don't think I even can. You are my security, Mark. You are what made me whole."

"But—" I want to bring up what she said before. About me being present in the nightmare since she placed me in the same picture of the worst day of her life.

"It's fixed."

"What's fixed?" I'm confused.

"You are my security again. I was wrong to see you as anything but, and I got some help."

"You've seen a therapist again?" I raise my brows, knowing she hated the idea of opening up to someone about what happened and how she feels about it. I know she'd been to therapy before but stopped going because it didn't help.

"Yes." She nervously bites the inside of her cheek. "It sucked." She chuckles. "But it helped."

"So, I'm not a boogeyman anymore?"

"You never were." I squeeze her hand again. "I just didn't see the Superman cap under all this hair." Her eyes twinkle with mischief as she circles her finger around my torso, making me laugh.

I grab her shoulder. "I love you, my phoenix."

"I love you too, my yeti."

"What?" I burst out laughing. "That's your pet name for me?"

"I think it's the best. There are a lot of babes and huns out there, but no yetis."

"The best," I agree, still laughing.

She pushes me back and climbs on top of me. Straddling my hips, she leans closer to my face. "I've missed you."

"I've missed you too." I lift my head, hoping for a kiss, but she pulls back.

"How many times did you jerk off this last month?" She's drawing lines on my chin, biting her lower lip. It makes me crazy when she does it because I know those teeth love to bite my neck, driving me up a wall. I know she asked me something, but I can't focus, so she repeats herself. "So how many times?"

And I freeze. How many times indeed? "Actually." I rack my brain. "Not many. A few, maybe."

"A day?"

"At all." I furrow my brows in concentration.

She instantly pulls back. "Really?"

"Yeah. To think of it, I've never had so much time between sessions before. Ever." I grab her chin between my fingers and turn her face toward me. So I can see her gorgeous eyes. And she can see mine. "You see what you do to me." And she loves what she does, judging by her smug look and wide smile. She loves that I get hard for her. Only for her.

"I see." Her eyes sober up and she pulls back. Again. Fucking fuck. When do I get to kiss her already?

"I need something. Can you help me?"

"Of course." I move to stand from the bed because if she needs anything, I'll do it. Move furniture right now, while my cock is hard? I'm here for it. Go get an ice cream at midnight during a snowstorm? Sign me up.

But she surprises me—as always—by pulling her shirt off and flipping on her stomach. "I need a massage."

I freeze. I'm shocked and don't know what to say. "A massage." I swallow. "On your back?"

"Yes." She looks up at me flirtatiously.

"But I'll be behind you."

"I know."

"But—" I struggle to find the right words. "But how? Like what if you—"

"I want to try it." She rolls her lips. "But I don't think I'm ready for anyone to touch me like that."

"I sure as fuck hope not."

She laughs. "I'm talking about a massage for starters. Without a happy ending."

"Oh, okay." I move closer to her and press my open palm to her back. The muscles under my touch contract, and I wait for them to relax. "You okay?"

"Yeah." Her reply is raspy, and I add another palm, waiting for a new wave of twitching to subside.

Then I move my hands. Her body eventually relaxes under my touch, and I can't even hide the proud smile at my girl bravely overcoming her fears. I lean and press a feather-like kiss to her shoulder, and she bucks. I stop moving.

"No, no. It felt good. Keep going," she muffles into the pillow, and I continue the exploration of her back. I can't believe she's letting me do this with her face in the pillow. I think it's more triggering for me than her, because my dick isn't hard—a very rare occasion when I'm touching her—and I'm scared shitless that I'll make a wrong move and spook her. I kiss her neck this time, and she lifts her butt toward me. All right, that was a clear sign if I've ever seen one, so I kiss her again, and she wiggles her raised ass, making me go to a full mast in seconds.

Being careful and ready to flee at any moment, I lean my body forward, letting my front touch her back. And wait. And wait until she lets out a loud breath and wiggles again. I press my pelvis against her ass, letting out a loud exhale. It's the sweetest torture.

Alicia turns her head to the side and whispers. "Keep going."

I keep peppering her shoulders and her neck with little kisses while pulling her pants down. I snake my hand between her legs and find her drenched. Another loud exhale. Hers or mine—I don't know. Then I make a move to help her out of her pants, but her hand shoots up and grabs mine. "Keep going. Don't let me think now."

I could make it perfect. A moment like this deserves to be perfect. I could undress her and myself and make it look good, but it will not be her 'perfect.' So I listen to her and return to my place and kiss her everywhere I can reach. I bite her skin and lick away the sting.

She gasps every time I glide my fingers along her drenched lips. I awkwardly unzip my pants and pull them down to my thighs. Taking my hard cock in my hand, I guide it to her center. Nipping and kissing her neck, I tease

318

her wetness with the head. Then I slip in, just an inch, and she gasps. Her muscles tense, and I stop moving.

"It's me, phoenix. It's your yeti." I bite her earlobe, and she lets out a cute half snort, half chuckle. My words seem to help, because she relaxes and pushes back against my dick, swallowing half of it inside herself.

My turn to gasp. I've missed this so much. This is the place where I want to be.

Chapter Thirty

MARK

It's Christmas at the Attleboroughs' house.

When the doorbell rings, Mary goes to open it.

"Hey, Alex! Hey, sweety." There're loud kissing sounds, and I peer at the hallway. Mrs. Attleborough's kissing Freya's super-red cheeks, the new-ish member of Little Hope town and a millionaire extraordinaire. I wanted to stop by her center for people with PTSD and see if they have any tips for me that might help Alicia, even though after the last few hours I've spent in Alicia's presence, I'm not sure she even needs it anymore.

I find Alicia. She's unwrapping a huge box, sitting on the floor by the Christmas tree next to her brother. Her hair falls down her shoulders in long soft waves. She woke up wearing only me wrapped around her body. She smiles shyly at something Justin told her and pokes him in his ribs, making him burst out laughing. His eyes dart to me, and he winks. It's fuckin' disturbing. I get a full-body shudder, and he cracks up more.

"Thank you," their father says quietly from somewhere on my left, but I don't pay attention. It clearly isn't directed at me. "For bringing my girl back."

My back stills as he chokes on the last word.

"I didn't know what to do, you know. I'm her father, and I didn't know how to help my little girl." He swallows roughly. "It's any parent's worst nightmare—to see your child suffer like that and not able to help her. She never told anyone. We thought she wasn't ready, so we waited, but I know my baby girl. She just wasn't ready to tell her story to us. She was waiting for you." His voice drops lower, and I turn toward him. His eyes are trained on my face, the corners of his lips point downward. "So yeah." He clears his throat. "I'm happy you are here, son."

His last words crack me from the inside. I've been dreaming to hear those words all my life but never got to. Until now. I don't know what to say, so I just nod. Gentle hands land on my shoulder with a quiet squeeze. I lift my eyes and find Alicia's mom with misty eyes. I cover her hand with mine and give her a gentle squeeze. She wipes the corner of her eyes and walks away.

I relax in my chair, and we watch everyone opening their gifts. Alicia and Justin constantly bicker like me and my sister do when we're together, but they somehow seem closer. Maybe it's a small age difference. Maybe it's a normal family thing. I don't know.

Justin's eyes dart toward me from time to time, and

there is not even a single twinkle of malice in them. I never knew I'd see a day when we can be in the same room, but here we are.

"Anyone want some mulled wine?" Mrs. Attleborough asks, and Alicia cries out.

"Mom, it's not even eleven in the morning."

She waves her off. "Let's talk when you're my age."

"I'll take some." Freya smiles from the floor where she's leaning on Alex's legs as he sits on the couch with an ever-present scowl on his scarred face, but no cap in sight. It's an improvement. There are only a couple of occasions where I've seen him without that awful cap since he returned from the service.

Freya's phone chimes in, and she pulls it from her jeans. She reads something before saying, "Oh, wow."

"What happened?" Kayla asks.

"Apparently, the local law enforcement got some serial rapists. Like real bad ones who've been doing it for years." Her eyes are on the lit screen of her phone, and she doesn't notice how everyone looks at Alicia.

She pales as Freya keeps reading.

"It says two Springfield citizens were caught in action by a friend of a victim. The unidentified source also provided police with the video proof.

"One of the criminals is the nephew of a local judge, who's currently under investigation because several old, clearly covered-up cases were brought to light. A few victims already came forward and are giving their testimony.

"The criminals are being released from the hospital this morning, where they've been treated for severe injuries, caused by two unknown Caucasian men in their early thirties, as per their testimony. They're not going to press charges since there are no witnesses to their claim. The only witness, who happened to be the victim's friend, claims not seeing anyone."

My eyes dart to Justin, who's already watching me, unblinking.

When he sees me watching him, he gives me a nod and the side of his lips quirks up in a secretive smile. I try to keep a stern look on my face, especially when Alicia's about to lose her cool. I find her again and see that her eyes are darting between me and Justin.

I look around the room and notice everyone's gaze on me and Justin, while Freya's oblivious to it all and keeps reading the article.

When she's done, Alex barks out a laugh. "I wonder who they are."

"Some monsters, obviously," Kayla spits out with disgust.

"No, I mean the vigilantes." He pokes the inside of his cheek with his tongue, trying to suppress the smile.

"Yeah, I wonder that too," Mr. Attleborough says, rubbing his chin and looking at me and Justin.

I feel uncomfortable under their attention but not guilty in the slightest. I'd fuckin' do it again. Over and over.

"Does the article have their names?" Alicia squeaks.

"Hold on," Freya says as she scrolls the article. She tells her the name of the two monsters who tried to ruin her life. They didn't succeed. She is fuckin' strong and indestructible.

"Does it say which police district is taking the statements?" she asks, a little more confident. Everyone watches her.

Even oblivious Freya says, "Fuck," as she drops the phone on her lap.

"Does it?" Alicia asks again, and Freya picks up the phone and responds, guilt on her face. "Yeah, it's the Springfield Police Department, since the first known crime was caught there." Her eyes fill with tears as she delivers the news.

I want to come and comfort Alicia, who fidgets with the hem of her pajama top, but I don't. She doesn't need me now, not really. She is strong enough on her own to face her demons, and if she needs me, she'll let me know, and I'll be beside her, fighting them off with her.

"Dad?" she asks.

"Mmm." His only response.

"Will you drive me there tomorrow?"

"I will," he answers with a choke and tries to clear his throat. A quiet sniffling comes from every woman in the room but my Alicia. She's holding her head high, her shoulders squared, ready for a battle that I know is not going to be easy.

Something bumps into the window with a loud thud, and we all jump. I swear to God, even I jump like a little boy scared shitless. Ghost lets out a loud bark and rushes toward the sound.

"Holy fucking shit!" Justin brings his hand to his chest. "My soul nearly left my body."

"Language!" Mrs. Attleborough reprimands him but doesn't really mean it. A light smile plays on her lips.

"What is that?" Freya stands from the floor and carefully walks to the window.

"Wait!" Alex is on his feet in an instant and reaches her in two big jumps. At the same time, I call out to Ghost to come over and stop barking.

"Chill, y'all." Kayla rolls her eyes. "It's Frank."

Frank? As in *the* Frank who was at Alicia's house?

Ariana Cane

"Seriously? How did he find us here?" Justin looks annoyed. "I swear he'll be the death of me."

Kayla waves him off. "Don't be a drama queen. I told him I'll be here tonight." She walks to the entrance door and opens it. "Frankie," she calls. "Frankie! Come to the door. Mama's here."

The hairy face of a big moose shows up in the opening, and I snort. *"That's Frank?"*

"Yeah, I had a similar reaction." Justin shakes his head in disbelief. "I still can't wrap my head around it. The dude is everywhere we go, and I mean it—everywhere." He points an accusing finger at the moose, currently nuzzling Kayla's shoulder. "Every time I say a word too loud, you know like, a little too loud, which I never do."

Now everyone snorts.

"What? I never do that." He looks around, and a few extra snorts with a few *yeah, sure, you don't*s follow. "So anyway, every time I do that, he's around, beating his damn hoof at me. And I'm telling you the motherfucker is scary."

"He's my boy, and he can hear you just fine!" Kayla yells from the door, still exchanging some weird hug with the moose.

"I think he's adorable." Alicia stands and walks to Kayla.

I must admit, it makes me a little uncomfortable, so I stand to follow her. Ghost is hot at my feet because he doesn't like the idea of sharing our Alicia with a dang moose.

When she notices our movements, she stops me with her hand. "Wait there. Frank doesn't get along with dogs." She smiles sadly at Ghost. "Sorry, buddy. I still love you."

Ghost lets out a loud growl, turns around, and walks back toward... *Justin.* Fucking Justin. *What happened with this family constantly stealing my dog?*

326

"Thank you!" Kayla exclaims with a laugh when the 'adorable' moose gives her sloppy kisses everywhere he can reach.

I turn toward Justin. "Will she take a shower after?"

"I sure as fuck hope so." His eyes widen and he shudders. Mr. Attleborough laughs.

The atmosphere lightens up, thanks to 'adorable' Frank. We all go about our business while Alicia and Kayla are doting over Frank. On any other occasion, I'd pull my phone and do some internet surfing, but here, right now, is what I was dreaming about since I was a little kid. A normal family. A little crazy, sometimes a lot, but the perfect one.

I look around the room and notice no one's pulled out their devices. Everyone's engaged in conversations or checking out their gifts.

My woman is laughing as Frank gives her a long lick on her cheek, and I laugh, hoping she'll take a shower too. I don't feel like kissing Frank.

A low chuckle comes from Mr. Attleborough, and I glance at him, noticing him giving me an approving nod. I smile back and settle in the comfy leather chair with my dog by my feet and my woman laughing happily—at something a wild beast snorts to her—surrounded by her friends and family with no more demons to haunt her dreams.

That's the definition of a perfect Christmas for me, the one I saw on a postcard but never thought I'd be a part of. Until her. The woman who gave me everything.

Epilogue

MARK

It's been two days since Christmas, and we're moving Alicia back to her place, even though we both know she'll end up staying at mine.

Justin understands it too. The moment she mentioned she'd be moving back, he tried to convince her to stay, shooting me nasty looks from across the room. I simply scratched my beard with my middle finger, and he picked his nose with his middle finger, making his father laugh.

"Leave them alone already," he said to Justin, rolling his eyes.

"Fine." He sulked, but no trace of malice was in his voice. It's like Justin wouldn't be Justin without being an asshole. Everyone understands that, including Alicia, who just rolled her eyes like her father, flipping him off too. That's my girl.

I carry her boxes to my truck so we can finally get moving and get her to my place, where she can be as loud as she wants. Mary and George come out to say their good-byes. Everyone hugs. Justin sends me a customary threatening stare and a smack on the shoulder. Kayla kisses my cheeks, secretly wiping tears away, and we finally get the hell out.

Don't get me wrong; I absolutely love her family, and I will never forget how they made me feel like one of them, but Alicia and I also have a lot to talk about. We need to discuss what we want, and I need to find courage to say what I want.

While Alicia chats away—I've never heard her talk so much, and I absolutely love it—I make a small detour to Donna's coffee shop. She has some secret recipe for Alicia's favorite chestnut praline latte.

I park the car, tell Alicia I'll be right back, and run inside. Three minutes later, I'm back in the car with the largest cup of her favorite coffee in hand.

She takes the cup from me and narrows her eyes suspiciously. "What do you want?"

"What do you mean?" I ask innocently, blinking at her.

She looks at the cup. "You brought me my favorite coffee while I know you'd rather go home and fuck like rabbits. It's like a thirty-minute detour." She looks back at me. "What do you want?"

I've been caught. "Take a sip first." I smile, and she squints even more. "C'mon, you want to." I laugh.

She inhales the aroma and closes her eyes. "Cheater." Then she takes a sip and moans. I love her moans. I love everything about her. With closed eyes, she asks, "Fine, what do you want?"

"Another sip?" I suggest, and her eyes fly open.

"Oh my gosh, Mark!"

"Don't think I don't know that you feed me before asking something I might not like!" She has the decency to look guilty, because her cheeks and the tip of her nose turn pink. Perfect timing. "Move in with me."

"What?" Her eyes just about pop out of her head, and her mouth forms that cute little *o* I love so much. "With you?"

"Yes." I swallow before diving into the explanation I've rehearsed five too many times. "We were practically living together anyway. You can still keep your place if you want. You know, if it makes you feel safe." I swallow again, preparing myself for a refusal.

"Okay." She shrugs and sips her coffee.

She stunned me by agreeing so quickly and without a fight. "What?"

"I wanted to live with you." And then she says with a smirk, "You didn't have to bribe me with coffee, even though it's much appreciated. I told you, you're my safe space. Pretty much my home at this point, so..." She shrugs. "Who cares where we live as long as we're together?"

I blink a few times. "Alright then."

"Alright." She turns away, hiding a happy smile.

I love this woman.

Acknowledgments

This time, I decided to put acknowledgments at the end, trying not to stir anyone's opinion about the book. Smarty pants here, ha-ha.

The first 'thank you' goes (runs, pretty much) to my PA Sarah Crouse. A person extraordinaire. If you want to steal her from me, I'll fight you with a frying pan, just like Alicia. Thank you, Sarah! I'd given up on writing and publishing a long time ago if not for you.

Moving on, there will be a lot of names, and they will be mentioned one by one, even though they hold the same importance.

Thank you, Steph. A therapist slash deputy mayor of Little Hope. Highly recommend. I don't know what I'd do without you constantly feeding my imagination.

Thank you, Jennifer. I don't even need to say anything —you know it all by now!

I appreciate every single person who picks up my books. Every single one of you. Without a reader, there will never be a writer.

Some readers are also bookstagrammers, and without your help my stories would never be discovered, and I appreciate every single one of you. Some readers go an extra mile and send you uplifting notes, usually when you need them the most. Preet and Meaghan, I'm looking at you. Darlene, Josie, Hailey, Traci, Sovaria, Trinity, Anshul, Zakerah, Crystal, Cheryl, Jenn, theoutgoingbookworm, deviant_book_queen, cookiereads, and everyone else who helped and supported me. If I didn't mention your name—most likely, I had a brain fog after all the editing—but you were meant to be here.

Symone, thank you for your tough love. I need it sometimes (a lot of times).

Andrea, you are probably expecting to be named because you're the first person (most likely) to get a discreet cover? Not this time. I'm putting your name here as a 'thank you' for your support, not because you bought the book.

To my sensitivity reader (no name will be named), who saw the book first. Thank you. You inspired me to tell your story. I hope it will help at least one person.

To my readers (meaning YOU). Again. And forever. Thank you, thank you, thank you!

~with love,

Ariana

Afterword

Welcome to Little Hope or Welcome Back! Thank you for reading this book.

I didn't know I can love my characters more than I already did (yes, even Justin, I love him too). Turned out, I was wrong. I cried so many times while I was writing this book, and the characters became a part of my family.

I hope you loved them as much as I did.

Guess who is going to be in the next story?

insert evil laugh here

Yes, Ar-r-rchie.

But who is going to be his half? Find Easter eggs in my group on Facebook.

If you want more books and news and freebies from me, you can find me on Social Media by typing this address to your web browser: https://linktr.ee/ArianaCaneAuthor. Or you can check out my website arianacane.com

I'm happy to see you here!

~Ariana

Also by Ariana Cane

The World of the Fallen Gates series

Dystopian, paranormal, urban fantasy romance series

Tale of the Deceived, Book 1 of the duet

Story of the Forsaken (coming soon), Book 2 of the duet

-vampires, werewolves, faes

-true enemies to lovers

-the life after the World has ended

-super slow-burn

-one bed

-true series

-scorching tension

-tons of secrets

Little Hope Series

Small town, slow burn, contemporary romance stand-alones.

Haunted Hearts, Little Hope Series, Book 1

Alex and Freya,

-one bed

-grumpy-sunshine

-strangers to enemies to lovers

-an ex-navy veteran with PTSD

-woman on the run

-woodchopping

-cabin in the woods

-damaged MMC

-all the bears of Maine

Guilty Minds, Little Hope Series, Book 2

Justin and Kayla

-true bully romance

-groveling

-tattoo artist-waitress/mechanic

-miscommunication for a good reason

-wildlife of Maine

Broken Souls, Little Hope Series, Book 3

Mark and Alicia

-fireman and author

-strangers to neighbors to lovers

-hurt/comfort

-trauma recovery

-man's best friend

-protective MMC

Fragile Lives, Little Hope Series, Book 4

Archie and Leila

-enemies to lovers

-one bed

-cabin in the woods

-age-gap

-brother's best friend

-the most beloved character

-wildlife of Maine

-trauma recovery/PTSD (MMC)

-lots of tattoos and piercings (MMC)

Book 4, Kenneth's story, is coming soon...

THEY SAY YOU SHOULDN'T LET THE PAST
DEFINE YOU. BUT WHEN THE PAST BECOMES
ALL YOU ARE, SOMETIMES YOU JUST NEED A
BLANK PAGE.

Broken Souls

Little Hope Series, Book 3

ARIANA CANE

Made in the USA
Coppell, TX
23 August 2023

20666083R00193